T0283374

CURVEBALL

A NOVEL

ERIC GOODMAN

Post Hill
PRESS

A POST HILL PRESS BOOK
ISBN: 979-8-88845-459-6
ISBN (eBook): 979-8-88845-460-2

Cover design by Jim Villaflores

Post Hill Press
New York • Nashville
posthillpress.com

Published in the United States of America
1 2 3 4 5 6 7 8 9 10

For my brothers Mike and Frank
Mets siblings Danny, Lamar, Rich, and Mary Jean
And for Mets fans everywhere
who every year
bleed orange and blue

The world is very old

But every spring

It groweth young again

And faeries sing

—Cicely Mary Barker

PART ONE

SPRING TRAINING

CHAPTER ONE

Jess Singer was tall, and he was fast. Like, really fast. Sophomore year, when he still flashed more acne than lip hair, he touched ninety. Six-two at sixteen, six-five as a senior, long-armed, broad-shouldered, long-legged as a ladder, Jess viewed the world through his mother's pale eyes from under his father's dark floppy hair and, as time would reveal, through his famous dad's ability to pitch up and in.

Remarkably, when the baseball gods and good fairies fluttered over Jess's crib, they not only blessed him with size and strength, an easy repeatable motion, and the hand-eye coordination the child of a beach volleyball star and a major league pitcher might expect, those same beneficent imps had made him left-handed. Left-handed! With fingers that would grow long and strong enough to enclose a ball in the web of his left hand, helping Jess master the curveball his father, Jewish Joe Singer, had forbidden him to throw until he was eighteen.

Four years later, as Jess toed a slab on the twelve-pack in the spring training complex in Port St. Lucie, most minor league scouts considered his curveball the best in the minors. Not only plus, but elite, a 12 to 6 tumbler, evoking comparisons to the famous hook thrown sixty years earlier by his co-religionist, the legendary Sandy Koufax, and more recently by another Dodger southpaw, Clayton Kershaw.

Jess's agent had explained to Jess and his parents, and to Grandpa Jack too, who'd groused about the lousy cheapskate bastards, that Jess could expect a call to the Show in late April or May, once the Super Two deadline had passed. Until then, he needed to hone throwing heat up in the zone and bouncing his curve when ahead in the count to produce more swings and misses. *Work on your Charlie,* Jack had whispered early in high school, when his father still forbade it. *And keep away from the slider. More elbows been blown out by that shit than anything.*

Sweating under the Florida sun, Jess hummed a heater homeward. Then another. Knee high, letter high, inside and out, ticking targets in all four quadrants set by Rah Ramirez, Jess's catcher the previous summer in Double-A. *Bing, bop, and zing. Bing, bop and zing,* the ball disappearing from Jess's fingers to materialize nanoseconds later in Rah's mitt.

Mac Davis, his father's catcher and best friend in their glory days in the '80s and '90s, and now the major league bullpen coach, stood behind Rah with several team officials Jess didn't recognize.

"Four more," Mac called.

Jess threw four four-seamers, then half a dozen two-seamers, which cut hard, left to right. Jess could see Mac and the others nodding, Mac's creased face round and tanned as a well-oiled mitt.

"Now the two," Mac said.

Jess nodded, reflexively rolling his glove hand forward in the universal meme for a curve. Rah set a low target and waggled two fingers. Jess positioned his glove in front of his face the way Jack had shown him long before Dad allowed him to throw a curve. His whole life he'd had his grandpa in one ear while with the other he feigned attention to Dad, who was kind-hearted if not, everyone said, very smart.

Jess had always felt closer to Jack, who had nicknamed him in middle school as he strode off a travel team mound, a head taller than his teammates.

"Look at him," Jack shouted. "Big as two fucking Jews."

The nickname stuck. Sanitized, but enduringly odd: Two-J's Singer.

Jess dug in his mitt and gripped the ball across the seams, supporting it with his flexed thumb. *Hide your face,* Jack had counseled. *Scare 'em shitless.* This was his advice when Jess was ten and twelve, not even

Bar Mitzvahed. *You're the Chosen One of the goddamned Chosen People. They'll be gunning for you, Two-J's, just like they did your dad.*

Jess rocked into motion, hiding his lips, nose, and the ball as well as he hid his secret self. *Release point,* he thought, *release point,* torqueing his wrist and snapping off a Charlie, aiming at the head of an imaginary left-handed batter, then watching his curve break sharply down and to the right, crossing the dish just above the batter's imaginary knees to settle in Rah's very real mitt like a white bird on a wire.

Yes, Jess thought and smiled. *Yes, sir.*

Sixty-four miles south, in Delray Beach, Jack was doing push-ups. Twice a day, he knocked out forty, followed by forty crunches. If it was good enough for Paul Newman, a good-looking Shaker Heights Yid, it was good enough for Jack, a *tummler* from East New York. Five years ago, he'd eliminated most red meat and cut way back on the hooch because as he always told Joey, *Take care of your body, and it'll take care of you.*

Unlike most old boys in South Florida, Jack could see his own dick without a mirror. A few years ago, after the second love of his life died and left him comfortable, Jack became known in Huntington Pointe as Viagra Jack, gray-haired Lancelot of old ladies. As he liked to assure Joey, and now Two-J's, the old man was one in a million. But even one in a million, old was old. On Jack's next birthday, an imaginary calendar would flip to eighty.

Thirty-six, Jack counted in his noggin, *twice Chai. Thirty-seven. Thirty-eight,* feeling the ache in his shoulders and arthritic thumbs as he fought to keep his gut flat and ass sea level, burning biceps, delts and lats. And now the whole truth and nothing but. Forty years ago, Jack began lying about his age. This was before Joey signed his first contract, not that he took a penny from the kid; he didn't. Jack wasn't seventy-nine, turning eighty the last day of November. He was eighty-two, turning eighty-three, but couldn't tell no one.

He finished his push-ups and collapsed gut down on the rug. Every other *alter kocker* in Huntington Pointe had tile floors. That's how condos were built down here, where it was *Schvitzville* six months a year. But now that he was four score and halfway to three, Jack feared falling more than black mold, so he'd had the tile ripped out and replaced with a rug.

When the doorbell chimed, Jack ignored it. Getting up and down was harder than the crunches and damn if he was going to struggle vertical, crab to the door, get down again to finish the set. Besides, he had a pretty good idea who it was.

Again, the bell.

Fourteen, fifteen, eighteen. Christ, he loved staying in shape. Fifty years ago, when he was raising Joey alone after his sweet first wife, may her name be a blessing, had to be put in a nut house—what sorrow, what shame—his gut was a plank, what the kids call an eight-pack. He used to encourage Joey, a sweet kid, to punch him hard as he could, just like Houdini. Joey's eyes would spin. *No, Daddy. No.*

Jack would taunt his own boy, and still Joey wouldn't punch until he'd threaten to send him to bed without supper. *Hit me if you know what's good for you.* Only then would Joey sock him. Eight and ten, he already packed a wallop, what a left arm! After every punch, Jack would remind Joey Houdini died because some anti-Semite bastard gut-punched him when he wasn't looking. A magical Jew, gone too soon.

Not Jack, still crunching in Delray Beach.

The bell rang a third time.

Thirty-six, thirty-seven.

"I know you're in there!"

Forty.

Jack pushed himself up on the coffee table, joints cracking like a dead man's bones. He approached the door and peered out the peephole. *Just like I thought.*

Gladys Goldberg, fully made-up at 10:00 a.m., fake lashes and platinum hair coiffed like Carol what's-her-name, Channing, cheeks smooth at seventy-six, eighty, eighty-five, who knew? stepped through the door. Glad surely shaved years off the real number, but who was he to hurl pebbles from inside the glass house of eighty-two? She must have had some nips and ducks, Jack thought, casting a knowing eye: quality work. She offered up a covered dish.

"I knew you were here, Jackie. I could hear you grunting."

"Whatcha got?"

"Your favorite."

He followed her to the kitchen where she set the *kugel* on the counter, then moved her hand to his cheek.

"You're sweaty."

"I need a shower."

Like wings, her lashes whirred. "Want me to scrub where you can't reach?"

She was a wild one, Glad. "You'll get wet."

"What if I do?"

He grinned and followed Mrs. Goldberg to the shower.

Joe eyed Frannie in profile on the patio. Only because he knew her, as he liked to say, better than she knew herself, could he detect the limp that had never completely gone away. Only Joe could see it. It made him feel guilty and sad and as full of love as he'd been since they met a quarter century ago in Hermosa Beach. Back then Frannie was the uncrowned queen of beach volleyball, everything about her larger than life. Her height, six-one; her ability to leap and spike; her loving heart; the crushing sorrow she'd survived as a girl. As Joe liked to say, you can't tell a book by its cover, nor a wounded girl by her beach bunny bod. Now that age and circumstance had reshaped the exterior—her long hair shorn at fifty, her leaping ability taken by the drunk who had hit them head-on twelve years ago—her loving heart and fierce, principled soul shone through even brighter.

"Breakfast, Joe."

Joe cast a long last look at the fairway and the green hills enclosing it. For the past four months, they'd been living on the ninth hole of a golf course in Sonoma County. This was the first time in years they hadn't wintered in Florida near Jack, or in Southern California, where they met. This year, feeling at loose ends with Jess away, they'd decided to try someplace new.

"I'll be right in."

Frannie disappeared inside the house, still long, still lean, which made Joe feel like a hippo. He'd gained twenty-five pounds since Christmas, padding his waist and ass. His face was rounder too, Semitic cheekbones sunk in goo. And though he hadn't lost any hair in front, there was considerable shine on the back forty: a two-and-a-half-inch circle a yarmulke would cover if Joe were that kind of Jew.

Joe watched a golfer proceed slowly up the fairway pushing an oversize handcart. He looked seventy-five or eighty, Jack's age. The old man selected an iron, swung mightily, and topped the ball ten feet.

"Fuck a duck!"

Joe turned, pretending he hadn't seen or heard the outburst. Inside, he found the bowl of steel-cut oats Frannie had set out for him, but no Frannie.

"I got tired of waiting," she said when he found her in the bedroom, putting on a warm-up jacket and tights for her morning bike ride. Ruby, her black mutt, the latest in a thirty-year-long line of rescues, crouched beside her, eying Joe suspiciously. Ruby was ten or twelve; she'd been with them only since the move to Sonoma. Short-legged, stout, and ill-favored, with a white muzzle and bulging eyes, Ruby rarely barked or wagged her tail. Her teats and belly sagged. There was nothing ruby-like about her except the name she'd come home with.

"Why'd you let Frannie adopt her?" Jack had asked when he visited.

"After Randy died, you remember Randy?"

Jack nodded.

"Ruby was the only dog she showed me with four legs."

"What is it, Joe?" Frannie asked.

"What's *what*?"

"You're not here."

"I am."

"Only in body."

Fair enough. "You going for a ride?"

Frannie nodded.

"Want company?"

"Sure, Joe. Only, you don't own a bike."

Joe felt flummoxed.

Frannie hugged him, and he glanced over her shoulder at Ruby, who, with her protuberant eyes, looked like a dog in a comic strip. After a moment, Ruby looked away just as Frannie added, "I'm going for my ride now, but when I come back, let's talk about what's bothering you."

Joe started to say, *Nothing,* but knew that wouldn't float.

When Joe returned, hours later, hiding from his wife and the looming conversation, it was 3:30 and drizzling. It had been a wet winter, rain every few days since November.

"Are you hungry?"

Joe shook his head. "I ate."

"I'm sure you did," Frannie said, then looked embarrassed for fat-shaming him. More gently, she asked, "How about tea, to take the chill off?"

Joe's eyes filled with sadness. It was easier to face Frannie's anger than kindness.

"I think I'll lie down."

"What about that conversation?"

"Later, okay?" Joe fled, guiltily, down the bedroom corridor, opened and closed the door behind him. What would Frannie think of his strange behavior? That he was having an affair? But he'd been the most loyal of husbands, even in his playing days, when women were all over him, like shell on a hardboiled egg.

Joe sat on their unmade bed, arms crossed, staring out through the sliding glass door at the rain and the puddling fairway. He tried to think about as little as possible, in fact, to think about nothing at all. Suddenly, the bedroom door burst open, and Frannie landed in front of him on the bed.

"What is it?" she demanded. "What is it, Joe?"

"Let me get this right," she shouted sometime later. "You've known *how long?*"

Frannie now sat beside him on the couch. Beyond the wall of windows and sliding glass doors, plump geese waddled up the wet fairway.

"Two months," he admitted.

"Two months! Two months ago, you had a blood test that said you might have cancer, and you didn't tell me?"

Joe nodded.

"Why the hell not?"

At first, he'd felt embarrassed. Then scared. Finally, after letting months slip past, he felt unable to act. "I couldn't."

"What the hell is wrong with you?"

"I told you. High PSA might mean prostate—"

"I *know!!*" Her eyes fired body-piercing blue missiles. "Why didn't you tell me?" Frannie's hands balled into fists larger than most men's. "Don't you love me? I could punch you in the face!"

I wish you would, Joe thought. "Go ahead."

She socked him. Eyes smarting, cheek throbbing, Joe declined to strike her back or, like a plunked batter, to rub the sore spot.

"Feel better?"

She nodded. "What about you?"

"I feel great," he said. "You hit like a girl."

"Fuck you, Joe. I suppose you haven't gone for tests, or anything?"

"I was scared, Frannie. That's why I didn't tell you. I didn't want to know."

"You think not knowing will save you?"

She was right. Frannie was always right.

"You're such a dope sometimes."

"But I'm *your* dope," he said hopefully. "Right?"

"Forever and a day."

He kissed her and she kissed him back. For a heartbeat he thought they might end up in bed, where they hadn't been in a really long time.

"Maybe later," Frannie said. "Right now, you call that doctor."

Joe thought about explaining he'd decided to pretend it was all a mistake or happening to someone else, that for two months he'd done nothing but eat because that would make him strong enough to fight off whatever was happening down there. But she'd only call him a dope, or invoke Jack's favorite insult, *the dumbest Jew in America*. Instead, he went looking for his cell phone.

And just like that, the nightmare began.

CHAPTER TWO

Jess was scheduled to pitch an inning in the big club's spring training game, so he'd slept badly. Fearful he was too keyed-up to keep food down, Jess decided to skip breakfast, but realized that was crazy. Energy! Fuel! He forced down four eggs, six slices of bacon, and an English muffin, then fretted, *What the hell? I'll be too full to pitch!* He considered making himself hurl like the gymnasts and cheerleaders did in the second-floor bathroom in Redondo High.

Oh, how he'd longed to join them in the girls' room—to learn the secrets of applying eyeliner—although Jess, all-county then all-state and destined, everyone said, to follow his famous dad to the Show, would never dare wear any.

At least not in public.

He arrived early at the park, stretched, and got his running in before the mandatory game-day meeting. Greg Gallagher, the pitching-savvy manager, not even forty, blue eyes, close-cropped beard starting to gray, took Jess aside after the meeting.

"Remember, Jess, pound the zone. Strike one, strike two, every batter. And don't be afraid to come inside." Gallagher, whom some of the vets called Gigi (sometimes singing it in a French accent, though not, of course, to his face), but whom Jess could only think of as The Manager, dropped his hands onto Jess's shoulders. "And do yourself a favor. Don't shake off Furillo."

In this way, Jess learned he'd be throwing to the Mets' starting catcher, rather than Rah or one of the other minor leaguers he'd known coming up. He was scheduled to pitch third—likely the fourth or fifth inning—depending on how long the starter lasted. No matter what, he wouldn't pitch for at least two hours. He exited the meeting room and passed a poster for *The Natural*: Redford as Roy Hobbs, winding up left-handed, grinning sexily. Why a movie poster and not one of the team's former pitching stars, Jess couldn't say. When he was in middle school, some of his teammates' fathers called him The Natural, but Dad wouldn't allow it. He never knew why. What Jess did know was that for as long as he could remember, he'd loved Redford's blond good looks, so different from his own. Just thinking about Redford, Jess felt a tingle downstairs. Growing up, if Jess could have looked like anyone, it would have been Robert Redford.

He picked at the training table lunch, then headed to the minor league side of the complex to run sprints on the outfield grass. He tried to remember if they'd been using these same fields when Dad played, and realized, of course not, how many years ago was that? Twenty-five? Thirty? Jess pulled his cap down and closed his eyes, visualizing strike one, strike two, just like Gallagher suggested. Then Jess heard his name, and when he looked up, Grandpa Jack was coming towards him.

"Two-J's," Jack said, "you ready?"

The old bookie wore a short-brimmed straw hat, which looked like the unnatural child of a Panama and a fedora; a red feather waved from the hatband. The moustache, now white, that Jack had worn Jess's entire childhood supported his hooked nose.

"Whatsamatter, Jess, cat got your tongue?"

"Grandpa, you're not supposed to be on the field."

Jack waved his fingers as if shooing gnats. "I slipped the mook a fiver. Anyway, they know me." He grinned, then his expression flipped serious. "Trust your stuff. And remember where you come from." He raised his right arm for a fist-bump. "The Chosen Ones' Chosen One." Jack pointed at his chest: one of Dad's old jerseys. Then he ambled towards the stands, like he owned the place.

Jess returned to the major league side of the complex. He shagged flies with the other pitchers, then stood in the semicircle of players watching Randy Vermouth, the club's number five starter, warm up on the practice mound halfway down the left field line. Vermouth was thirty-four, in the last year of his contract. Never overpowering, Vermouth's greatest virtue, from the team's perspective, was durability. Unlike most of the big club's pitchers, he never went on the IL. Instead, he took the ball every fifth day and gobbled innings like salted nuts. From Jess's perspective, Vermouth's greatest value was his expiring contract; there was a spot in next year's rotation.

When the game started, Jess sat in the bullpen beside Rah. They were the same age, and for the past three years had played on the same minor league affiliates in Low-A, Advanced-A, and Double-A. Rah, whose full name was Pedro Torres Ramirez, buzzed his hair on both sides, but grew the center part long enough to curl. He hailed from Cuernavaca, Morelos, Mexico, not Venezuela or the DR. Like his hero, Yadier Molina, Rah often dyed his central swatch of hair blond. He was six-one, with medium-brown skin, large hands, a great arm, broad shoulders, and a rollicking sense of humor. Everyone said if Rah could just hit .240 he'd reach the Show.

Rah had signed at sixteen and reached the US at eighteen, which was when he and Jess met. Four years ago, Rah spoke badly broken English and hung out only with other Latins. Since then, he'd learned English, mostly, he said, by watching *Friends* re-runs.

Maybe because of his devotion to sitcoms, or maybe it was the other way around, Rah laughed often, and the world laughed with him. His large, perfectly formed teeth were as well-matched as a box of Chiclets, which Rah pronounced, *Chick-lay*. Privately, Jess thought Rah was cute as the Eveready Bunny, and he sometimes feared he was half in love with his batterymate.

"*Cabrón.*" Rah banged his right fist on Jess's knee. "You ready?"

"You know it."

"Little Prince finally gonna pitch for the big club."

For years, Rah had been calling Jess "Little Prince," intimating he was baseball royalty because his dad had pitched in the Bigs, while he was a *campesino* from nowhere, his dad a security guard. But while he might have come from Nowhere, Rah had signed for 500K—dollars, not pesos—and bought his Mom and Pops a new house, or as Rah said, *una casita*. As Jess liked to remind him, he wasn't from nowhere no more. What Rah didn't understand was that because of the whole gambling thing and the way his career ended, Dad wasn't exactly baseball royalty, more like the star who fell from the sky.

"Someday," Jess said. "I'm gonna pitch in New York and you're gonna catch me."

"Think so?" Rah asked, eyes dreaming.

Jess considered leaning in and hugging Rah, which happened all the time with teammates, although usually after some on-the-field achievement. Instead, he settled for a fist bump.

"You know it, *cabrón*."

A moment later, Ray Gibson, the major league pitching coach, told Jess to warm up.

Jack wanted a beer, but decided no. Then, he thought, as he often did, *Fuck it!* Two-J's was throwing to big leaguers for the first time ever. Finishing a Bud Light served in a commemorative blue and orange plastic cup, Jack considered a second, but thwarted his own desire. He was seated in the sun, six rows behind home, and needed to provide an accurate scouting report to his son. Why wasn't Joey here? Some cockamamie excuse about trying out life in Northern C-A. Why didn't he and Frannie visit wine country after spring training, or better yet, after the season? But Jack had never understood how and why his son did half of what he did, no way.

Pretty soon, though not soon enough for Jack, it was the top of the fifth. Jess, wearing a bush leaguer's number, 72, stepped onto the mound. He looked like a baseball god: six-five; broad shoulders; narrow waist; long, ropey arms. He bounced the resin bag once, twice, on his palm then once, twice on the back of his left hand, then dropped it to the ground, where it emitted a faint puff. *Christ*, Jack thought, did

Two-J's look the part or what? What a shame Frannie and Joey never had another, or maybe four more; he never understood why not.

Jess finished his warm-ups, popping Furillo's mitt, then broke off a couple dipsy-doodles. What must the kid be feeling as he turned his back to the plate, displaying the 72 on his jersey to the box seat fans? The ball wove its way around the infield as if on a thread: catcher, short, second base, third then back to first, from there landing in Two-J's lefty mitt.

The PA announcer announced: "Now pitching for your New York Mets, Jess Singer."

Two-J's set up on the first base side of the rubber and peered towards home, shielding his face with his glove, just like Jack had taught him when he was a kid. For a moment, Jack saw Two-J's at eight or ten, toeing the rubber in Little League, so precocious, so serious. Then Two J's in his present form fired home, and the ump's right thumb and index finger shot up, signaling Strike One.

When he poured in Strike Two, Jack struggled not to stand and echo the ump's call. Then, after wasting a fastball inside that knocked the batter off the dish, Jess broke off a curve that dotted the outside corner—who expected a twenty-two-year-old to have such a pitch?—Jack jumped up and shouted, "Atta boy, Two-J's!" as the ump raised his right fist punching out the batter.

"Who's pitching?" asked some geezer, nose like a hatchet, three seats to Jack's right.

"Joe Singer's son," said his friend, both of them wearing Jewish stars. "'Member him?" Both *alter kockers* wore Mets caps, their forearms as dotted with liver spots as an ocelot's ass. "What a damn shame he got caught up in gambling. He was never the same."

Jack started to say Joey was never caught up in gambling, not ever, and he wasn't the same on account of getting shot. But for once he closed his pie hole and watched his grandson throw filthy four-seamers, two-seamers, and curveballs as if he were starring in a video game: *Born to Pitch.* Two-J's Singer: bigger, brighter, and purer than a dozen old men.

CHAPTER THREE

The morning after he threw for the big club—two innings, three strikeouts, one walk, one hit, no runs, thirty-six pitches—Jess lay in bed, savoring how well he'd done. He remembered a very different time, his first pro season, when he pitched in rookie ball, also here in Port St. Lucie. He'd just turned eighteen, his first time away from home. All summer he pitched like crap, and what was worse, he nearly died of lonely. Things got so bad his parents moved out to support him. Dad wore a disguise to the ballpark, a black slouch hat and dark glasses— what Jack called *The Midnight Jew* because Dad didn't want to talk to reporters or have the focus on him instead of on Jess. Growing up, Jess was grateful, although that first summer—when he was trying too hard, overthrowing his heater, losing his release point on the curve, in general performing like a scared little bitch—he would have been happy to have Dad suck up some of the attention that came with being Jewish Joe's son.

He'd returned to California that first September—rookie leagues played a short season—and pulled a psychic blanket over his head. Rookie ball was the first time he hadn't clearly been the best athlete on the field. Surrounded by players from the DR and Venezuela who knew each other from the Dominican Summer Leagues, Jess not only nearly died of lonely, he came to know with a loud and final clang, as if a prison door was slamming shut, that he was queer, twisted, gay.

And not just for now, but as Mom liked to say when she was tucking him in as a little boy, assuring him she would always love him: *Forever and a day.*

Yes, Jewish Joe's son would be queer forever. Not just curious, as he told himself in eighth grade when he discovered gay porn sites. Or going through a phase, as he believed in high school, as he jerked off over and over while fantasizing about Ricardo Valdez, the team's center fielder. He liked girls too, didn't he? *Didn't he?* And weren't girls crazy about him? So tall, so cool, so good-looking. No, no, as the Latin players said, and they said it all the time when they were clowning around, *Maricón, eres maricón.* And poor Jess, unlucky, lucky Jess, Latin dudes were his type. Smooth-muscled, dark-haired, dark-eyed. *Maricón, maricón.* Unless it was *Faggot, faggot, faggot,* the first English word they seemed to learn. Faggot this, *maricón* that. *Your fastball sucks my cock, maricón.*

If only, thought Jess.

Frannie stood beside him in the dining room as he dialed the doctor's office, both to make sure he called, and because after that drunk hit them twelve years ago and blew up her leg, they both knew how important it was to have someone beside you, not just emotionally but physically, *right there*, when you were negotiating scary medical business. So she stood beside him while he dialed his family practice office, which had called several times three months ago to schedule a follow-up, then stopped when he didn't return calls. He hadn't told Frannie that and didn't plan to. The receptionist placed him on hold—Frannie asked him to put his cell on speaker—and moments later, Dr. Hardy, his primary care physician, came on the line.

This was bad, Joe thought. Doctors never spoke to you directly. But maybe Hardy was making an exception. Maybe he was a baseball fan, and now that Joe had resurfaced from the pool of the medically missing, he wanted an autograph. But no, the gravelly, no-nonsense voice on the other end announced he needed an appointment *pronto* with a urologist and probably an oncologist too, and there wasn't a moment to lose, don't you see, and why the hell didn't you call sooner?

You need an x-ray, then an MRI. Depending on the results, you'll need a biopsy, likely followed by a bone scan, but those will have to be ordered by one of the specialists, although, Hardy added, it wouldn't hurt to have the x-ray and MRI available when you first go, especially since the clock was ticking, and had been for months.

By the time he hung up, Joe felt, and probably looked, he thought, like a steer led onto the killing floor, or perhaps like a middle-aged pitcher smacked with a bat. When he turned her way, Frannie's anger had dissolved into worry, which, Joe realized, was what it had been all along.

While they were trying to decide which specialist to contact first, Joe's phone rang. What if it was Hardy's office calling back with even grimmer news, but no, it was Jack calling to re-hash Jess's pitching performance.

"Two-J's looked GREAT!" he shouted.

Jack was getting pretty hard of hearing, but he was too vain, or perhaps too cheap, to buy hearing aids.

"Like a MAN among boys, just like in LITTLE LEAGUE."

"That's great, Dad," Joe said.

"So when the FUCK you coming EAST, Joey?"

Joe looked at Frannie. She shook her head, *No.*

"I don't know."

"Whatcha MEAN, you don't KNOW?"

"There's some things—"

"WHAT THINGS?"

Frannie pressed a finger to her lips.

"Things."

"Get your FINGER out your ASS, Joey! Two-J's was throwing LIGHTS OUT! You need to get DOWN HERE!"

"Medical things," Joe said.

Frannie looked like she wanted to punch him again. The last thing they wanted was for Jess to know anything before they knew what there was to know.

"What medical things?"

Frannie grabbed the cell phone. "One minute, Jack." She held the phone as far from Joe's big mouth as she could. "What is it," she hissed, "you don't understand about this?" She smacked her index finger across her own pursed lips. Into the phone, she said, "Joe's gotta take some tests."

She put the phone on speaker so Joe could hear. *Who wanted to hear?*

"What tests?"

"If we wanted you to know, Jack, we would have told you." She glanced at Joe. "The last thing we want is for you to tell Jess."

"Why would I tell Jess?"

"I don't know why you say or do half the things you do."

"No fair stealing my line about Joey." Jack laughed. "I'm the SPHINX OF DELRAY. I won't say a fucking word. What's wrong?"

She glanced at Joe, who nodded.

"You see," she began.

Joe blew her a kiss, then slipped out of the room.

In the morning, Joe tried to stay positive about how quickly the urologist and oncologist were willing to schedule him, Jewish Joe Singer! But the truth was, and he knew it, the relevant facts were not his moments of athletic glory, which were twenty-five years in the past, but his PSA, which two months ago was 12.8.

Two days later, Frannie accompanied him to Dr. Perlman's office in the medical arts building in downtown Santa Rosa. Frannie, who'd insisted upon driving, remained in the waiting room when the nurse called him in. Joe was glad Frannie had come along, although it made him feel like an idiot that she'd felt she had to drive him to ensure he'd keep the appointment. Ever since he was a little kid and his mom got sick, he'd felt more comfortable taking care of someone than being cared for. Better get over that, he thought, and winked at Frannie, then followed the young Latina nurse to an examination room. He'd barely settled in after having his vitals taken when there was a knock on the door and Doctor Perlman entered.

Perlman was short and tubby, five-six or seven. Short gray hair, hazel eyes, plump cheeks. Above the left breast pocket of his white lab coat, *Dr. Perlman* was stitched in Dodger blue. A stethoscope slung casually around his neck gave Perlman the look of a small-town doctor, although the diploma on the wall was from NYU.

He extended his hand. "Paul Perlman."

"Joe Singer."

Joe took the much smaller hand in his own.

"I know who you are," Perlman said. Then he sandwiched Joe's right hand between both of his, a gesture that reminded Joe of his father's generation, though not, of course, Jack.

"You've been bad, Joe." Perlman shook his head. "Letting two months go by."

Joe nodded.

"Lucky for you, I'm a fan, a native New Yorker."

Joe nodded a second time, unsure where this was going. Twenty-five years ago, his so-called *fans* were the angriest.

"I pulled some strings, and you'll get the tests you need in the next two days. Boom, boom, boom."

"Thank you."

"Back in the day," Perlman continued, "when I was in college and med school, you were my hero. Got me through a lot of late nights. You know, the only member of the Tribe. We were all so proud."

Joe had heard variants of this before, and it always made him uncomfortable. During the year he was suspended, it was often his own who turned on him most viciously, insisting he'd disgraced them all. *Hey, scumbag. Don't you know what the goyim think of us?*

But Perlman was on the level.

"And now," the little doc said, eyes twinkling. "I need to examine you, so please drop trow and bend over the examination table."

Joe felt his expression change.

"I know," Perlman said, "everyone's favorite part."

"Not really."

"Whenever you're ready, Joe."

Joe unbuckled his belt. Dr. Perlman pulled on disposable gloves and smeared lubricant over his index finger. Joe dropped his pants below his knees and bent over the stainless-steel examination table. Joe wondered what sort of man, with options, *a Jewish doctor!* would choose this as his occupation. He tried not to tense up. Then he felt the doctor's finger slip into his anus, *Oh God*, and root around like a truffle-hunting pig.

When the examination was over, the doctor looked worried, before a curtain of professional distance descended.

"I'm sure you have a million questions, Joe," Dr. Perlman said, "but let's wait until the tests come back before we jump to conclusions."

In Delray Beach, at 5:30 p.m. on a Tuesday, Jack was settling into K'ee Grill with Glad Goldberg for an early bird dinner. K'ee was one of the swankiest local joints, and during Season—before the snowbirds flew north—it was packed every night, early bird and regular seating. Jack generally avoided early birds; hell, most nights he didn't bother going out, preferring to dine from his fridge while watching sports. But the Joey news had knocked him ass over teakettle, and he felt the need of companionship. Holy shit, he'd been thinking since the phone call, Joey's got the Big C.

So Jack called Glad, who seemed surprised; she generally just stopped by with a casserole the mornings she woke up frisky. Glad was flattered by the invite, she said, but only if they went Dutch and therefore only for an early bird. When he offered to pick her up, she asked, "You still drive after dark, Jackie?"

"You know it."

"You really are one in a million."

K'ee Grill was packed, but he'd asked for and they'd been seated at one of the romantic deuces, under a white canvas umbrella. Jack, who favored white shoes, white pants, and Hawaiian shirts year-round, Memorial and Labor Day injunctions be damned, fed the young hostess a fin for her kindness. K'ee was a white tablecloth kind of place with fishing nets and a stuffed marlin on the wall, grouper and yellowtail on the menu. Except for two miserable-looking grandkids, the clientele averaged seventy-five, easy. Near the maître d' station, half a dozen folded walkers lined the wall, trusty steeds awaiting their masters' returns.

Framed by swooping platinum hair of a shade existing nowhere in nature, Glad's heavily made-up eyes regarded him with cool blue intelligence. "So, Jack, to what do I owe the honor?"

"I thought it'd be nice to break bread."

Glad walloped her pinot. She stood five-one or so, worked out two hours a day, and weighed a hundred and ten dripping wet. Her body wasn't exactly dried up, but there wasn't an extra ounce of meat nowhere.

"Nah," Glad said. "There's something on your mind."

Before he could confirm or deny, their tall pecker of a waiter, all elbows, legs, and curly black hair, zoomed up for their order. Glad requested a Caesar, extra anchovies and grilled chicken, while Jack, breaking his usual injunction against red meat, opted for the double-cut baby lamb chops, medium rare, baked potato, sour cream, chives, and the house special, creamed spinach.

When the server shot off towards the kitchen, Glad observed, "Eating like that at our age will kill you."

"What do you know about it?"

"I buried two husbands."

"That all? I figured you for four or five."

"Don't be an ass." She drained her wine.

"I was kidding."

"Thank God your other jokes are funnier." Glad raised her right hand—red nails a half inch past her fingertips—to recall the waiter.

"I've buried two wives."

"Is that why they call you a lady-killer?"

"Okay." Jack sipped his scotch. "We're even."

"People like us," Glad began.

He wasn't sure where she was going, and maybe she wasn't either.

She continued, "In case you're wondering, I'm not going be anybody's nurse ever again." She captured his hand under hers. "Besides, I like what we got."

Just then, Mister Penis Hair rushed up and took their second drink orders. When he left, Jack said, "I'm not looking to nurse anyone again neither."

"I'm glad we cleared that up. So, why'd you ask me out?"

Jack considered and rejected bullshit. "My son's got prostate cancer."

"The famous one?"

"The only one."

"How bad?"

"We don't know. I'm guessing pretty bad."

"That's tough." She reached across the table and laced her red, razor-tipped fingers through his. "That's the worst, when your kids are sick."

The waiter returned with their second round, and Jack raised the single malt to his lips.

On Wednesday, Jess pitched on the major league side of the complex for the second straight outing. Four innings, two runs, both coming on a fastball he left middle-middle, which Rivera deposited so far beyond the left-center field fence, Jess didn't bother to look. Except for that one mistake, he thought, all good. Five strikeouts, two walks, two hits, seventy pitches. When he strode off the mound to the dugout, Gallagher met him on the top step.

"Good job, kid." Gallagher pumped his hand. "Real good."

Jess walked the length of the dugout as if it were a receiving line, getting and returning high fives; fist bumps; *Atta-boys*; *Ándales*; *Fucking-As*; *Way to Go, Pendejo*; *You Rock, rook*; *Pinche Cabrón*, multi-lingual male music from the men he hoped would someday be his teammates. At the far end of the bench, just past Rick Heynen, the team ace, his father's catcher and old friend, Mac Davis, grasped Jess's right hand. Mac's meatier one still felt to Jess as it had his entire childhood: large and leathery enough to be the mitt he'd worn for so many years with such distinction.

"Two-J's," Mac said softly. "Sit with me."

Mac looped an arm over Jess's pitching shoulder.

"Take care of that money-maker, son." Mac grinned and squeezed Jess's biceps. "The way you threw today? Reminds me of your dad."

"Coming from you, that means a lot."

Mac gazed at the field, where the Astros infielders tossed a ball around while their pitcher warmed up. The old catcher filled his mouth with sunflower seeds. "Ya know," he drawled, extending two syllables into three or four, all the while cracking and spitting shells on the dugout floor. "I woulda thought Joe and Frannie might woulda been down to watch you throw 'fore now."

Jess would have thought so too, but Mom and Dad had become less regular about calling, and when they did, they were hard to pin down.

"My grandpa's here," Jess said. "He never misses."

Mac's heavy lids fell once, then a second time, like a blinking cat. He sprayed shells, slowly and moistly, as if aiming a brown stream of the chewing tobacco he'd enjoyed in his playing days. Jess suspected there was bad history between his godfather and grandfather, and he regretted bringing Jack up and spoiling the happy moment with Mac.

"Two-J's," Mac said *sotto voce*, extending *Two-J's* into three syllables. "You didn't hear this from me. Gallagher wants to bring you north, but the front office says not so fast." He sprayed black and white shells at the dugout floor. "My guess, you start the year in Syracuse. But hell's bells, son, I been wrong before."

Jess thought about starting the year in Queens, how cool would that be! But he told himself, *Nah, that wouldn't happen.* He glanced at Rick Heynen, who was seated just on the other side of Mac. Heynen was tall and lean, same body type. So far, Jess hadn't managed more than *Hello* and *Goodbye*. Heynen had won the Cy Young two years ago, and Jess felt more like his fanboy than a teammate.

He thanked Mac for his kind words and headed to the trainer's room to ice his money-maker.

CHAPTER FOUR

In the end, these tests weren't all that different from tests Joe had taken in his playing days except the stakes were higher, as if he'd been promoted from the medical bush leagues to the Show. A lot of sitting and standing, holding his breath and holding still; removing and replacing clothes, pushing and prodding, unspeakable invasions, snipping, needling, hurrying and waiting, listening and nodding without understanding, then drinking eight glasses of water for days on end. Frannie remained at his side whenever the technicians permitted. Nothing was obviously torn, fractured, or broken, and the area in doubt was neither a limb nor a ligament, nor even an ulnar nerve, but a one-and-half-inch, three-quarter-ounce gland accessed through his bottom. Joe felt frightened and embarrassed, as if even the possibility of *this* cancer was too unmanly to mention.

Barely a week after he confessed to Frannie, they were back in Doctor Perlman's waiting room. This time, when the Latina assistant came out to call him, Frannie accompanied Joe to the examination room. He'd dropped a few pounds, which was good; he'd been trying. But he was so scared about what Dr. Perlman was about to tell him, the first time the nurse checked his BP, it was 160 over 96; his whole life it had been 120 over 72.

"Would you try his other arm?" Frannie asked. "That's much higher than usual."

Nurse Carla glanced from Frannie to Joe, then nodded. This time, he concentrated on controlling his breathing and racing heart, much as when he was pitching, he'd try to stay still and focused, blocking out everything except Mac's glove.

"One thirty-five over eighty-four," Nurse Carla announced. "Much better."

Then she left the room, and Frannie took his right hand in both of hers.

"Your pressure's up because you're scared shitless."

Joe nodded, wondering what he had done to deserve such a loving wife, when there was a soft knock. Before he could say, *Come in*, Doc Perlman entered, wearing the same lab coat as last time. With Frannie beside him, Perlman looked even smaller than Joe remembered, a Munchkin physician. One look at Perlman's expression, and Joe nearly shat himself.

"You must be Mrs. Singer."

Frannie stood and shook the doc's hand. "Call me Frannie."

"Paul Perlman," Perlman said, grinning goofily despite, Joe thought, what he had to say next. Over the years, Frannie had had a similar goofifying effect on many men. "I'm your husband's biggest fan in the North Bay." He glanced at Joe. "I wish I had better news."

Frannie returned to the chair beside him. Dr. Perlman sat on the rolling stainless steel physician stool. Joe did not glance at his wife because that, he thought, would make things worse.

"As we suspected, it's cancer. No surprise given the DRE—"

"The what?" Frannie asked.

"Digital rectal exam. His PSA is up to thirteen, which is very high."

"Oh," said Frannie.

"To complicate matters, although neither the biopsy nor the MRI show the cancer has spread outside the prostate—"

Thank God, Joe thought.

"—the Gleason score is seven."

Gleason? Joe wondered. "Like, Jackie Gleason?"

Perlman smiled. "Spelled the same, but not as funny. The higher the Gleason, the more aggressive the cancer. A Gleason score of eight or nine is quite high, seven not quite as bad, but cause for concern."

Pow to the moon, thought Joe.

Frannie squeezed his hand in what he knew was a gesture of support, but he couldn't bear to look at her.

"So what does this mean?" Frannie asked, from a place beyond Joe's vision.

"It means Joe needs to see an oncologist and a surgeon to choose a treatment plan, because the last thing we want is for the cancer to move outside the gland."

Joe let out the breath he didn't know he'd been holding.

"I can recommend two different oncologists," Perlman said, "and I've contacted their offices to make sure they can see Joe soon."

"Thank you," Frannie said, "that's very kind."

"There's one more thing. I've ordered a bone scan, to confirm the cancer hasn't spread to his bones. I don't think it has. The MRI shows it hasn't spread to nearby lymph nodes or other soft tissue. But you can never be too sure, right, Joe?"

He nodded.

"And now," Perlman said, "I'm sure you have a million questions."

Frannie squeezed his hand again, and this time he turned towards her. She looked like he felt.

"I have a question," Joe said, surprising himself. "If the cancer has moved to my bones, am I a dead man walking?"

"Not necessarily, but it would change the treatment plan. Other questions?"

He knew Frannie would have questions, and as she began to ask them, he retreated into silence. For Joe, there was really only one question, and he allowed his thoughts to carry him away.

That night they made love for the first time in what seemed like forever.

After dinner at a Santa Rosa restaurant where portions were standard but flavor combos Wine Country weird—kimchee and chopped liver; schmaltz and sushi—Frannie encouraged Joe to shower in the guest bathroom then meet her in the bedroom. Tonight, she said, was going to be about their lives together—twenty-five years!—and of course, their bodies. Tonight, would be about the simple pleasures of flesh on flesh.

Joe showered quickly then put on the Hawaiian shirt and shiny silver silk boxers he saved for nights like this: old friends in the fucking game. Then he lit a scented candle and waited in bed for Frannie. She appeared in a Valentine-themed bustier and see-through bottoms, cut low on the hips and open from behind.

She climbed into bed and lay down beside him, the flame from the frangipani candle showing faintly in his eyes. He kissed her softly, the merest nibble, until she caught his lip between hers and began to *suck*. That drew his hand to her crotch, which already felt familiarly warm and slightly moist. Maybe he should try to slow things down, but it had been so long, and they were both so deprived. While he was trying to decide what to do, Frannie moved her mouth to his ear, teasing his lobe with her tongue, then *biting* him, and he thought, *What the hell!* He slipped his finger, then fingers, deeper inside her.

"Oh, Joe," she murmured, her tongue and teeth and lips no longer nibbling. She reached into his boxers, and he shied away.

"What's wrong?"

"I'm not sure I can."

She got up on her knees, breasts rolling forward into her bustier, her lips sliding down to his shiny silken boxers, which she threaded past his knees. Taking him in her mouth, she commenced ringing then wringing his cock between her fingers.

For a long scary moment—*nothing*. On her knees, bent forward sucking, her ass exposed through the silly see-through panties, she did her best, while Joe offered a prayer to the God of Pitchers and Catchers, who giveth and taketh away fastballs and hard-ons. And then, just before he despaired, his cock stiffened. His hands tangled in her hair, encouraging her mouth to slide up and down his cock harder and faster. A sound began in the back of his throat, and surely, she knew what that meant. Then it was coming from her throat too, and just before he exploded, she did the cruel thing and spat him out.

"Please, Joe, come inside me."

He rolled her over and pulled her panties down. And sometime during the luscious fucking, she climbed on top and rode him home. After he'd come and she had too, *My God*, he thought, they lay together, spent. When Joe could form words again, he thanked her.

"What are you thanking me for?"

"Getting the ball rolling?"

She laughed, then padded off to the bathroom to clean up. Waiting for Frannie to return, he turned on the bedside lamp and spotted a drop of blood on his penis. That couldn't have come from Frannie, he thought, her period had stopped two years ago. The blood must have been in his semen. Dr. Perlman had warned that could happen after a biopsy.

Oh God, he thought, *cancer really is in our bed.* Joe found a Kleenex, wiped the blood, and switched off the lamp. When Frannie returned, she blew the candle out and climbed in beside him. Inhaling the dying puff of frangipani, Joe wrapped her in his arms and held on.

CHAPTER FIVE

Jess, Rah, and two other players likely headed to Triple-A decided to take advantage of their last unscheduled afternoon—morning practice, no game—and headed to the beach when practice ended at two. The Atlantic hadn't warmed enough by the third week of March for extended swimming, but the sun blazed and the guys splashed and flashed their bods. All those well-defined pecs and lats, glutes and biceps, were lovely to behold but also a challenge. Who could gaze upon such sensual physiques—like athletes in the first Olympic games who competed nude—and not be beguiled?

Not Two-J's Singer, and not the group of college girls on spring break from somewhere up north: Katie, Taylor, Emily, and Tiffany, who found them near the beach volleyball court.

"You guys are really something," Tiffany said.

Tiff was the leader of the four-girl pack. Big brown eyes and the oversized breasts straight guys liked, but which Jess found particularly off-putting. Emily was the prettiest: blonde, tall, blue-eyed, and freckled, an American beauty rose.

"Are you, like, athletes or something?" Tiff asked.

Big Barnes, a right-handed reliever destined for Triple-A, or possibly straight to the Show, started snickering. Big was nearly as tall as Jess, but big all over, built, as Grandpa Jack liked to say, like a brick shithouse. Barrel chest, beer belly, and a head like a granite block with eye holes. Jess had played with and competed against Big at three different levels of the minors and didn't much like him.

Big said, "We play for the Mets."

"Or will someday," Jess added, not wanting to mislead the girls.

"We're *bush* leaguers." Rah winked. "But hopefully, not for long."

Katie and Taylor didn't know a bat from a bazooka, but Tiff and Emily, call-me-Emmy, proclaimed they were fans.

"Then maybe"—Rah had such a great smile that when he smiled the world and these cute girls smiled with him—"you hear of Jess's father, Joe Singer? He pitched in the big leagues."

All four girls looked impressed. Emmy, who hadn't taken her eyes off Jess since the girls wandered up, said, *Oh yes*, she'd heard of him, *wasn't he famous?*

By then, the group was walking up the beach approaching the boardwalk.

"Hey," Big said, "wanna get a drink?"

"We'd love to," Tiff replied, "right, girls?"

The others nodded, including Emmy, who continued to ogle Jess. "Only," she said, "you know a place that doesn't card? We're not all twenty-one."

"Doan worry," Jorge Escobar said. "*Yo tampoco.*"

Jorge was from the DR, and no surprise, a shortstop.

"Doan worry," Jorge repeated. "They always serve us."

They agreed to change then meet at Big Wave Dave's, a dive bar and restaurant overlooking the Atlantic. There was live music on the deck, and two-for-one drinks until nine. The guys cleaned up and headed out in Jess's Land Rover, looking for love and trouble. Jorge smelled like he'd showered in cologne. Rah used so much product his hair stood up like a shark fin. Big, all 250 pounds of Big, called shottie and rode beside Jess, who wondered what the hell he was doing.

"That blonde," Big said, "was *hot.*"

From the back, Jorge yodeled, "*Mamacita!*"

Big added, "I'd fuck her in a minute."

"More like twenty seconds," Jess said, and the other guys laughed.

Rah called from the back. "She outta yo league, Big. You see how she lookin' at my boy Yess?"

"Just saying," Big replied. "I wouldn't throw her outta bed."

I would, Jess thought, turning into Big Wave's parking lot.

They found the girls sipping *mojitos* on the deck, squeezed into short skirts and tank tops. Emmy was really something: not just pretty, but beautiful, and tall enough for Jess, five-ten or eleven in heels. She kept smiling in a way that made him uncomfortable, and as often happened when he was pretending to be straight when out with guys, he couldn't think of anything to say. Not Big. He was grinding with one of the brunettes a few feet away on the dance floor, Katie or Taylor, Jess couldn't tell them apart. Little Tiff, big breasts and the gift of gab, smiled at Rah and Jorge, two stools away from Jess.

Emmy's long, straight hair smelled like Juicy Fruit. She laid a finger on his wrist.

"So, I looked up your dad. You look just like him." She wrinkled her nose. "Only cuter."

Jess felt his face grow hot.

"I hope you don't think I'm, like, some crazy stalker." She smiled and shrugged. It was a Pretty Girl shrug—both tanned shoulders rose towards her ears—a gesture Jess remembered from Redondo High. Emmy, who had clearly been gorgeous her entire life, would have fit right in at Redondo.

"I mean, usually, it's guys hitting on me. It's just..." She bobbed up on her toes and kissed him, then stepped back and Pretty Girl shrugged again. "There." She smiled. "I've been wanting to do that since I saw you."

"*Wow.*" Jess felt like a possum in headlights. Big caught his eye and winked. Jess glanced at Rah but couldn't gauge what his friend was thinking. Rah's eyes burned with an indecipherable message. Then the normal bar noise kicked in and the band began to play. Or maybe it had been playing all along.

"You want another drink?" Jess asked.

"Sure," Emmy said. "But you know what I really want?"

Oh no, Jess thought. "Wanna dance?"

After drinks and more drinks, burgers and grouper sandwiches, dancing on the deck and goofing around, it was getting late. Someone had to make the next move. For Jess, the only acceptable move was heading home. But Big was drunk and necking with one of the brunettes on the dance floor. When the song ended, Tiff suggested they move to the girls' condo and continue the party.

Big and Jorge thought that sounded super and arranged to ride in the girls' car. Jess agreed to tail them, driving with Emmy up front and Rah in back with Tiff, who was describing where they went to school: some small college outside Ithaca.

"Wait a sec," Emmy shouted.

Then she laughed, and Jess, who was struggling to steer between the white lines, glanced her way.

"Didn't you guys say you were going to be at Syracuse?"

"That's right," Rah said. "Mos likely."

"Well, Syracuse," said Tiffany, "is like fifty minutes from where we go to school. We could see you play!"

"Thas amazing," Rah called from the back.

Jess agreed. He glanced at Emmy, who smiled and dropped her hand on his knee. She really was pretty; if he had any interest in girls, he'd be interested in her.

Later that night, driving home, with Rah beside him, Jess contemplated the future. Big and Jorge had stayed with the girls. They said they'd Uber home in time for practice. Or maybe later that night. Or who knew when; Jess didn't care. Big was a douche. Jess was surprised Rah hadn't stayed; Tiff seemed hot for him.

Rah asked, "Yo, Yess, you got a girl in Cali?"

Jess considered lying. "Nah, I'm staying single till I get to the Show. What about you, a *novia* in Cuernavaca?"

"No way." Rah smiled, and his teeth flashed in the dark. "So, where you picking up your Spanish, Yess?"

"From my *chingalera amigos, pinches cabrones*," Jess replied, stringing together every Mexican swear he knew.

Rah laughed. "My agent warned me, girls in the minors wanna be your Baby Mama, collect a big check every month."

Jess had been warned about the same thing. "So, you think Tiff?"

"*Que curvas,*" Rah said, "*y yo no tengo frenas.*"

"What does that mean?"

"What curves, and I ain't got no brakes."

"You think little Tiff and her curves wanted some of your dick?" Saying *dick* to Rah, Jess felt a tingle. "So she can carry your baby?"

"*No se.* What about Emmy? Girl was all over you."

"I think she *just* wanted my dick."

"Why didn't you give it to her?"

For a millisecond, Jess almost told Rah the truth, but decided, *No way. Not now, not ever.* He said, "Not my scene." Then, worried Rah might get the wrong right idea, he added, "Not with Big and Jorge all fucked up and the other girls around. I'm more private."

"*Yo también.*"

"Also, I don't want to show at practice hung over." He glanced at his friend. "I know it's a long shot, but I'm hoping they'll take me north."

"You think so?"

"Not really, but I'm gonna make it hard to send me down."

"You never know. A vet gets hurt, and they need you. You on the forty-man roster?"

Jess nodded.

"*Yo también.*"

Then they didn't speak until Jess stopped in front of the complex where Rah and a bunch of the other Latin players lived during spring training.

"Thanks for driving."

"No problem."

Then, just as Rah was getting out of the car—later Jess would wonder if he'd been planning this, or if the question had popped out of his mouth spontaneously and unplanned: "So, if we both end up in Syracuse, you wanna room together?"

The light from the dome lit the strong angles of Rah's face. "I'd like that. But we both know you're not gonna be there long."

Jess grinned. "Neither are you."

"Long enough to teach you more Spanish."

"*Gracias.*"

"*Hasta mañana.*"

Rah closed the door, and Jess drove home.

When Jack answered at nine in the a.m., his son said, "Hi, Dad."

Uh-oh, Jack thought. *This is bad.* "You're up early, Joey."

"Lot on my mind."

Jack waited for Joe to explain, but he didn't, which was just like him. "I'm sure there is."

Joe began, "The cancer—"

Jack held his breath and looked around the condo, which he'd bought decorated and had never bothered to re-do. The fake potted plant next to the breakfront. The glass chandelier he wouldn't have picked but was too lazy to change.

"—is pretty bad."

"How bad? Has it, you know, moved?"

"They don't think so. They want to do some test."

"What test?"

"I don't know. Something about Jackie Gleason."

"What the fuck you talking about?"

"I don't know!" Joe shouted and for a moment or two, maybe a dozen, they sat wreathed in silence, thousands of miles apart. Finally, Joe said, "Whatever this score is, and maybe it's Groucho, not Gleason, means the cancer is more likely to *met—*, to *meta—*. Fuck, I can never say it right."

"I know what you mean."

"Anyway, I gotta start treatment."

"What kind?" Jack asked, but he didn't ask what he really wanted to know. The kind where afterwards your dick don't work and you piss your pants all the time?

"I haven't decided yet. We meet with the surgeon this afternoon."

"So, you're having surgery?"

"I told you, we haven't decided."

We, Jack thought. *He means Frannie.*

"The reason I'm calling."

"Aintcha calling to tell me about the big C?"

"I'm calling about Jess. You've been seeing a lot more of him than we have."

"You ain't been seeing him at all."

There was a long pause, and Jack wanted to hit himself for being such a putz.

"Before I start treatment," Joe said. "I want to tell Jess in person."

Jack thought about all the things he might say. How Jess was doing great. How he might make the club and needed to focus like a mother-fucker, so now was no time for distractions. Then he considered what Joey was facing.

"So," he asked, "when you coming?"

"We'll be there tomorrow, Pops. Frannie too. On the red-eye."

Later, Jack sat with the phone in his hand, trying to remember the last time Joey called him *Pops. A long goddamn time.* He set the receiver in its cradle and headed to the john for an old man whiz, which was like water torture, drop by effing drop. Then he started his morning workout, forty push-ups, forty crunches. If it was good enough for Paul Newman, super-Yid, it was good enough for Jack Singer, one in a million.

CHAPTER SIX

After surviving the red-eye, San Francisco-Atlanta, then a regional jet, Atlanta-West Palm, Joe and Frannie rented a full-size from Avis and drove north towards First Data Field in Port Saint Lucie. During Joe's playing days, the stadium complex was brand-new and wasn't called First Data, but damn if he could remember its former name. Occupying the passenger seat, Joe was lost in thought. He had a great deal to think about, most of it upsetting, but he was looking forward to surprising Jess. Jack, whom they'd sworn to secrecy, was driving up from Delray to join them.

Last night, while they waited to board at SFO, Jack had called to say Jess was scheduled to throw a few innings today. Which, Jack added, was unplanned so maybe the Mets were considering taking Jess north when the team broke camp.

Joe remembered heading north for the first time with the big club. He was twenty-four, still married to his first wife, Sarah, who later betrayed him with the first baseman, Perez. What a piece of work, Sarah. These days, he didn't know where she lived, or even if she was alive. Thirty-three years ago, Joe was so clueless he didn't realize he was with the wrong woman until it was too late. To be honest, he didn't know much of anything back then, but man, could he bring it. Even prone as Joe was to self-doubt, at twenty-four he was not only cocksure, but cocky. He was *that* gifted, blessed by the God of Pitchers and Catchers, who giveth and taketh away fastballs.

Joe glanced at Frannie. She'd come along to the surgeon yesterday. Unlike Dr. Perlman, Dr. Slocum had the warm and fuzzy rating of a six-foot iguana. Thirty seconds into the consult, Joe's brain shut down. Afterwards, all he could remember was that Slocum, a surgeon, had recommended surgery. *That way, you'll grow old with your beautiful wife, without having to worry about the cancer spreading.*

Or getting a boner, Joe thought.

He remembered their fabulous lovemaking three nights ago. Man, if he could bottle that and take a swig when he needed a pick-me-up. He reached across the center console and laid a hand on Frannie's thigh, midway between waist and knee. She glanced his way and smiled.

Jack was outside the main gate watching the crowd filter in when Frannie appeared. She still looked like a million bucks, his daughter-in-law. Extra tall and lean, maybe some wear on her tires and gray in her hair, but still so big and shapely, with spooky light blue eyes, everything about her austere and symmetrical, like that Jewish Wonder Woman actress. Jack reached up to kiss her cheek; she was a good five inches taller than he was, now that he'd started shrinking. Another few years, if he didn't croak, she'd be looking down at the top of his head.

"Hey, Jack," she said in his embrace. "Great to see you."

"Likewise." He stepped back. "So, where's Joey?"

"He went in the players' entrance."

"He's not going say nothing to Jess?"

"Not until after the game."

"So what's he doing in the clubhouse?"

"He wanted to see Jess. He misses him."

What about me? Jack wondered.

"And he wanted to say hi to Mac."

Jack could feel Frannie's spooky eyes pin his, as she weighed how much to say.

"He doesn't tell anyone what's bothering him. Not even me. I blame you for that."

He knew what she meant. *Like father, like son.* "Let's find our seats."

Frannie fell in beside him. After they passed through the turnstile, she took his arm. He guessed all was forgiven.

"Hey, Jack." She smiled. What a looker, once and always. "Buy me a beer?"

Joe couldn't find Jess. Not in the locker room, where half a dozen young guys Joe didn't recognize were dressing. Not in the trainer's suite, empty except for the familiar scents of gauze and Icy-Hot. Not in the corridors or weight room, with its glistening array of free weights and ellipticals, bikes and treadmills, iso devices for every muscle. None of this, back in his day. Above every machine a screen, and mirrors, mirrors everywhere, covering the walls and even part of the ceiling, as if the weight room were a high-tech whorehouse, which did exist in his day, though he'd never been to one. He was just about to abandon his plan and head for the stands knowing it must be getting near game-time when he heard footsteps. Soon enough, he spied the Mets' new manager, Greg Gallagher, whom Joe had never met, as well as several members of his coaching staff, who were older and less fit than the manager, including his old friend, Mac.

"I heard you was here," Mac drawled, wrapping Joe in a manly embrace, followed by an equally manly shoulder thump.

"Who'd you hear from?" Joe stepped out of Mac's arms, embarrassed, because Gallagher and the others were watching.

"Rizzo, the equipment manager," Mac replied. "Who else been round long enough to know your sorry ass?" Putting his mouth near Joe's ear, Mac growled, "About damn time too."

"Joe," said Gallagher, hand extended: smart dark eyes, kiltered sideways; well-barbered graying beard. "Glad to meet you."

Strangers often tongue-tied Joe, and he couldn't find a single inoffensive sentiment, settling for, "Likewise," which fell with a thud on his embarrassed ears.

"Guess you're here to see Jess throw," Gallagher said. "You must be proud of him."

"I am," Joe said, pleased to be able to answer two questions with just two words.

"Well, we've got a game to play."

Gallagher and his coaches headed towards the field entrance. Mac called over his shoulder, "See you after the game, Joe."

Mac disappeared with the others. Joe looked around the weight room. He wished he'd said more to Gallagher, but what did it matter? This wasn't about him. Joe inhaled the comforting stink of jockdom, then went to find Jack and Frannie in the stands.

By the top of the fifth, Frannie and Jack had each finished two ginor-mous Bud Lites. Joe had decided not to drink, so while his wife and father were getting loud and tipsy, Joe was simply enjoying the sun-shine. Unlike the past month in Santa Rosa, where it had been nothing but rain, rain, drear, and rain, matching his mood, here the day was so nice and warm, Joe felt almost happy. Jack was in fine, aggravating form, joking with the fans around them. From time to time, he'd razz Joe about the weight he'd gained by calling him *Buttercup*. So what? He was used to Jack's needling, and even Jack being a dick gave him some-thing to think about other than his prostate and what to do and what was going to happen to him. Then, wonder of wonders, Jess strode in from the bullpen. He hopped over the third base foul line, a good luck tic since he was fourteen. Mid-hop, the PA announcer announced, "Now pitching for your Mets, Jess Singer."

Jess looked mature and grown-up, so tall and lean, all business, all magic, as if he'd become a different person since Joe last saw him, though his ball cap was still tugged characteristically low on his forehead. If Jess knew he and Frannie were there, which he must—Mac must have told him—he gave no sign. Jess focused on the plate and poured in his warm-ups; then he stood behind the mound while the ball whistled a happy tune around the infield. Jess bounced the resin bag on his palm then the back of his hand, and a candle of paternal pride ignited inside

Joe. He'd done the exact same thing when he pitched, except it had been his right hand, not the left. Frannie glanced at him, eyes bright, and Joe knew what she was thinking: *Rosin bag just like you.*

Jess settled on the rubber. Maybe he didn't know they were watching, or didn't care, or didn't know where they were sitting. Jess peered towards home for the sign. Joe grabbed Frannie's hand. He almost couldn't bear to watch. Jess covered the lower half of his face with his glove, rocked forward and back then forward, and the ball shot towards home almost too fast to see. The overmatched batter swung and missed—and not just the first pitch, but the second and fourth ones too. *Strike three!*

"Two-J's!" Jack shouted.

Joe wanted to shout too, but Jess's teenage years, when parents were *so embarrassing!* had trained him to zip his lip, not just because parents were a source of shame, but because everyone knew who he was. Frannie kept quiet too, expressing her emotions by squeezing Joe's hand. Jack was the designated family shouter, and over the next six pitches, there was a lot to shout about. A weak tapper to third for the second out, and four pitches later, a called third strike on a curve that must have had a foot of drop. Jess punched his mitt with his left hand and started towards the dugout, only then turning slightly to glance over his shoulder, looking straight at their section.

"He knows we're here." Frannie squeezed Joe's hand again.

"Of course," Jack thundered. "He's not an idjit."

"What do you think, Joe?" She glanced directly at him for the first time since Jess retired the side. Joe was crying. Tears of joy, he hoped, but he wasn't sure.

CHAPTER SEVEN

After the game, combing their hair in the mirrors above the row of locker room sinks, Jess asked Rah if he'd like to meet his parents.

"Who wouldn't wanna meet Joe Singer?" Rah met his eyes in the mirror. "But, ya know?"

Rah winked, and Jess's heart just about melted.

"We already meet, two years ago. He probably doan remember. I also meet your *abuelo loco.*"

Jess ran a comb through his dark wavy hair. Why didn't he remember? "You met my mom?"

Rah shook his head. "I hear she very *bonita.*"

"Where'd you hear that?"

"Coach Mac." Rubbing gel into his short, dyed hair, Rah grinned. "So how come you so *feo?*"

Before he could work up an appropriate insult, Big Barnes, trailed by a couple minor league relievers, crossed behind Jess, and clapped his bare shoulder.

"Hey, Singer. Great outing."

"Thanks."

Big and his crew slid out of the room. It seemed to Jess, and he'd been over and over this, that if Big broke camp with the big club, he wouldn't. And if he went north, Big wouldn't. Or maybe neither of them would. Either way, it was out of character for Big to say what he did.

Rah asked, "You like that guy?"

Jess shrugged.

"*Muy pendejo.*"

Jess said, "I thought *you* liked him."

"Nah, he Jorge's friend."

Jess thought back to the college girl night. The next day and for days after, Big and Jorge had boasted how they'd nailed some coeds.

"Big's okay," Jess said with more conviction than he felt since he didn't trust the fucker one bit. "My mom,"—he grinned—"used to be some kind of hottie."

Later, Jess was sitting with his parents and Grandpa Jack at a steak house favored by team brass, when Mac entered, spotted them, and headed for their table. Jess watched Dad stand and smile. He didn't have many friends from his playing days, but he was always glad to see Mac. Then Mom stood.

"Hey, good-looking." Mac kissed her. "Whatcha been feeding this guy?"

Jack said, "I been asking the same damn thing."

Dad ignored them. "Can you join us?"

"Not tonight." Mac slung a heavy arm over each of his parents' shoulders and widened his button eyes, which always reminded Jess of Little Orphan Annie's eyes. He inclined his head towards the far corner of the dining room. "We got a working dinner, and I gotta tell you, Jess is making it hard as billy-goat turds to send him down. Was he lights out or wha—aaat?"

Mac set out for the corner table, leaving Jess with a big grin on his face.

"Did I tell you!" Grandpa Jack cried, then waved for the waitress, Jess thought, to order drinks.

Mom and Dad sat down. "You're probably wondering," Mom began, "why Dad and I haven't been here."

"Christ," Jack muttered. "Can't you let Two-J's enjoy what Mac said?"

"I *have* been wondering."

"I got a little medical problem." Dad looked down, embarrassed. The waitress arrived.

"Stoli rocks," Jack said. "Twist of lime. Make it a double. Anyone else?"

"Goose Island IPA," Jess answered.

Mom shook her head and so did Dad. The young waitress bustled off, and Jess watched his grandfather's eyes follow the metronome of her bottom.

"What Dad's trying to tell you," Mom began.

Jack muttered, "In his own ridiculous way."

Jess looked at his wonderful, one-of-a-kind dad, Jewish Joe.

"I got cancer."

Jess felt his world unhinge. *Dad! Cancer! Jewish Joe!* When the world stopped whirling and up was again up and down was down, he asked, "What kind?"

Just then, Rah Ramirez, hair gelled, cheeks and eyes shining, wearing gray slacks with a matching gray silk shirt, top buttons open to reveal a double-stranded gold necklace—clearly, Rah's top-of-the-line outfit—drew up beside them and smiled his killer smile, waiting to be introduced.

After dinner, Joe and Frannie followed Jess to his apartment where they provided details. What kind of cancer? *Prostate.* How serious, Dad? *We don't know yet. But I'm pretty high on the Gleason scale.*

"What's that?"

Joe shrugged and watched his son try to process this scary information, which he knew was a lot to lay on a twenty-two-year-old. Jess's long, lean face, much like Joe's own, had always revealed his emotions.

"Tell me the truth," Jess said. "You're not going to die?"

"Someday."

"Dad's going to be fine." Frannie patted Jess's knee. "It's just, you know, scary."

"I didn't want to upset you," Joe said, "when you're pitching so great and have a chance to go north."

Fear then tears spread across Jess's cheeks.

"Family hug," Frannie announced, standing. Jess and Joe stood too. *Family hug!* They'd practiced it since Jess was little. Hugging his family muted the drumming in Joe's chest. Looking up into his son's eyes, he marveled at how tall Jess had grown, six-five, at least. When they walked together on the street, everyone else was so much smaller. He sometimes thought they were a separate species: *Athletus Erectus*.

"Jess," he said, "that curve you froze Suarez with, to end the fifth? Better than I ever threw."

Jess raised his head off Frannie's shoulder. "Thanks, Dad. But we're talking about you, not me."

"You know Dad doesn't like talking about himself."

"I mean it," Joe continued. "One hell of a hook."

Frannie laughed. "See what I mean?"

"What happens next, Dad?"

Joe shrugged. He didn't know which treatment to pick, so he chose to play the fool, a familiar and comfortable role. "I still think they'll keep you in Syracuse until after the Super Two deadline."

"You know I was talking about you, right?"

"Of course, I know." He looked closely at Jess. Still so young, he barely needed to shave. None of the Singer men, despite their dark hair, could raise much of a beard. "How dumb do you think I am, Jess? And don't say, 'The dumbest Jew in America.' That's Jack's line."

Joe's plan was working. Jess smiled.

"When I know, you'll know. What you got to do is keep pitching lights out."

Later, Jess invited them to stay over, offering to sleep on the couch, but Joe and Frannie were exhausted from the red-eye and looking forward to the king-size bed waiting in their beachside Westin. As they were walking out, Frannie said, "Jess, I almost forgot to mention. Your friend, Rah, seems really nice."

"And he's got a cannon for an arm," Joe added.

Jess smiled, clearly pleased to be talking about his friend. "I'm glad you like him. He's my Mac, best friend and catcher."

Something moved in Jess's eyes, which Joe couldn't read or understand. But he suddenly felt so tired from the long day, the uncomfortable conversations, and who knew, maybe the cancer, he feared he would pass out standing up.

"If we're both sent to Syracuse, we're gonna room together."

"How nice," Frannie said. "I really did like him."

They walked out to the rental car. Barely able to keep his eyes open, Joe asked Frannie to drive. The next thing he knew they were in the hotel parking lot, and she was jostling his shoulder to wake him up.

After breakfast in the lobby, they sat on their balcony holding hands. On the beach below, whitecaps tumbled towards shore. Above, puffy clouds tufted a bright sky.

"I've been thinking," Joe began. "What to do."

"So have I."

"You first."

"You bum." Frannie faced him. "As much as I love your Little Big Man."

"What?"

She dropped her hand on his crotch and smiled. "And what he can do. And despite how much sex has meant to us, we're still young."

"No," Joe said, "Jess is young."

"Young enough. And I want you around," Frannie finished, "for a long, long time."

"Even without?" Joe couldn't make himself say it. "You know."

"Between you and your cock, I choose you."

Joe peered into his wife's eyes. "So you're saying have surgery and not radiation."

"I want whatever gives you the best chance of living a long time. I can't lose anyone else."

Then she was in his arms, and in this moment of his greatest distress, Joe was characteristically more concerned with giving than receiving comfort.

"It's okay." He rubbed Frannie's back. "It's just…"

"What?"

"I hated that surgeon."

"So did I. What a bastard."

"Why don't I call Doc Perlman to see if he can recommend a different one?"

"Or maybe," Frannie said, sounding more like herself. "He could recommend a surgeon near here? With all the old men in South Florida, prostates have got to be big business. Maybe Jack knows someone."

"No way," Joe said. "Nothing ever goes wrong with Jack. And he doesn't know any men, just women."

"Your dad."

"I know, one in a million." He placed his hand on Frannie's knee. "I wonder," he said, "if you might throw a fella a bone."

"A fella with a boner?"

"I can't believe you said that."

"I can't either."

Frannie stood, and Joe followed her inside.

CHAPTER EIGHT

Jack was finishing his crunches when Glad arrived. Climbing off the carpet, Jack wondered, not for the first time, if she'd hidden a spy-camera in his apartment that alerted her when he was flat on his back and sweated up because half the time that was when she appeared. It wasn't always the same time of day. Jack didn't keep a schedule, regularity having always been, in his opinion, the nobgoblin of puny minds. Sometimes first thing, sometimes later, crunches and pushups. The only thing Jack liked to do the same time each morning was move his bowels. Eight-sixteen, boom-down.

Glad seemed to like him sweaty. Or maybe she liked washing the sweat off, or really, who knew what old broads in general, and Glad in particular, wanted from him? Maybe just to feel they ain't dead yet, just like Jack.

So, he opened the door, and after he gave Glad what she had coming—or maybe it was Glad giving it to him—Jack wondered when she was going to take off? Joe and Frannie were driving down from Port Saint Lucie for lunch, and he needed to pine up the place. Unbury dishes from the kitchen sink, tidy the toilets, sponge moustache trim from the guest sink. But Glad wasn't going.

"Surprise." Jack climbed out of bed. "My son and daughter-in-law are stopping by for lunch."

Before he could finish, *So you gotta scram, cause I gotta clean,* she replied, "I'd love to meet them."

He shot Glad a stink eye, which missed the mark.

"I ever tell you I saw him pitch?"

Jack turned back on his way to the head. "No shit."

"My first husband Artie—"

First time she mentioned his name.

"—the original Mister Goldberg, was quite the fan."

"How'd he do?" Jack asked.

"How'd Artie do what?"

"How'd Joe pitch?"

"You think I remember?" Glad widened her mascara-ed eyes. "It was thirty years ago."

Women, Jack thought. "I gotta clean before they arrive."

She stared straight at him, as if daring him to ask.

"Maybe you could make the bed? Or something? On account of your *arrival"*—Jack winked—"I'm behind schedule."

He ducked into the john before she could say something smart.

Jess, Rah, Big Barnes, Jorge, and a group of younger players with non-roster invites to big league camp were out to dinner. These supremely gifted young men had learned to think of themselves as selected by destiny, because how else to account for their abilities, so far beyond those of the boys they'd grown up with? Surely, it was Fate, or the hand of God, that had raised them up, not just from American towns no one had heard of, but increasingly from islands and countries far to the south where the only way out was *beisbol.*

And even if some of the young men suspected their success didn't exclusively depend on the blessing of the God of Pitchers, Catchers, and Batters, realizing that their abilities might have to do with DNA, they'd all been taught to believe there were athletes and there were politicians, and you couldn't be both. MLB ran training sessions that emphasized it was best to keep your yap shut. Look what had happened to Colin Kaepernick. Dude never played again. Even Black Lives Matter and the murder of George Floyd only changed things for a minute. MLB-mandated training prepped young players on how to deal with uncomfortable questions. *No matter what reporters ask about this, that, or the other thing, just say, I'm here to give 110 percent for the team.*

Jess was thinking about politics, because since they'd arrived at Wings N Things to watch a Heat game, a message had been scrolling across the bottom of the screen about a school shooting not far from where Grandpa Jack lived. Did Jess remark on it to anyone? *No.* Did anyone mention it to him? *Of course not.* Just for a moment, Jess fantasized about coming out after he was done playing and becoming an advocate for gay rights in baseball. That got him so upset he nearly choked on an Infernally Hot wing. He looked around to see if anyone had noticed. No way. Too busy sucking down suds. After several flocks of wings chased with an equally large number of pitchers, the guys were considering which burgers to order when Big stood and waved his massive arms.

"With cut down coming this week—"

"And next," someone called from the periphery.

"Right." Big grinned. "*Final* cut is next week. I got a little wager to propose."

Big paused, and Rah, seated to Jess's right, translated for some of the Latin guys.

"Whoever survives this week's cuts buys dinner here Friday night, okay? Whoever survives next week, takes everyone out for steak!"

Big's blocky head, his cheeks and neck black with stubble, swung toward Jess. "Hey, Singer, if you make it, you gonna pay up?"

"Why wouldn't I?"

"I don't know," Big replied, "too frugal?"

Jess stood up from his high-top table and stepped towards Big. What was this? A Jew joke? Fuck this guy.

"*Frugal?*" he asked. "I didn't know you knew big words."

"Sure," Big replied. "Frugal's the same as cheap. All you—"

Jess took another step towards Big, who out-weighed him by forty pounds.

"—guys who signed for big bucks, still got every penny. Dontcha? The son of *Jewish Joe*?"

"Don't worry," Jess said, and from the corner of his eye, he could see Rah getting ready to stand up beside him, just in case. "If I make the *big* club, I'll buy steaks *big* as your fucking head."

"That's two Bigs in one sentence, Singer. Don't wear out my name, okay?" Big grinned at the other players. "*Dude*, I'm just yanking your chain. We cool, okay?"

Jess nodded. In addition to being a total douche, Big just might be an anti-Semite. Still, he wasn't as dumb as he looked. "Yeah, we cool."

"Don't worry, Singer. There's no way you're buying my steak 'cause you're not going north. But if you're not too *frugal*, how about another round right now?"

Jess started towards the bar waving a credit card, as the players around him whistled and clapped.

CHAPTER NINE

Despite his splendid spring, Jess was assigned to Triple-A Syracuse. In his hidden heart, he'd known it was coming, and he wasn't the only one. The day before final cuts, Joel Grant, a columnist for the *Post*, opined, "Having Jess Singer start the season in Flushing would be tantamount to malpractice."

Keeping him in the minors past the Super Two deadline would give the club another year before he'd qualify for arbitration; Jess understood that. But what his heart knew and what his mind accepted were gloves of a different leather. Hadn't he put up the best numbers of any Mets pitcher except Rick Heynen, the team ace? Wouldn't the manager—and if not the manager, the Mets' long-suffering fans—want him there from day one? All the pundits said the NL East was going to be a three-or-four team race, and every win, including April wins, was important, helping to determine which team would reach the promised land of the post-season and which team wouldn't.

Even so, the Mets had assigned him to Syracuse. He understood. If he made it—hell, dream big, if he became a star—the Mets would save millions, maybe twenty million on his sixth year's salary. He understood: baseball was a business. What really, really, *really* pissed Jess off, however, was that Big Barnes was going north with the club.

Jess's final morning in major league camp, Greg Gallagher called him into his office. "Jess," the manager said from the other side of his desk, his eyes not quite making contact, maybe twenty degrees off, which was damn disconcerting. "We're expecting great things from you, you know that, right?"

Jess nodded.

"A baseball lifer like you."

Gallagher grinned, knowing Jess would get the joke. *Baseball lifers* were grizzled ex-players like Mac, who'd stayed in the game their entire life. Dad wasn't a lifer.

Gallagher continued, "So I don't have to explain why you're being sent down."

"No sir." Jess felt his features darken. "An extra year of low-cost control for the club."

The manager's eyes narrowed, and for a second, he seemed to peer directly at Jess as if he could not only see the frown on his face but hear the angry beat of his heart. "The worst thing you could do is go down and sulk. You understand what I'm saying, son?"

Jess nodded.

"You may think, after how you pitched this spring, you deserve to go north." Gallagher squinted again, and fine lines, like cracks in sheer ice, shot from his eyes across his cheeks towards his ears. "Tell me, is that what you think?"

Jess wondered where Gallagher was going with this? Like every other aspiring big leaguer, Jess had watched *Bull Durham* dozens of times and knew the correct response. "No sir, I don't think that at all. I just want to get better every day, give one hundred and ten percent." Jess grinned. "And help the team win."

Gallagher grinned too. "I bet you do."

"I do. But if you're asking if I think I'm one of the thirteen, or even, twelve best pitchers, yes sir, I do."

"To be honest," Gallagher said, "so do I."

Jess couldn't believe his manager had said that, and inside his nearly hairless chest, Jess's heart beat faster. He wanted to thank GG, but that didn't seem manly, and Jess was very careful about potential dings to his manhood.

"Keep working on throwing your four-seamer up and bouncing the two when you're ahead in the count. Your change could be better to righties, you know that. And work on adding and subtracting, like we discussed."

"Yes sir."

"You know you don't have to call me *Sir.*"

Jess couldn't remember when he'd started *Sir-ing* his managers. Must have picked it up from Dad, who was always respectful. He certainly hadn't learned it from Grandpa Jack.

"Yes sir," he said. "I mean, okay."

Gallagher squinted in that quizzical way he had, half thoughtful, half myopic, his eyes directed somewhere past Jess's ear. "At Syracuse, Rah Ramirez will catch you. I already spoke to Dusty Rhodes. You guys are friends, right?"

"We agreed to room together, if we both started in Syracuse."

"So, you're not surprised."

"No," Jess admitted, remembering to swallow the *sir.* "But I don't like it."

"I wouldn't expect you to."

Yet there was a part of him, Jess realized, which was looking forward to starting in Syracuse—not that he had any choice. That way, he'd get to share an apartment with Rah.

Jack wasn't sure about this new intimacy with Glad. For months she was all about *Slam bam, thank you, Jack. Here's a kugel for your trouble.*

Suddenly she'd maneuvered into meeting Joe and Frannie, and not just once, two days out of three. And now she was greasing the rails without being asked, very nice, of course, but out of left field, for Joe to see some fancy doc at Sloane Kettering, the friend of her own fancy doc son, whose name and profession Jack hadn't known until two days ago. Accustomed to more rigorous boundaries, Jack could feel himself getting sucked into Glad's slipstream, and Glad getting tangled up in his business. Emotional tentacles were attaching themselves everywhere, the exact sort of involvement he swore he'd never allow again after losing Shirley three years ago, not to mention his first wife, Joey's poor mom, in the eighties.

But here he sat in the Huntington Pointe Café, sharing a late breakfast with Glad, Joe, and Frannie, conversing like two old married couples. And while he and Glad were sure as hell old, even after snipping a few, they sure weren't married, not like Joe and Frannie, twenty-five years and counting. So why were Glad's silver glitter fingernails nestled in his left palm? Why was her bony knee nuzzling his under the table? He shot her a look like, *What the hell?* But she only batted her lashes, which were black as licorice, then went right on chatting up Frannie. Ostensibly, this was so Jack could talk to his son, only sometimes conversing with Joey was like pulling molars: Joey hadn't said more than eight words since the meal began.

Their waitress, Eileen, no spring duck herself, emerged from the kitchen balancing platters of eggs, pig meat, and home fries, toasted bagels and schmears for the Singers, a sad little scoop of cottage cheese and sliced tomatoes for Glad, who ate like a nuthatch, which was why she weighed a buck-five, buck-ten, tops. Joe and Frannie set upon their food with intent. They hadn't said much all morning; some sort of tension between them. One thing Jack had always admired about Frannie, in addition to her physical gifts: she didn't eat like a girly-girl. Of course, being taller than most men, she needed fuel.

Glad was cutting her tomato slices into bird-size nibbles. Every once in a while, she'd drop four nodules of cottage cheese onto a square of tomato and pass it through her bright pink lips. Jack smeared cream cheese on his Long Island, sliced into his over-easies, and watched as golden yolk oozed into his mound of paprika'd potatoes. He larded his fork with potatoes, egg, and sausage, swallowed like a trout hitting a fly, then followed up with a bite of bagel. He glanced towards Glad, who was staring at him amused or horrified, maybe both.

"What's a matter? Ain't you never seen a man eat before?"

Joey tapped Jack's wrist and passed his hand across his own upper lip.

"*What?*"

Glad said, "He's trying to tell you there's enough cream cheese on your stache to schmear half of Boca."

Jack glanced from Glad to Joey, then napkin-ed his lip. Looking up from her food, Frannie said, "Glad, I want to thank you for reaching out to your son about Joe."

Glad said, "I was happy to do it. It's no big deal."

Frannie answered, "It's a very big deal."

She turned towards Joe, who looked up from his food, embarrassed. After a moment, he said, "Yes, thank you so much."

All the thanking brought Joe's prostate to the table and turned Jack's stomach. He sipped his coffee, which was just the way he liked it, not like the sludge they served at Starbucks.

Frannie said, "You must be really proud of your son, a doctor at Sloane Kettering." She smiled. "Every Jewish mother's dream. Not that I would know."

"I *am* proud of him." She glanced at Jack. "But compared to an all-star pitcher, Jewish doctors are a dime a dozen. Isn't that right, Jack?"

Of course, that was right. There weren't hardly any Jewish pitchers, everyone knew that. So what was Glad saying? That he wasn't proud enough of Joey? Of course, he was proud of Joey. Wasn't he?

CHAPTER TEN

Joe and Frannie flew to New York Tuesday afternoon. The next morning Joe arrived at the Sloane Kettering medical arts building for his first appointment. Frannie sat beside him in the crowded waiting room, which was loud with whispers. Several nearby patients were clearly mid-treatment. Gaunt and bald, male and female, some wearing wigs, some not bothering. The large room obviously served a range of specialists; the women couldn't be there for prostate cancer.

Joe leaned towards Frannie, whispering like the other waiting whisperers. On one hand, it was comforting to be at Sloane Kettering; on the other, it horrified. No longer could Joe deny, as he had for months, that he'd boarded the bus for an away game in the League of the Sick and Maybe Very Sick. He'd even caught the especially morbid thought, and Joe didn't know how or why it had found his mind's mitt, that Sloane was where you went if you were going to die.

They hadn't been waiting long, certainly less long than many of the others, when a door opened at the front of the room and a nurse announced, "Joe Singer, for Doctor Bernstein."

Joe started forward. Why was he being summoned so quickly, in effect jumping the medical line? Joe was always embarrassed when his name was announced in public, not only after the betting scandal all those years ago, but before it too, when he was the nearest thing to a folk hero in the City; the only recognizable Jewish sports star in a generation, and the first since Koufax moved west with the Dodgers. The mantle of fame had never rested easily on Joe's shoulders; it was more like a yarmulke of thorns. He tugged at his broad-brimmed hat and, trailed by Frannie, followed the nurse from the waiting room, fearful that on *Page Six* of tomorrow's *Post* there'd be a picture of Jewish Joe Singer at Sloane Kettering.

They were led to an examination room in which a bank of high-tech equipment and light boards covered one wall. The nurse took Joe's vitals then disappeared. From his perch on an examination table, Joe glanced at Frannie, wondering if he should thank her again for coming, and what sort of examination this would be and if he'd have to ask her to leave? But before he could speak, a soft knock was followed immediately by the door opening inward.

"Mr. Singer." An older man in a lab coat extended his hand. "Avi Bernstein, radiation oncologist. I'm pleased to make your acquaintance."

Bernstein's hands were veiny and spotted, and his face looked as if he spent every day at the beach. He spoke formally, with a faint but discernible accent, which, because his name was Avi, Joe assumed was Israeli. Avi turned his hazel eyes towards Frannie.

"And this lovely lady must be Mrs. Singer."

"Please Dr. Bernstein, call me Frannie."

Bernstein inclined his head of white hair. "If you *vill* call me Avi. Joe," he continued, "I hope I didn't keep you *vhaiting* long."

"Actually." The truth raced out of Joe's mouth like a rabbit. "Some of the others had been waiting a lot longer, and"—he hesitated, wondering if he were fishing for a compliment—"they looked a lot sicker."

"Such a man of the people." He grinned at Frannie. "If you *vhant*, next time, you'll *vhait* two hours. Look here."

He opened Joe's chart. Fearing he was about to see a new piece of terrible news, Joe's heart fell to his feet.

"*Vhat* do you see?"

"D.N.W.," Frannie answered.

"Does Not Vhait," Avi pronounced the third word somewhere between *Wait* and *Vait*. "You might think it's because you are the famous pitcher, Jewish Joe Singer, you receive special treatment. Am I right?"

Joe nodded.

"But here." Avi raised his right palm in front of his face. "*Here*, I am the celebrity. I'm seeing you on short notice, without allowing you to *vhait*, because my close friend and colleague, Doctor Goldberg, asked me.

"I don't know Doctor Goldberg."

Frannie explained, "Joe's father is friendly with Dr. Goldberg's mother."

"I've known Glad thirty years." Avi smiled. Then he was all business. "I've looked at your chart, Joe, and the biopsy your doctor sent."

He was no longer smiling.

"Yours is a very interesting, and one might say, puzzling case. Your PSA was twelve point eight in January, now it's approaching fourteen."

Frannie squeezed Joe's hand, and he felt once again what a dope he'd been.

"But your Gleason score is seven, which isn't so bad."

"Excuse me," Frannie asked, "what is a Gleason score? Joe's California doctor mentioned it too."

"Gleason measures how aggressive a tumor is, in Joe's case, how likely it is to move out of the gland. For the treatment I propose, which is only done at an institute I run in Portugal, a patient's Gleason score cannot be higher than seven. So, Joe qualifies. But because Joe's PSA is high, he must have a PET-CT scan, to make sure the cancer hasn't moved into the seminal vesicles or anywhere else." Avi looked from Frannie to Joe. "Any questions?"

Oh boy. Joe felt so befuddled, he wanted to weep. "Portugal?"

Frannie said, "If what we most care about is for Joe to live a long, long time, wouldn't surgery be better?"

"Joe," Avi said. "Let me ask you, and please excuse my candor. You're sexually active? Impotence is not a problem?"

Joe glanced at Frannie.

"No," she said. "It's not."

"Good." Avi smiled. "Prostate surgery nearly always changes a person as a human being because of the serious side effects. Impotence. Anal leakage."

Joe grimaced.

"Yet recent studies indicate radiation and surgery are equally effective, and that's not taking into account what we have discovered in Portugal."

"What's that?" Frannie asked.

"Side effects result from the proximity of the prostate to other organs. But because the prostate is located at an outlet of air, feces, and urine, we realized the prostrate must be quite mobile, which we confirmed by introducing a GPS. We decided, 'Let's do what nature does.' Introduce a balloon into the rectum and move the prostate out of the way."

Joe thought, *You want to put a GPS in my ass?*

Frannie patted his hand.

Avi continued, "This process enables us to cure locally contained prostate cancer, with one treatment and no side effects. In Portugal, we have had one hundred patients with one-hundred-percent cure rate. One treatment, one day."

Frannie smiled. "I see why *you* are the celebrity."

Avi looked, Joe thought, like a cat that had swallowed a very tasty bird.

"But first," Avi continued, "we must schedule a PET-CT scan, to confirm the cancer is contained." He smiled at Joe. "And now, to answer questions you have not asked. You fly from here to London, and the next morning from London to Portugal. You can leave the same afternoon. Or maybe, you and Frannie will *vhant* to stay and enjoy the beach."

Frannie nodded. Joe hoped she'd come with him. He also hoped she'd understood more than he had. He couldn't get beyond the GPS in his ass. Who would believe this? One treatment, one day, 100-percent success rate? It sounded too good to be true. Yet for the first time in months, Joe could breathe. "Thank you."

"Yes," Frannie echoed. "Thank you."

"Don't thank me yet." Avi shrugged. "Yet, I haven't done anything. If you *vhant* to thank anyone…"

There was a knock at the door.

"That might be Stu now. He said he'd stop by."

The door opened, and a dark-haired, dark-bearded doctor entered. He looked sixty, give or take. For a doc, Joe thought, he wore his hair long, over his back collar. And he looked familiar, though Joe was certain they hadn't met.

"You must be Doctor Goldberg," Frannie said. "You look just like your mom." She smiled. "Except the beard."

"I hear that all the time." He extended his hand to Joe. "My mother speaks well of you *and* your father. And if you know my mother—"

I really don't.

"—you know how rare that is."

"Doctor Goldberg," Frannie said, "thanks for arranging for Joe to see Avi."

Joe watched Dr. Goldberg's eyes register the use of Avi's first name. Frannie must have noticed too, because she added, "He asked us to call him Avi."

From across the room, where he was entering examination notes, Avi said, "Of course, I did."

Dr. Goldberg took Frannie's hand. "Call me Stu, or Stuart, if you're feeling formal." He turned towards Joe. "I don't know if my mother told you, but I've been a Mets fan my entire life. So, I feel like I already know you."

Joe never knew what to say at moments like this. *Thank you? You don't know me?* "That's great."

"My mother tells me your son is on the verge of joining the Mets."

"We hope so," Frannie said.

Stu replied, "Maybe we can see a game together."

If all this medical crap worked, Joe thought, he'd owe Stu Goldberg a lot more than a ticket. "Sure."

Avi approached Joe and shook his hand. "Keep your phone handy. We're trying to schedule the PET-CT for later today."

A moment later, Avi left trailed by his colleague, Glad Goldberg's son. Joe turned to Frannie wondering just how grateful he had to be that Jack was one in a million.

After the game, Grandpa Jack said it best. *Two-J's! You stunk up the joint like you been eating beans!*

Jess's line for his first start back on the minor league side of the complex was embarrassing: three innings, five runs, four walks, two strikeouts, one hit by pitch. But after being sent down, Jess couldn't focus. He knew where he was headed, and it wasn't Flushing. Syracuse? He'd never been, having spent last year in Double-A Binghamton, but what he heard wasn't great unless you liked homemade sausage. Actually, he did, but what the hell? Why had he thought the front office would let him skip Triple-A and call him up before the Super Two deadline, thereby granting him an extra year of arbitration? *Stupid.* Maybe he really did think, like Rah said, he was the Crown Prince of Baseball, and standard rules didn't apply because he was Jewish Joe's son. Just shows how fucked up a boy could be.

Honestly, he was pretty fucked up, sitting alone at Big Wave Dave's, sucking down margaritas. Now that he'd farted up the joint, maybe the Mets brass wouldn't promote him even after the Super Two deadline. Maybe he'd toil on the Syracuse sausage farm all year. Jess threw back the bottom two inches of his third margarita, which Big Wave served in sixteen-ounce water glasses, narrow on the bottom, wide at the mouth, with lots of ice and salt.

Jess glanced down the bar towards two good-looking guys, early to mid-twenties, one blond, one Latino. They were sucking suds, three or four stools to his right. The Anglo, further from Jess, leaned towards the Latino, put his mouth near his friend's ear. Jess watched his lips, felt as much as saw the hot Latin guy lean back and laugh, his black hair and chiseled cheek obscuring Jess's view of the blond. Somehow this window on their intimacy—were they friends, or possibly, lovers, stopping for drinks before heading to a motel room, where they'd get it on in ways that Jess could only imagine (and imagine and imagine)? This vision filled Jess with such longing it was all he could do not to put his head down and weep. He'd had a few one-night stands, but he'd always been so afraid of being found out, he'd never had a boyfriend, or for that matter, slept with the same guy twice. What was wrong with him? If he wasn't such a scared little pussy, he'd walk down the bar, put his arms around both their shoulders and whisper, *Hey guys, why don't we all go back to my place and get it on?*

Instead, Jess ordered a fourth margarita and told himself not to look at them. Why torture himself? His plan was to get to the Show, have an All-Star career, and then and only then, would he come out. So what, if he'd be in his late thirties? Back in Redondo his parents knew this rich businessman who didn't come out until he was seventy-two, because his family was long-lived, and he was waiting for his father to die. Jess didn't think his own parents would care, certainly not Mom, and probably not Dad either. But the rest of the baseball world? Fucking-A.

Jess kept stealing glances at the hot guys. Then their dates arrived, hotties in tube tops, who planted wet kisses on their cheeks. Poor Jess, bound for Syracuse and homemade sausage.

When Joe and Frannie had been gone forty-eight hours and still hadn't called, Jack began to worry. He was deep in his cups, up to and past his eyeballs, because he'd broken his rule about hooch, and not only hooch but drinking alone. What sort of dumbbell doesn't follow up after bad news? His dumbbell! Maybe because Joey was his one and only, and after Joey's mother died, may her name be a blessing, he poured all his love and hopes and dreams into his son, though you wouldn't know it sometimes, the way it was between them. But if anything happened?

Jack didn't think he could stand it. He slammed down his scotch glass, now mostly rocks, picked up the remote, and began flipping through the forty-eight sports channels he paid for. What sort of man outlived his son? An unhappy one. *But who was talking about dying?* No one said nothing about dying.

All right, Jack thought, *call them again.*

He dialed Joe's number. Straight to voicemail.

Then he called Jess, who'd really pitched like crap today. Not that Jack blamed him. It was so unfair, and stupid, really stupid and short-sighted, to save the Mets money years from now when he was the best thing they had going this year.

Two-J's answered the third ring, and right away Jack could tell he was shitfaced.

"How much you had to drink?"

"Plenny," Jess answered. "Mebbe more."

In the background, bar buzz, laughter, and whatnot. At Jess's age, he loved chasing in bars. Caught his fair share too. "You looking for a woman, Jess, help you forget how bad you pitched?"

"Grandpa," Jess replied, "there's sumpingotta tell you."

"What's that?"

For a moment, nothing. Then moaning, or sobbing, something. "I'm going be sick."

"Don't get in a car!" Jack shouted, thinking about police, DUI's, and Two-J's future. "Take one of them Uppers!"

The line went dead, and when Jack called back, it shot straight to Jess's cheery voice, sounding like an ump, "*I'm out!* Leave a message."

Jack switched off the television, walked to his modest bar to pour himself a final drink, thought better of it, and settled for a glass of the Italian fizzy water Frannie had left in his fridge. The rest of the night, Jack slept, except when he needed to quench his need for water or to pee, falling back, time and again, into a shallow, troubled sleep.

PART TWO

THE MINORS

CHAPTER ELEVEN

Through the Syracuse clubhouse manager, Jess and Rah arranged to rent a two-bedroom unit in Applewood Suites, a newish, they were assured, all-suites hotel a short drive from NBT Bank Stadium in downtown Syracuse. Applewood's amenities included an indoor pool and fitness center. A buffet breakfast served seven days a week. Free wine and hors d'oeuvres Wednesday evenings, which Rah thought sounded great, although Jess pointed out they probably wouldn't be there often to enjoy it.

Jess was trying not to think about Syracuse. He hoped he'd be promoted soon, a month, maybe six weeks, though he was more excited than he wanted to admit about rooming with Rah. For years, since he'd admitted to himself he was gay, he'd arranged to live alone whenever possible. It was safer; the less people knew about him the better. He had enough saved from his signing bonus—one point eight million—he could do what he wanted. If some of the other players, like that dickhead Big Barnes, thought he was stuck-up, fuck 'em. *Better to be safe,* Jess thought, in a joke he could only tell himself, *than outed.*

Anyway, he was too busy preparing for his final Florida start to devote much brainpower to Syracuse. This afternoon he would throw a bullpen, likely watched by major league coaches, to work on adjusting his change-up grip. And there was all the energy he had to expend *not* to think about Dad's cancer; man, that was something else. Jess couldn't even talk about it, because anyone he confided in might tell Mac or a reporter, and Dad wouldn't want anyone to know. He was weird that way, almost like he was afraid of the press: Jewish Joe, the anti-celebrity. Dad didn't tweet or use social media. In many ways, Jess thought, Dad was in the closet, just like his son.

That evening, fresh from a shower and a successful bullpen, Jess drove south on I-95 to visit Jack in Delray. A few nights ago, when he'd been so trashed and upset about how badly he'd pitched, he'd called Jack just before he got sick. He was really messed up, and now, driving, he couldn't remember what he said, but with Jack it didn't matter. The old outlaw loved him. Jess had a sense that when he'd called Jack from the bar, he might have been planning to come out to him, how crazy was that? Grandpa Jack, the horniest hetero in Florida, still going strong at seventy-nine. *Still,* Jess thought, moving to the right lane and signaling to get off at Woolbright, the exit closest to Jack's condo, *wouldn't it be great to tell someone in his family? To be honest just once, and not feel so alone.*

After driving several miles west on Woolbright, he turned south onto Jog and began passing a sprawl of gated communities and strip malls. Just after the Lake Ida light—in middle school he'd asked who Ida was, and Jack said some old gal he'd been *schtupping*—Jess turned left again into Huntington Pointe, joining a queue of cars at the guard house. Ten annoying minutes later, a young African American rent-a-cop approached his driver-side window.

"Jess Singer," Jess said to the young woman, "to visit Jack Singer, apartment one-oh-four, building one-twenty-eight."

"I.D., please." She was short and short-haired, about his age.

"That's the thing." Jess gave her his best smile, the very one that appeared on all the top prospect websites. "I can't find it. I think I left it home."

The guard was unmoved by his smile and annoyed by his explanation. "Then I can't let you in."

"I've been coming here," Jess said, "my whole life to visit my grandfather, Jack Singer, apartment one-oh-four. Can't you do me a solid"—Jess smiled again—"and let me in just this once?"

His use of *Do me a solid*, an expression favored by several African American teammates, seemed to piss her off even more.

"Not a chance. Now get out of line so I can help the next person."

It occurred to Jess that *Do me a solid* might be off-limits unless you were Black. "Please. My grandfather's expecting me."

"Then get outta my line and ask Grandpa to *Do you a solid*."

"You're being a real asshole."

"No, I'm doing my job."

She spun on her heel and started towards the guard house. Jess wanted to shout, *I'm not moving, goddamnit!* and it was all he could do not to blare his horn, just to see her jump. Then he thought, *What the hell!* He got out of line, pulled over and called Jack.

A half hour later they were seated at The Sea, and Jack was laughing at him.

"Stunt like that is the kind your dad pulled." He took a big belt of his margarita, no salt, he said, in deference to his age. "Dumbest Jew in America."

Jess wished Jack would cut it out. It didn't seem right, and nowhere near as funny as it used to be now that Dad was sick. Jess sipped his own margarita, which Jack had paid for, saying, *Only one. You're pitching tomorrow, aintcha?*

Of course, he was pitching tomorrow, and of course, Jack knew. Jack kept better track of Jess's schedule than he did himself.

"I don't know if they told you, but it turns out Glad's son is this really big deal doc, whose friend invented this special new treatment for prostate cancer, only available in Portugal."

Jess took a big hit of his joy juice. "Why does Dad need a special treatment? Is he really sick?"

Jack's eyes narrowed, and he turned towards the open kitchen, displaying in profile the hooked nose he liked to say had been broken twice, once by God and once by a big wop in East New York.

"Maybe," Jack said, "and maybe he ain't. But I don't want you should worry."

Jess gulped his margarita and felt the self-inflicted stab of a brain freeze. "How can I not worry?"

"You want to help your dad? Pitch your ass off and get to the Show soon as possible."

Just as he'd feared. "Why?" Jess lowered his voice. "Is Dad going to die soon?"

Jack's jaw clenched. "Fuck." And then, almost to himself, he added, "I told Frannie we shouldn't tell you nothing."

"Why would you even consider keeping something this *important* a secret?"

"That's what Frannie said." Jack slammed his drink, not an old man's careful sip, but a wide-mouthed gulp. "Jess," Jack continued, "I got no problem keeping secrets. To get to the Show? You don't need no distractions."

If you only knew, Jess thought.

When Jack returned from the bathroom—*When you're my age,* he'd quipped, *when Nature calls, you better hop to it*—he discovered Two-J's had ordered each of them a second margarita. Jack lowered himself carefully into his chair, feeling every one of his eighty-two-plus years in his balky right knee.

"I told you, only one drink night before you pitch."

Jess quaffed the top half inch of his margarita, which, given the size of the tall, rimmed glass, must have packed a wallop.

"What the fuck, Jess?"

"I got something to tell you."

Jack took in his grandson's movie star looks, face long and lean, hair so dark it was nearly black, with a touch of midnight blue. Like Superman in the old comics. Two-J's eyes were large and almond-shaped, just like Joey and his mother, may her name be a blessing, but blue like Frannie's. "So spill."

Before Jess could answer, their waitress arrived with food. Raw tuna and sushi for Jess—*Yuck,* Jack thought—and took a bite of his nice piece of teriyaki salmon. Jess mixed up the *watusi* in a small dish of soy sauce. Using chopsticks, he dipped and raised a raw tangle of tuna to his lips.

"I'm gay," he said.

"What?"

"I'm queer."

Jack looked at Two-J's, so big, so strong and good-looking, a world-class athlete. "You're kidding, right?"

Jess dipped a round of California roll and ate that too. "Why would I be kidding?"

"I thought," Jack began, "because you're eating raw fish like one of them, you're pulling my leg."

Jess dipped another square of raw fish in the *watusi* and fed it through his lips. "So, you think if a guy likes sushi, he's gay?"

"Sure." Jack knife-and-forked a piece of salmon. "Everyone knows that."

Jess set down his chopsticks and tossed back a bolt of margarita. "Grandpa, let me say this so you'll understand. I'm a faggot."

Jack recoiled as if punched. "You got no call to talk so crude." He looked hard at Two-J's. *Really?* He'd seen no sign, no mincing around or playing with Barbies. Then again, he couldn't remember Jess having a girlfriend. "Maybe you ain't met the right girl?"

Jess leaned forward. "My problem is, I ain't met the right guy."

Jack felt again as if he'd been sucker-punched, like Houdini. "I ain't prejudiced, you know." He considered what it must be like for Jess to be a faggot ballplayer. *Terrible.* "So," he continued, after a moment. "Who knows? Your mom? Your dad?"

"No one."

Oy, Jack thought. Kid musta been so lonely. He dropped a hand on Two-J's wrist and waited for his eyes to rise towards his own. "Don't worry. Your secret's safe with me."

Two-J's smiled, but only his lips.

"Although maybe," Jack added, "you oughta tell your parents."

"They have enough to worry about."

What a great kid. Jack sipped his margarita. *Wow, never to know a woman's love.* Jack thought about all the women he'd known and how much love and carnal pleasure had meant to him for almost sixty-five years. A woman's scent! Resting after sex, half-asleep in your lover's arms. Then he thought about Jess, who hadn't known that, or had had to hide it, because being a gay pitcher was, like, no way.

"Don't worry," he repeated. "I'm the sphinx of Delray. Your secret's safe with me." Then, unable not to nudge Two-J's about his parents, he added, "For as long as you need it to be."

"Thanks, I knew I could count on you."

They finished their meal in silence, Jack thought, as if they hadn't said nothing about nothing.

CHAPTER TWELVE

Joe's PET-CT came back clean. Thirty-six hours later, he and Frannie stood in front of the Macouba Centre for the Unknown, which looked more like a movie set than a medical facility: weird steel and glass geometric forms, stacked one on top of each other, seemingly at random. They'd flown all night—New York-London, London-Lisbon—and Joe felt adrift.

"You ready?" Frannie asked.

He nodded.

Later, Joe wouldn't remember much. In the morning, radiation technicians did some sort of dry run. In the afternoon, the real deal. Although he felt nothing, they must have placed the mini-GPS in his ass and *boom!* He was cured. How could he be cured so quickly after being worried so long?

None of it made sense. But four days later, jogging beside Frannie under the hot Portuguese sun on Praia do Cascais, one of the Atlantic beaches west of Lisbon, Joe was trying to assess his good fortune. The sand was hot, white, and hard to run on. Behind dark glasses, even Joe's eyelids were sweating. Frannie ran on his left, further from the water, tonguing sweat from her upper lip.

Twenty-five years ago, the summer he was suspended for stonewalling the commissioner about who introduced him to the disgruntled gamblers, he and Frannie used to run like this on Hermosa Beach.

She was with Des then, and they were volleyball partners, nothing else. God, was she something! Frannie didn't know or care who he was; she didn't know about the suspension. Meeting her on the beach volleyball court was the best thing that ever happened to him. One thing led to the next, and here they were, still jogging together. Back in January, what had scared him most wasn't cancer, or even dying, but losing Frannie.

If he'd truly dodged the bullet, it was clearly better to be lucky than good. His whole life, Joe had tried extra hard to be good, because he never thought Jack was. He still hadn't forgiven him, not for what happened to his mother, or the gamblers. Decades later, he could see it wasn't Jack's fault his mother died in a public asylum. Jack didn't have money for someplace better. Joe didn't remember much about the place, except the smell. That was enough. As for the gamblers, they'd barely discussed what happened. But now that he had Jack to thank for the connection to Avi, he guessed they were square.

Joe glanced at Frannie, who smiled. She looked great, he thought; she wasn't even breathing hard. And Joe looked, he hoped, now that he'd lost some weight, like an athlete again, which was all he'd ever wanted to be.

They arranged to eat dinner that night, their last in Portugal, with Avi Bernstein, who met them at the hotel restaurant dressed all in white: shirt, pants, and shoes. His tanned face glowed above the white garments and below his mostly white hair, which, Joe noted, was thicker than his own. Avi ordered a bottle of *vinho verde*, which, he explained, meant the wine was released young, three to six months after harvest.

"Like a rookie," Joe quipped, and Avi laughed.

They were seated at the front corner of the restaurant balcony. The weather was perfect. The sky blazed with stars. It was past nine, later than Joe and Frannie had wanted to eat the night before a long flight, but Avi assured them everyone in Portugal ate late. Restaurants didn't open until eight, and only Americans ate that early.

"Avi," Frannie asked. "I hope you don't mind my asking."

"Ask anything."

"How old are you?"

"Eighty-two."

"And still working full time?"

Avi smiled proudly. "More than full time."

He sipped his *vinho verde*. So did Joe. The wine tasted more like alcoholic grape juice than the Chardonnays he drank with Frannie, and it went down easy with the seafood Avi had ordered for the table. They were on their second bottle.

"I like to work, always have," Avi continued. "And when my wife died six years ago?" Instead of looking away as Joe would have, Avi looked straight at Frannie. "Work kept me going. A recurrence of breast cancer."

"I'm sorry," Frannie said. "How old was she?"

"Seventy-three." Avi cut an inch of grilled octopus and consumed it. "We were married forty-eight years."

"I'm sorry," Joe said, echoing Frannie. And then, perhaps because of all the *vinho verde*, he asked, "You think I'll live that long?"

"Your father's going strong and from what I hear, remains quite vital."

"Nothing," Joe replied bitterly, "happens to Jack."

"Ah." Avi refilled their glasses. "You are asking for your prognosis."

"I guess I am."

Avi stalled, Joe thought, by spooning a second helping of seafood rice onto everyone's plate. He took a bite, chewed, and cleared his mouth, then asked, "Do you remember what I told you in New York?"

Joe laid into the rice and seafood, stalling like their host. The dish tasted like paella, but *not* like paella. It was hard to explain. "No." He felt a rush of shame. "Not a word."

Avi smiled at Frannie. "Joe's very honest, isn't he? That's a rare quality."

Frannie returned Avi's smile. "Yes, it is."

"Or maybe just not very smart," Joe admitted. "Medical stuff just won't stick in my head."

A cloud shifted over the bright moon suspended over the dark ocean, and for a moment, Avi's face was swallowed in shadow. Then the moon reemerged. "Many years ago," he began, "before there were many good outcomes for the kind of cancer Joe has, we conducted a study in which I told patients and a family member in great detail the truth of their condition. Two weeks later, when the patient and family member returned, we'd ask if they remembered. Overwhelmingly, the family member did, but the patient? The patient denied and denied."

Joe wondered what Avi was trying to say, and as often happened when Joe felt confused, he felt even more confused. "I promise, this time I'll remember."

"You probably won't. It's only human."

I'm more human than most, Joe thought.

"But I bet Frannie will."

"I will," Frannie said, "don't worry." She squeezed Joe's hand.

"There's a slight chance, Joe," Avi began, looking mostly at Frannie, "that when Joe's tumor was biopsied, one of his lesions was higher than Gleason seven, and we missed it. A *very* slight chance, because we repeated the biopsy you brought from California. But because of his high PSA, we can't rule it out, you see."

Joe didn't see.

"It's important," Avi continued, "to monitor Joe's PSA carefully post-surgery. It should gradually go down and not go back up."

Joe took another bite of seafood rice. Squid, he thought. And scallop. Two Jews and a *shiksa* eat in Portugal, and every bite more *traif* than the next.

"So," Joe said, feeling like a small dog attempting to chew the same rather large bone. "You think I'll be okay?"

Avi shot him a strange, not entirely benevolent look. He set his knife and fork down and looked out towards the ocean and the black night sky before turning again towards Joe. "In all likelihood, you'll be okay."

Good, Joe thought. *I'll be okay.*

CHAPTER THIRTEEN

Jess's final Florida start was a semi-stinker. He'd get ahead but couldn't put batters away. Lefties and righties kept fouling off pitches. It was all about location, location, location, as he remembered his mom's best friend, Laura, a Santa Monica realtor, saying about her business. Instead of painting with heat, he'd miss by two inches; not middle-middle, but enough plate to produce a crop of foul balls. Instead of swings and misses, or soft contact with his curve and change-up, he'd leave the ball up, or bounce it too far in the front of the plate. The result? Seven or eight pitch marathons with hitters he should have put away easily. He was pulled with one out in the fourth instead of finishing five, which he'd needed to make a final good impression before shuffling off to Syracuse.

And now it was moving day. Jess felt sour and pissed at himself, but also excited because he'd be rooming with Rah, who felt REALLY excited about being promoted to Triple-A, just one level below the Show. Of course, it was Rah's nature to be excited.

That was good because when they landed at Hancock International it was forty-two degrees and raining. The Syracuse forecast for the entire week was high forties, nighttime lows in the thirties, snow flurries possible Opening Day. Four or five other players were on the same flight, and not one was appropriately dressed for Syracuse; West Palm was eighty and sunny when they left. *Mucho* laughter and *pendejos*, directed at Rah, who'd flown in shorts and sandals. None of the other guys were staying at Applewood Suites, so they'd said goodbye at baggage claim. Jess rented the same SUV he always rented. Rah, who didn't have an American license, offered to share expenses, since Jess would be doing all the driving.

Applewood Suites looked like one of the dozens, or maybe hundreds, of motels Jess had slept in during his four professional seasons. Their suite consisted of two small bedrooms (each with a queen bed) and a functional kitchen. Jess selected the bedroom on the left side of the living room/kitchenette, and let Rah have the slightly larger bedroom on the right. Each had its own television and bathroom. They unpacked, and Rah changed into sweats. Team meeting was 8:30 in the morning—the stadium was ten minutes south—but they were free until then.

"What do you want to do for dinner?" Jess asked. It was past six, and they hadn't eaten since lunch. "I'm starving."

"How about Mexican?"

"Man," Jess said. "You always want Mexican."

"Dude, *soy Mexicano.*"

"You know it's gonna suck, right?"

Rah smiled his sexy Cuernavacan smile. "How bad could a taco suck?"

Man, Jess thought, *I love this guy.* "Okay, Mexican, long as they serve margaritas."

Fifteen minutes later, they were sliding into a booth in Otro Cuatro, a hip-establishment with Southwestern-themed murals on its brick facade and three different margaritas on the drink menu. Jess ordered a pitcher of the Cuatro, made with reposado Herradura, poured them each a large one in a salted-rim glass, and thought about the last time he'd been drinking margaritas: the night he came out to Grandpa Jack. He still couldn't believe he'd done it, although he'd been fantasizing about telling someone for years. And now? Maybe it wasn't a good idea. They hadn't spoken since, and he wondered if Jack would really keep his secret.

Jess sipped his margarita, dipped chips in fresh salsa, and gazed happily at Rah, who was studying the menu as if there was going to be a test.

"Jess," Rah said, pronouncing it as he always did, somewhere between *Yess* and *Jess*, "this ain't Mexican. I mean some. What is this shit?"

Jess grudgingly shifted his eyes from Rah to the menu. "It says, Mexican and Spanish."

"Oh." Rah grinned. "That explains it."

Rah ordered enchiladas with salsa verde, and Jess, though he was tempted by the paella—which he'd learned to eat in his parents' favorite Spanish restaurant in West Hollywood—chose his go-to Mexican: *carnitas*, out of loyalty to his best friend, Rah. After half a margarita and a full basket of chips and salsa, Rah said, "I bet you ain't gonna be here long."

"I hope not too long. But it's going to be fun, you know, rooming together."

"I think so too." Rah grinned. "You know how to cook?"

"Call Grubhub. What about you?"

"I'm pretty good. My big sisters taught me."

"You got brothers?"

"Only girls." His eyes came to Jess. "Except for me."

"I'm an only." And then, imagining them sitting around their apartment some evening without a game, he said, "Maybe you can cook for us sometime? I'll do the dishes."

Later, back at Applewood, perhaps influenced by the pitcher of top-shelf Otro margaritas, Jess dried off after his shower, changed into the boxers and Rumble Ponies t-shirt he slept in, and went looking for Rah to say goodnight. Found him in his bedroom, wearing nothing but boxers, doing curls with the forty-pound free weight he'd borrowed from the motel gym. His hairless chest and bulging biceps were the color of creamed coffee. The image of Rah half-naked and working out so seared Jess's retinae he started getting hard. *What if Rah sees?* Jess backed out, calling, "Night, Rah, see you in the morning."

"Hasta mañana, man," Rah answered.

Oh God, Jess thought, lying in bed, touching himself. *What now?*

Jack was walking, as had become his morning routine, around the ring road inside Huntington Pointe. It was half past ten: post-break-fast, early for lunch. With spring training over, he had nothing going until televised sports came on after dinner. Opening Day tomorrow would change that, but with so few day games, he'd already decided to keep up the walking, which in turn would keep down his gut. The past month, especially the last five days since he saw Two-J's, he'd been falling pretty damn shy of his resolution to limit the hooch. Once he got started, and he'd been getting started every afternoon, he couldn't seem to stop. All he had to do was remember the look on Two-J's face and the ugly words coming from the kid's mouth, *I'm a faggot*, and he'd need another drink and then another. His gut was bigger, his ass wider. He was caught in a real con*dumb*drum. He needed to tell someone, only he'd promised up, down, and sideways he wouldn't.

Instead, Jack circled Huntington Pointe in his Panama, madras Bermudas, and dark glasses. Funny how fast what he thought he knew became what he didn't. What he believed was stable ground had shifted. He'd been certain Jess's life was golden: 1.8-million-dollar bonus; mov-ie-star looks; best curve since Kershaw. But now, like it often did, life had chomped him on the *tuchas*.

Jack looked up at the Florida sun dripping orange juice out of the pale blue sky. The vision so disoriented him he didn't know which end was up, then he snapped back into himself in the no-bullshit way that had gotten him through hard times before. Jack knew exactly who and where he was: across from a palm-tree-lined side street of *villas*, which was Huntington Pointe's pompous word for houses. Third one in was Glad's, who had her reasons, he supposed, for never inviting him over. She showed up at his place with a casserole, or they went out to eat. But even when he dropped her off, she never asked him in. He used to think it was cute, and he'd tease her about the skeleton she was hiding, but now he wasn't sure.

Jack raised Glad's knocker and let it *klunk* once then again. He heard movement, and maybe the curtain twitched, but no Glad. He leaned on the bell as if it were the only thing keeping him from falling off the planet. A moment later, she cracked the door and peered out, hair tucked under a straw hat with embroidered purple flowers on the brim. This was Glad unadorned: no shadow, mascara, or lashes; no powder, lipstick, or blush. She looked like a much older woman.

"This better be good, Jack."

"You want I should come back?"

"Too late," Glad growled and opened the door.

She parked him on the couch and went off to become the Glad he knew. During his wait, Jack considered making himself a Bloody Mary to settle his nerves, but no, she hadn't offered. Besides, it wasn't even noon. He sat on the uncomfortable couch, studying family photos of people he didn't recognize, except for what was likely a much younger Glad standing beside the original Mister Goldberg, their arms around a boy and a girl, maybe twelve and ten years old. There was another one just the son, likely the future Dr. Goldberg, in a *yarmulke* and *tallis*, smiling like the precocious Bar Mitzvah boy he must have been.

Joey hadn't been Bar Mitzvahed, not officially. Jack didn't have the money for a reception, or maybe the focus, not with his first wife in the nut house. Looking at Glad's *boychikel*, all dolled up in his *tallis*, Jack felt the pang he always felt for being such a shitty dad.

There were other pictures of the future Dr. Goldberg, and pictures of grandchildren too, but no other ones, Jack realized, getting up for a closer inspection of the shelves of family photos, of the daughter. Just then, Glad appeared looking very much like herself.

"So, what was so damn important? And don't say you missed me."

"I'm not supposed to tell no one."

"Too late for that, Jack."

"My grandson Jess, the pitcher?"

"Yeah?"

"Before he went north with his team, to Syracuse?" Jack looked into Glad's perfectly made-up eyes. Blue shadow, false lashes, mascara, the whole she-bang. "He came over to tell me he's gay."

Glad didn't bat a false eyelash. "What's the big deal? It's the twenty-first century, Jack."

"Trust me, in baseball, it's the 1950s. You know how good Jess is, right? Likely to reach the majors soon? Well, there's never been a gay player in the majors. At least not one who admitted it."

"If you say so."

"Hell," Jack said, "he hasn't even told his parents."

Glad's features softened for the first time since he'd barged in. "So why'd he tell you?"

"Me and Jess, we always been like this." He held up his second and third fingers, pressed together.

Glad stepped towards him. "If you weren't supposed to tell anyone, why'd you tell me?"

Suddenly Jack was fighting tears, which had not fallen in decades. "I'm so worried for him, Glad." He stepped into his lover's arms and allowed himself to be comforted. After a moment he asked, "You think I could have a drink, like a Bloody Mary or something?"

"So, why'd you tell *me*?"

He started to say, *I had to tell someone.* He almost said, *Who else would I tell?* But that wasn't it. Instead, he told the truth. "Because I trust you."

"I'll get you that drink now." She kissed him on the mouth. "And I'll have one with you."

CHAPTER FOURTEEN

It was so cold at their first practice, the players kept handwarmers in their boxers. So cold, frost glistened in the outfield grass. So cold, the bases were frozen. When Raul Valdez slid into third, he slid right off, crashed into the stands, and had to be helped off the field. So effing cold, the guys told *It was so cold/ Tanto frio* jokes for days, like the *Yo Momma's so fat* jokes Jess recalled from middle school—although everyone knew *his momma* was tall and beautiful.

The night after the third frozen day was what Jack called *Erev Opening Day*, as if Opening Day was a Jewish holiday, which in the Singer household, it was. Jess and Rah were sitting around Applewood Suites knocking back beers when Jess's cell rang and a vaguely familiar voice asked, "Hiya, is this Jess the pitcher?"

"It is." The voice was neither high nor low. "Who's this?"

"Emmy Williams?" The girl's voice went up at the end, as if she didn't know her own name, but that couldn't be the explanation and it wasn't. The question mark pertained to what came next. "I don't know if you remember me, but I'm, like, hoping you do?"

"Give me a hint."

"Tiff and I met you and your friends Rah and Big, and I can't remember the shortstop's name—"

Bingo, Jess remembered: Emmy, the long-stemmed American beauty, corn silk hair, blue eyes, rising on her toes to kiss him. "Of course, I remember you."

Through the phone line he could feel her smile, such a pretty girl, with that Pretty Girl shrug. *Oh man*, he thought, *are you barking up the wrong tree.*

"Anyway, me and Tiff, our school's less than an hour away. We thought maybe this weekend we could drive over and watch a game if you're pitching. We just *love* baseball, like we told you. Maybe afterwards, we can hang out? If you want to."

"Hold on," Jess said, thinking he should ask if Rah wanted to see them, but of course Rah would want to see little Tiff with her big eyes and big chest; just the kind of girl straight guys liked. Without quizzing Rah he answered, "I'm pitching Sunday, a 1:00-p.m. start. I'll leave tickets at the box office. You better dress warm, it's cold as shit here."

"It's cold as shit here too."

She hung up, and Jess told Rah.

"The *rubia* who was all over you, and the little one with the big *tetas*?"

"Yep."

"I thought you weren't interested?"

"I thought you were." He watched Rah's face. *It's better if you're with a girl. Might help me stop fantasizing about you.*

"Right now, Jess"—Rah shrugged—"I'm more interested in our game plan for Sunday." He started towards the kitchen. "*Compai*, you wanna nother cold one?"

Sunday broke cold and sharp as a Kershaw curve. Frost quilted the Applewood lawn. The ice on Jess's windshield was so thick, he borrowed a scraper from the hotel desk.

Oh man, he thought, scraping, *I can't feel my fingers.* But the low sun slicing through the bare trees promised warmth by game time. When Jess returned to the apartment to see if Rah was ready for breakfast, he checked his phone and thought, *Dumb fuck, it's only seven-thirty, go back to bed!* But he was jumpy as a kitten, so he waited for Rah, who liked to sleep in, to wake on his own. Jess pored over scouting reports on his iPad, visualizing the first batter: *Strike one, strike two. Take a seat!*

At eight-thirty, Jess pounded on Rah's door: enough sleeping! When Rah didn't answer, Jess entered to pummel his friend's shoulder; they were supposed to be at the park by ten. Rah lay in bed, fast asleep, spikey blond hair standing straight up, eyes closed, a smile on his full lips. For half a sec Jess devoured Rah's features and thought about bending down to kiss his lips like Sleeping Beauty's, wondering what that would feel like? Instead, he shook Rah's shoulder until his brown eyes opened.

"*Pendejo.*" Jess grinned. "*Despiertas!*"

Although his eyes were open, Rah still seemed asleep. And dreaming. "*Yess*, you talking fucking *mucho* Spanish."

"It's eight forty-five. Breakfast!"

"Why didn't you wake me sooner?" Rah smiled the smile Jess loved, but still Rah didn't move.

"You getting up or do I leave your sorry ass here?"

"If you leave"—Rah glanced at a spot approximately halfway to his feet—"I can get out of bed."

Jess didn't understand, then he did.

"*Metedura de pata.*" Rah laughed. "Your Spanish word for the day!"

By then, mortified, Jess was headed for the door. Later, he'd translate *Metedura de pata* on his iPhone: boner.

It was forty-four degrees at game time. But the sun blazed and the badass wind that had blown through NBT Bank Stadium for the past four days had finally subsided. Standing behind the mound prior to the first pitch, bouncing the rosin bag on his palm then the back of his hand, Jess could feel his fingers. He stepped onto the rubber for his first pitch of the new season, picked up Rah's sign, a single finger wiggling like a plump brown worm. Jess darted one across the heart of the plate, and the next thing he knew, the ball was banging around the right field corner and the batter was sliding into second with a double. The next batter singled on the next pitch; two offerings into the season that was supposed to carry him to the Show, and Jess and the S-Mets were already behind.

Jess paced behind the hill rubbing up a new ball. Rah started out to parley, but Jess waved him off, climbed back on the mound, and toed the rubber. Then, from behind the home dugout, he heard *girls' voices*. It was the college girls he'd left tickets for: Emmy in a white bubble parka and white stocking hat, Tiffany in something electric blue.

"You can do it, Jess!"

Oh, Christ, he thought. *How can I even hear them?*

He shook Rah off until he dropped two fingers for a curve.

"Jess, you can do it!"

He blocked out the world, the girls, the importance of the start, and focused on his release point: eleven o'clock, just beyond his left ear. He hid his face, aligned his fingers in the curveball grip he'd learned all those years ago from Jack—left thumb bent underneath, fingertips gripping the seams. Stepping towards the plate, left arm rising to eleven, thumb pressing up to spin the ball, index finger pulling down, he let it fly.

In Joe's day, every season opened in Cincinnati to honor the first professional baseball team, the 1869 Cincinnati Red Legs. A parade snaked from Findley Market through downtown to Riverfront. Kids skipped school, and the game was sold out months in advance. The only season Joe's Mets opened in the Natti, he threw seven innings of one run ball for the win.

Major League Baseball killed the Cincinnati Opening Day tradition some years back. Too old-timey, Joe thought, sitting on his couch in Santa Rosa, flipping through games on MLB Network. Too nostalgic and not enough about the bottom line. No bean counter would support giving a small market team like the Reds Opening Game every year. He couldn't remember exactly when MLB changed it, a decade or more, and now the season sometimes started with a night game, on *Erev Opening Day*. On Opening Day itself, there were games around both leagues. If the change made financial sense, Joe thought—and don't even get him started on the pitch clock and universal DH—it didn't make emotional sense to throw away such a fine tradition. And if that made him a fuddy-duddy, maybe that's what he'd become. An old-timer, who hadn't been back for an Old-Timers' game since he retired.

This year the Mets had won on Opening Day, which they usually did, but lost the next three games. Now, on the first Sunday of the season, which was the same day Jess was starting in Syracuse, the Mets' fifth starter, Randy Vermouth, was throwing, and Joe was planted in front of the large TV in their living room feeling conflicted. He was loyal as loyal could be and always wanted his former team to win, and he certainly didn't want to root against anyone pitching for the Mets. But Vermouth had had a rocky spring, and if Jess was going to take anyone's place in a month or two, it was most likely Vermouth's. So the proud poppa in Joe wanted Vermouth to give up a three-run bomb in the first.

"No, no," Jack had said just a few minutes ago on the phone. "That old fuck needs to pull a hammy."

Joe and Jack spoke much more frequently during baseball season than the rest of the year, when they couldn't find a subject. It had been this way their entire lives. Not exactly oil and water; more like cats and dogs, or Katz and Jones, their warring neighbors in Brooklyn when Joe was growing up. Whatever Joe said, even when he was a star, pissed Jack off unless they were talking sports. After Joe's suspension, things were even worse, and they barely talked for a couple of years, until Jess was born. So, Joe had lost the habit, if he'd ever had it, of confiding in his father.

In between the first and second inning, Joe got up to fix a sandwich; Frannie was out, he wasn't sure where. When he returned, the Mets were behind 2-0, and Ruby wasn't in her usual spot on the corner of the couch. *Uh-oh*, Joe thought, *she better not be pissing*. They'd been having a hell of a time with Ruby. Joe set down his plate and went to look for the dog. By the time he found her, there was a wet spot on the battered bedroom rug, and Ruby had assumed her guilty psycho position: face and neck hidden behind the bedroom curtain, just her black rump sticking out.

"Goddamnit, Ruby, what's wrong with you?"

She burrowed deeper into the curtain. Poor Ruby. Joe believed he knew what was wrong with her: something bad, something fatal. Why else would an old dog start pissing indoors? But Frannie didn't want to hear it. She insisted Ruby's problems were emotional. *We left her in the kennel for three weeks, Joe!* Not only had it cost a fortune, the kennel had brought back the trauma of Ruby's early abandonment. According to Frannie, Ruby suffered from doggy PTSD; Joe agreed, with an emphasis on *Pee*.

The problem wasn't only *where* Ruby was pissing—she was pissing everywhere—but that he couldn't tell Frannie what he really thought. How do you tell the love of your life her pet needs to be put down? What if he started having bladder trouble, caused by cancer? Would Frannie want to put *him* down?

So Joe had zipped his lip. Kneeling, he squirted cleaning solution from the Little Green Machine on the pee spot, then heard his cell phone ringing in the living room.

"Joey," Jack said, when he finally picked up. "Where you been?"

"You don't want to know."

"Ain't you been watching Vermouth get shelled like a walnut?"

Joe glanced at the screen. *Phils 6, Mets 0.*

"Vermouth sucks," Jack continued. "Maybe they'll call Two-J's up sooner than we thought."

Joe had met Randy Vermouth once or twice and liked him. That was one of the things he'd always disliked about sports: one man's success required another's failure. "You have any idea how Jess threw today?"

"A run in the first, then four scoreless."

"How do you know that?"

"I stream the Syracuse games on my computer. What, you don't?"

Joe wouldn't admit it to Jack, but he'd never streamed anything. "For an old guy—" Joe began.

"Whaddya mean, old?"

"You're pretty good on that computer." Thousands of miles away, Joe could feel his father's pleasure in the compliment.

"Two-J's showed me," Jack said. "It ain't hard."

"Maybe not for you," Joe said, feeling inadequate, which was how Jack had made him feel his entire life. "Talk later, okay?"

Joe hung up and settled in to watch the game.

Emmy and Tiff texted to say they'd wait outside the players' entrance after the game. Rah, Jess thought, looked completely pumped. He'd banged out two hits, called his usual great game, and threw out a baserunner. Jess was excited too, not so much about the girls, but about how he'd pitched: no runs after the second batter, and hardly any barreled balls. Ray Suarez, the S-Mets manager, shook Jess's hand after taking him out, said something about how Jess wouldn't be around long if he pitched like that. And though Jess demurred, said, *No, he wasn't really that sharp*, he felt good about his performance. Showering after the game, feeling the hot spray on his left arm, which he'd iced for half an hour, as he did after every start, he could clearly remember how hearing Emmy shout, "Jess, you can do it! You can do it!" calmed him down in the first, when things really could have gone sideways.

So Jess was feeling grateful as he and Rah, whose hair was slick and wet from his shower, walked down the corridor towards the players' exit. Jess had decided to take everyone out to a nice dinner as a way of saying thanks—although he wasn't sure he would tell them what he was thanking them for, since he wasn't sure he wanted to see them again. When Jess and Rah emerged from the clubhouse, the girls were leaning against the hood of a red Mustang, surrounded by other players, not all of them single. Emmy and Tiff's mouths exploded into smiles, and Jess realized he was glad to see them too. Emmy and Tiff, but especially Emmy, were so damned good-looking, and the other guys could see she only had eyes for him. That felt good, even though nothing could ever happen between them.

The girls pushed themselves off the hood of what he assumed was their hot car—one of them must have rich parents—and started towards them. For a moment, Jess wondered if Emmy was going to jump into his arms like the prime minister's plump girlfriend in *Love, Actually,* one of his and Mom's favorite movies. Or at least stand on her tiptoes and kiss him like she had in Florida. But no, she stopped in front of him and shrugged her Pretty Girl shrug.

"Hey, Jess, you pitched great."

Tiff threw herself into Rah's arms in just the way he'd fantasized Emmy would leap into his. From the corner of his eye, he watched Rah kiss Tiff, or maybe Tiff kissed Rah. *This is killing me,* he thought.

Then he realized Emmy was standing in front of him, in front of his teammates too, looking stricken, her smile beneath her white sock hat melting on her pretty face; he'd neither hugged nor kissed her, not like Rah and Tiff, and she'd come all this way. She was so great-looking, and he didn't want to hurt her feelings, not with all the guys watching. He stepped forward and hugged her, not a crush-her-breasts-against-your-body, but not a wimpy hug either, so no one would know he was queer.

Jess and Rah exchanged less robust hugs with the other's girl, Jess having to lean way down to embrace Tiffany, who was more than a foot shorter. There was the added impediment of her breasts, which made the embrace extra awkward. Then the couples, for that was how they must look to the other players, set off in both cars: Rah and Tiff in what turned out to be her red Mustang, Jess and Emmy in his SUV; first to the Applewood to show the girls their apartment, then out to dinner, or really, who knew where the hell they were headed when Emmy looked across at him from the passenger seat and smiled.

The girls returned to the apartment after dinner, where one thing led to another, and somehow when Rah and Tiff disappeared into his bedroom to *watch TV,* Jess found himself on the living room couch and then his bed, making out with Emmy. This wasn't the first time something like this had happened, though it was the first time in several years. In the past whenever he'd ended up with a girl, at first because he didn't know better, and later to keep everyone from guessing what he knew—*this was wrong, all wrong*—he'd fantasize about this blond Latino hunk on a porn site he used to whack off to. Rey's cock, Rey's mouth, Rey's long smooth muscles, Rey's lips. Now, kissing Emmy, who had wide but rather thin lips and an active tongue, and whose long, straight hair curtained Jess's cheeks when she rolled on top, it was Rah's face he fantasized about. Rah's cheeks, Rah's lips, Rah's fingers feather-stepping down his side and across his abdomen and finally onto his cock. Rah's fingers unzipping him, Rah touching him. Rah, Rah, Rah, as if his name were a prayer, because what if he couldn't get hard, and Emmy was such a beautiful girl, and then everyone would know. *Rah, Rah, Rah,* he thought, then she took him into her mouth. Rah's lips, Rah's mouth, and for a moment he tried to push her away, his fingers tangled in her hair.

"Don't worry about me," she said, surfacing and looking up at him. "Don't worry about me."

Then Jess wasn't worrying about anything, not even about how long it had been since he'd had sex with a real live human and not an image on a screen, not thinking about how wrong this was, not even about Rah and Tiff in the next room. Just the skillful tongue and mouth, and Emmy so sweet and beautiful. Then he was exploding, and she was making swallowing sounds. Emmy crawled up beside him, laid her head on his shoulder, and looked at him through the blonde damask of her hair, which after a moment she opened.

"Hope that was up to snuff." She grinned, looking pleased with herself. "I'm sure the groupies are all over you."

"Not really."

"I'll be right back. Okay, if I use your toothbrush?"

"Unless you think it's too intimate."

Emmy laughed and climbed off the bed. Jess watched her walk towards his bathroom, long, tall, blonde, and sexy. The entire time she was gone, Jess wondered what Rah and Tiff were doing in the next room.

The girls had morning classes and announced they had to leave. Maybe next time, they could stay over, or maybe the guys would visit them at school? Sure, said the guys, and they walked them out to Tiff's red Mustang where they kissed the girls goodbye.

"Great game," Tiff said.

"Yah." Rah grinned. "Great game."

Tiff and Emmy drove off, and Jess followed Rah inside, admiring how his shoulders bloomed from his narrow waist. Soon, they sat side by side on the couch, sipping, each of them, a Rolling Rock.

"Man," Rah said, grinning, "those college *chicas* are *locas*, no?"

Jess nodded, blushing, remembering how the entire time, he'd fantasized about Rah.

"Jess," Rah asked, "did you do it with her?"

Jess took a long sobering swallow of his Rock. "She went down on me. She didn't even take her clothes off."

"*Lo mismo!*" Rah's eyes widened. "Tiff said she doan have sex unless she knows a guy real well. That's fine with me, cause I doan want no baby mama. But she said a blow job was okay." Rah's mouth formed an O while his tongue slid out and in.

That was too much! Jess thought. He was tempted yet terrified of making the first move. But what if he didn't, and that's what Rah wanted? My God, Rah was pantomiming a blow job and *looking* at him. Why else would Rah do that? What if Jess missed his only chance because he was a chicken shit?

Jess could never say for sure who moved first and who responded, who risked rejection and who didn't reject, but suddenly, after years of longing, he was kissing Rah and Rah was kissing him, their lips and tongues and even their teeth knocking together. Jess's arms encircled Rah, whose strong catcher's hands pulled Jess into him. Rolling Rock bottles flew off the coffee table, spurting onto the couch and rug. The top of Jess's head was coming off, and then their clothes were coming off, and they ended up naked in Jess's bed. If there was any lingering scent of Emmy and her perfume, it served only as an aphrodisiac; the oh-my-God realization that less than an hour ago, Emmy was going down on him in this same bed on these very same sheets. And now Rah, who seemed to know what he was doing—yes, Rah knew what he was doing—Rah was inside him, and he was catching his catcher.

Thinking would come later. So would conversation. For now, Jess was only feeling, and what he was feeling was grand.

CHAPTER FIFTEEN

Over the years; Jack had watched Two-J's at every cow town during his rise through the minors. If the kid kept throwing like he'd done his first starts, he wouldn't stay long in Triple-A, the whole Super Two bullshit rules be damned. Five innings both times: the most they'd let a youngster pitch early in the season. One earned run each start, twelve strikeouts over ten combined innings, six hits, two walks, a WHIP under one, and all the new-fangled analytic statistics, FIP and Batting Average on Balls in Play, showed the same thing. Two-J's was pitching so lights out, it was a total eclipse for the batters. Plus, the kid sounded confident and happy, like Jack had rarely heard him. Even though Jess, like Joe before him, was so adept at throwing a ball it was like watching Michelangelo carve marble, Jess and Joe lacked confidence sometimes.

Those that can, Jack thought, do it. The rest just brag. The last time he spoke to Two-J's, after his second start, the kid seemed different.

"How you doing, Jess?"

"Great, Jack. I'm doing great."

Whoa, he'd thought, never heard you say that before. "What's got into you?"

"Everything's coming together."

Then he'd jumped off, said he was going out with his buds. When he spoke to Joey that night, Jack tried to explain. *Something's up; Jess has really turned the corner; we should go see him.* But Joey had a follow-up appointment with his prostate doc; not the fancy one in New York, the one in Santa Rosa, and he couldn't get away. So, Jack was going alone, or maybe with Glad, a possibility he'd been turning over in his mind like a shiny quarter.

"Syracuse?" she replied. "You're inviting me to Syracuse?"

He'd waited until they were luxuriating in bed, enjoying a moment of afterburn. "That's where Two-J's pitches next. After that, it's Wilkes-Barre. You rather go to Wilkes-Barre?"

"Well," Glad said, "let me think about that."

She slipped into a pink dressing gown with feathery white cuffs and set out for the bathroom. The last couple of weeks, she'd been inviting him over in the evenings, instead of just showing up in the morning with a pan of kugel.

The toilet flushed and Glad returned.

"All right, Big Spender." She batted her oversized lashes. "We're going to Syracuse."

Big Spender? She thinks I'm paying? Then a voice very much like his own answered, *Schmuck, of course she thinks you're paying, you invited her.*

It was twenty-six degrees with a bad wind when they landed in Syracuse; Glad was looking like Einstein for bringing her full-length mink. Jack, meanwhile, was freezing his *tuchas* off outside the terminal keeping an eye peeled for Two-J's. Then Glad came out and waited beside him grinning like the Cheddar Cat while Jack stamped his feet and blew on his bare fingers.

"Come inside," Glad said. "You want to catch pneumonia?"

"No way, let me borrow your mink."

"You're kidding."

He wasn't. Glad waited in the terminal, and Jack wore the mink, looking like Clyde the Glide Frazier, back when the Knicks won. A minute later, damn, but the coat was warm, Two-J's pulled up in an SUV.

"Hey, Jack!" Jess came around to the curb, hugged him, then hoisted their bags. "You look sweet."

Jack hustled inside, swapped coats with Glad, and they roared off to Applewood Suites, where Two-J's roomie, Rah, met them in the lobby. "*Señor* Jack." He crushed Jack's hand in his own. "Good to see you." "You too." *Christ, you nearly broke my knuckles.* "I'd like you to meet my friend, Gladys Goldberg."

"*Mucho gusto*, Mrs. Goldberg." Rah displayed about a million white teeth. "I admire very much your coat."

Two-J's entered, porting their luggage. "Jack was wearing the mink when I drove up, looking mighty cute."

"That's cause you were late, and I was freezing my nuts off."

Rah—whose muscles had muscles, a lot like Joey's catcher, Mac— and Two-J's grinned at each other. Two-J's said, "I paid for your suite already; it's down the hall next to ours."

"That's very nice of you," Glad said. "But you didn't have to."

"It's all right," Jack said, taking the key cards. "The kid's loaded."

Wrapped in her mink, Glad cut her eyes at him, and Jack took the hint.

"Thanks, Jess, dinner's on us."

They ended up at Café Citti, which wasn't shitty. Jack ordered veal parm with a side of penne in vodka sauce, just like the old days in Brooklyn. Glad pecked at a scampi, but mostly drank dinner, a martini followed by pinot gris. The boys started with mussels and margaritas, moved onto a second round of margs, and when Jess tried to order a bottle of cab sauv to sauce their steaks, Jack snapped, "Ain't you pitching tomorrow?"

"That's the rumor."

"Who do you think you are, Mickey Mantle?"

Rah asked, "Meekey Mantle?"

Jack couldn't believe it. "Greatest switch-hitter of all time? Center fielder for the Yanks?"

On Rah's face, incomprehension. Jack turned towards Two-J's. "And a big-time boozehound, shortened his career."

"Grandpa, you think I'm a boozehound?"

Jack glanced at Glad, who was trying to sink him with optical torpedoes. "No, it's just, everything is going great for you."

"Everything *is* going great."

"I don't want you to fuck things up."

"Who's more focused on how I do, me or you?"

Glad piped up, "He thinks he is."

Jess laughed. "I know he does."

For a moment, in profile, his long lean face, angled cheeks and nose, looked so much like Joey's, Jack could hardly stand it.

"Hey," he said to Glad, "whose side are you on?" He turned to Two-J's. "It's just, I know better than you, how fast things can go bad."

In the end, Jess ordered a glass of cab to go with his steak while Rah, a really sweet kid, even if he didn't know who the Mick was, said he didn't need wine. They got through the meal discussing the scouting report on the Lehigh Valley IronPigs' top hitters. Jack polished off his parm and penne, and when the white-shirted, bow-tied waiter—just like Brooklyn!—offered a shot of sambuca with their cheesecake and espresso, Jack thought, *Why the hell not?* Jess, however, held his hand up like a school crossing guard.

"No thanks." He grinned. "I'm pitching tomorrow."

Glad grabbed the substantial check, and after some face-saving protests, Jack relented. She could afford it, no problem. Jess drove them back to Applewood through the frozen tundra of Syracuse, Jack in the back with Glad in her mink, content with how the night had turned out.

After sex, Jess and Rah were sitting up in Rah's bed, trying to talk to each other in their new glowing reality. "You think your *abuelo*, he knows about us?"

Jess kissed the corner of Rah's mouth. "I doubt it."

"*Señora* Goldberg," Rah began.

"Glad," Jess said.

"I call her *Señora* Goldberg. You *pendejo norteamericanos* show no respect for your elders." Rah grinned. "You even call your *abuelo* Jack."

"Okay, *Señora* Goldberg."

"I think she knows."

"Why do you say that?"

"I see her watching how you look at me."

"And how," Jess asked, placing his hand on Rah's thigh through the bedclothes, "do I look at you?"

Rah pushed his hand away. "Like you want to have sex with me."

"That's not how I look at you." He replaced his hand on Rah's leg, closer to his crotch.

"No?"

"I look at you like I love you."

"Doan say that unless you mean it."

"I've never had a boyfriend, just one-nighters." Jess looked away then back at Rah. "What about you?"

"When I was fifteen, there was this older guy. We were together for three years, until I left Mexico."

"Weren't you afraid he'd tell?"

Rah laughed. "I doan think so. He was one of my coaches. He had a wife and two kids."

Wow, Jess thought. "You know when I was afraid?"

Rah shook his head.

"Ever since I met you, but especially this year. I was afraid you'd figure out I was in love with you, tell me to fuck off, and tell everyone."

"I would never do that. I've been afraid my whole life, just not about my coach, who had more to lose than I did."

Jess thought a moment. "I still can't believe you were only fifteen. I didn't even know I was gay when I was fifteen."

"I've known since I was ten. So, when did you first make love with a man?"

Jess remembered fumbling in the back seat of a car in Manhattan Beach, with a guy whose name he didn't even know. "I was seventeen. It was awful."

"When it comes to sex," Rah said, "you're a rookie."

"But I'm a fast learner."

Rah's eyes glistened. He moved Jess's hand to his crotch.

"We must take care," Rah said softly.

"Not to let anyone know?" They'd discussed this and agreed not to let any of the coaches or players know, especially not any of the Latin players. They'd also agreed to keep seeing Emmy and Tiff, to make sure no one got the wrong, that is, the right idea about them. The girls were coming to tomorrow's game, sitting in the same row as Jack.

"Nah." Rah grinned his killer grin. He moved his hand under the sheet.

Here we go again, Jess thought.

"Nah," Rah repeated, rolling onto his side to face Jess. "Careful not to make so much noise. Your *abuelo* and *Señora* Goldberg, they're right next door."

"Next time," Jess said, worrying if doing it twice on the night before he pitched was a good idea. "Next time," he repeated, remembering the *last time, and all the times before that,* "I'll get them a room on a different floor." Then he wasn't thinking about anything except his lover, Rah Ramirez, and how great his life felt at last.

In the morning, Jess woke in his own bed. That was something else they'd agreed to. Separate beds so no one would know, not even the maids.

By game time it was in the fifties, but Glad still wore her mink because it gave her and the college girls something to talk about. The tall blonde reminded Jack of a young Frannie, though not so *zaftig*; Emmy was thinner, more model-like. Five-nine or ten, rocking a Jess Singer jersey, number 32, just like Joe and Sandy, a line of Jewish pitchers wearing 32. She had perfect skin, Jack thought, a few freckles dotting her cheeks, and straight blonde hair drawn back in a pony through the opening at the back of her Syracuse Mets cap. During batting practice and warm-ups, Jack had struggled not to stare. The other girl, who was eight inches shorter, with a sizeable rack that made her body top-heavy, was nice enough, but not in the same league.

"Jack," Glad hissed. "*Jack.*"

"What?"

"Stop staring, you old goat. *I'm* your goddamned date."

He grinned at Glad, gorgeous in mink with her skinny ass on a blue wooden seat. "Of course. It's just…"

"I know." Glad leaned into him. "She's really beautiful." She inched closer. "I thought Jess was gay."

Jack moved his mouth to Glad's ear. "Maybe until he met her? Or maybe, you know." He looked past Glad at Emmy whose face shone in the sun as if she had a spotlight on her. "He's a switch-hitter?"

"Maybe," Glad said, though he could tell she didn't think so.

The thing about these girls, they really knew baseball. Watching Joey back in the day, Jack had sat with a lot of baseball wives; half didn't know one end of a bat from the other. But these girls, Jack thought. They'd seen Jess's last start, and Emmy, in particular, could remember which of Two-J's pitches was working ("The Charlie," she said and grinned), and how Jess had been able to pitch up and in with his heater, then down and away with his change.

"Filthy," she'd said, and Jack believed her.

They were seated four rows behind the third base dugout. Two-J's looked locked in. Jack was so excited, he thought he might piss himself. Two-J's threw his last warm-up, and Rah rifled the rock towards second. The ball darted from infielder to infielder, like a hummingbird sipping nectar from their gloves. Jess climbed the hill and looked in for a sign from Rah squatting behind the dish, though he had one of those PitchCom things in his ear. The IronPig leadoff batter tapped the plate with his bat and took two practice swings. Jack leaned forward and glanced past Glad at Emmy, who met his gaze.

"Ya think Jess starts him off with a hook?"

"No way. High heat."

Two-J's rocked into his motion, which had always been a dream, so easy and repeatable. The ball flashed towards home, and the batter spun out of the way. *High heat.*

Emmy turned her pretty face towards him. "Told ya."

Jack wondered how she'd known, then he wasn't thinking about Emmy. He focused totally on his grandson, who hid his face behind his glove just like Jack had taught him when he was in middle school.

CHAPTER SIXTEEN

Joe was putting in an hour a day on the putting green. Like many players, especially starting pitchers, who only worked every fifth day, Joe had taken up the grand old game once he got to the big leagues. He soon played to a six handicap and appeared at pro-am tournaments. He was paired once with Tom Weiskopf, another time with Lee Trevino, who was funnier than hell and had a much worse-looking swing than Joe's. But after the betting scandal, the invitations dried up. Even when he was reinstated, Joe never got back into the celebrity business, which he'd mostly hated anyway.

After returning from Portugal, Joe celebrated by purchasing a new putter: the red TaylorMade Spider Tour. He probably didn't *need* it. He already putted well. But with the weather improving and the cancer scare behind him, Joe had decided to see if he could drop a couple strokes closer to par. He putted and chipped every morning; four afternoons a week he played eighteen holes. Before dinner he lifted, core and upper body. Without consciously dieting, he'd lost all the weight he'd put on during the dark days of winter.

Joe stroked a Titleist with the big red head of the Spider; eighteen smooth feet later, it fell into the cup. He struck a second ball, which rimmed out, then a third, which followed the first into the cup as if it were its twin brother. When he crossed the green to retrieve his balls, a woman putting to the adjacent practice hole said, "Nice touch."

He fumbled for an appropriate response. "Thanks?"

She wore a visor, powder-blue golf shirt, and khaki shorts. She looked like an athlete: flat belly, toned arms and calves. Thirty-five or forty, Joe guessed, younger than most mid-week golfers.

"Has anyone mentioned you look a lot like Joe Singer?"

Joe looked up from the mallet head of his putter. Was she tugging his leg? "Who's Joe Singer?"

The woman, who looked vaguely familiar, shook her head, and smiled. Her light brown pageboy jiggled. "You're kidding. I thought you would have heard this so many times."

She was attractive, not exactly pretty, but nice-looking, and spoke with a slight accent. Dutch? Scandinavian? Kind of a button nose. Joe wondered, *Is she hitting on me?* That hadn't happened in a while. Suddenly, she stepped towards him, putter under her left arm, right palm extended.

"Carlie Johannsen, I'm the club pro."

Now he knew why she looked familiar; there was a picture of her, smiling just like now, in the pro shop, advertising lessons.

"I'm Joe," he said. "Joe Singer."

"Wait," she said. "What?"

"Yes," he admitted. "Guilty as charged."

She invited him to play a round on Monday, her day off, and Joe accepted. He generally played alone, not having made any friends in Santa Rosa. If he played in a group, there was the possibility of awkward questions; not that they always came, but Joe was habitually on guard. Even if his former glory and fall from grace didn't come up, random golfers were rarely competitive, and that diminished his pleasure in the round, and make it harder to go all out. With Carlie Johannsen that wouldn't be a problem, and Joe had to admit that golfing with an attractive woman—not as pretty as Frannie, of course—was kind of exciting.

He dropped his three practice balls on the green and knocked the first one in the center of the cup from twenty feet away.

With Jack, Glad, and the girls in the stands, Jess was untouchable through five: nine strikeouts, three hits, two walks, no runs. Suarez told him he wasn't going back out to pitch the sixth, which Jess already knew; he hadn't thrown six all season. Suarez asked Jess to sit beside him when Rah and the team took the field for the top of the sixth.

"You know, Jess." Suarez, who always had a mouthful of sunflower seeds, sprayed black and white shells on the dugout floor. "Keep pitching like that"—he glanced at Jess and grinned—"you ain't gonna be around much longer."

Jess, who was watching Rah squat to receive warm-ups from Arturo Gomez, the soft-tossing lefty who'd relieved him, said, "Thanks. I felt like I had it all working today."

"You did. Best sink yet on your change. You been working on it?"

"Yes sir. Every chance I get."

Suarez sprayed another moist mouthful of shells. "You got three plus pitches." He packed his mouth. "All you need."

From inside Suarez's closed mouth, Jess could hear shells cracking. On the field, Rah threw Gomez's last warm-up to second base. "Thanks, Skip. I'm glad you think so."

"It's not just me." Suarez looked meaningfully at Jess, then back out at the field. "Go ice that million-dollar arm of yours."

Jess started down the tunnel from the dugout to the clubhouse, heart pounding with his manager's praise. Since they'd come north, he'd worked hard with Rah on his change, and today he'd gotten four whiffs, and lots of soft contact. In Port St. Lucie, that's what Gallagher, Gib, and Mac had said he needed to be called up. Three plus pitches, and now he had them. It was Rah who had helped. Rah who called such a great game today, Rah who had fallen asleep in his arms last night before Jess went back to his own bed.

Halfway down the rank concrete tunnel, which smelled of mold, sweat, and who knew what else, the realization hit him. The better he pitched, the sooner he'd be promoted, away from Rah.

They ended up, the whole crew, at an upscale Mexican restaurant for an early dinner. This time when Two-J's ordered a pitcher of Patron margaritas, Jack didn't say boo, although everyone knew you couldn't taste good tequila with all the other shit in the pitcher. It was only a matter of time, and not very much time, before they promoted him. If Two-J's wanted to drink margaritas, Jack thought, why the hell not? He'd sure earned them today.

Meanwhile, young love was blooming all around their table. Little Tiffany was mashed so close to Rah her boobs bumped his elbow. And Emmy, who looked, except for the dusting of freckles on her nose, like that actress Gwyneth whatever, kept staring at Two-J's all goo-goo eyed. But she was too classy, Jack thought, to lay a finger, and certainly not a boob, on him in public, especially not in front of his grandpa. Hell, Jack thought, *he* was staring at Two-J's googly eyed. He'd never seen the kid pitch better. He'd never seen anyone pitch better. Well, maybe Joey once or twice, and Sandy, of course, and maybe Scherzer, that blue-and-brown-eyed freak.

Jack swiveled his margarita glass to bring a fresh stretch of salted rim to his lips. Two-J's pitched like a man against boys today, even though he was one of the youngest players on the field.

"Jack," Glad said and placed her red-nailed fingers on his arm. "The way those kids are drinking." He followed her eyes to Jess, Rah, and the girls. "You're driving us home."

"No problem." Jack couldn't exactly hear what Two-J's was saying to Emmy or what Emmy was saying to Two-J's, but he couldn't take his eyes off them. Like movie stars, they were.

"So maybe, that should be your only drink."

No way! Then he saw the iron in Glad's eye. "Okay. No problem."

By the end of dinner, and the grub was better than Jack expected, the kids were polluted as Love Canal. Everyone piled into Two-J's SUV—they'd left the girls' Mustang parked at the Applewood. Jack drove: Jess's long legs gave him shotgun; Rah and the women squeezed in back. Halfway home, and it was lucky he'd taken surface streets, Emmy began moaning she was going to be sick.

Jack snapped, "Stick your head out the window!"

"No," Jess shouted, "it'll blow back!"

"Jack," Glad commanded, "pull over."

The girls stumbled out the driver side rear door, and Emmy puked into some poor schlub's garbage can, with Tiffany holding her hair back from her face. When they climbed back in, Jack drove, double-time, towards Applewood with the windows open. One, it reeked, and two, Emmy, poor kid, kept apologizing for how drunk she was, so maybe she wasn't done yet. Sure enough, not two minutes from the motel, Emmy moaned, "Pull over."

This time, she barely got her head outside before she hurled in the gutter. Tiff and Glad, still in her mink, walked her around for a minute and tried to get her cleaned up. Jack glanced at Two-J's. "I guess you won't be French-kissing tonight."

"You don't have to worry about that."

Rah, the only person still in the back, cracked up laughing. Soon enough, the women returned. Jack caught Glad's eyes in the rearview. "I hope she didn't puke on your mink."

"Shut up, Jack."

Jess half-walked, half-carried Emmy into the Applewood. Rah walked beside Tiff without touching her, carrying Emmy's soiled coat. Jack and Glad brought up the caboose of the puke parade, stopping in front of their own room, while the youngsters fumbled to unlock their door.

"What a night," Jack said.

"Those poor girls," Glad replied, then opened their door, and disappeared inside.

Joe and Frannie arrived early for Joe's appointment with Doc Perlman, his first since his return from Portugal. He'd had blood drawn two days ago, and he was nervous about the results. The whole trip seemed unreal. *This*, holding Frannie's hand—he squeezed hard—and she met his worried smile with her own. *This* was real.

Inside the exam room, Frannie said, "I'm sure it will be okay."

The door opened. "Hey, Joe." Doc Perlman extended his small hand. "Hello, Frannie." Turning towards Joe, he said, "You look like yourself again." He fisted his hands and raised them above his head. "Really strong."

"Thanks. I feel like myself again."

Perlman looked from Joe to Frannie and back again. "I won't keep you in suspense. Your PSA is heading down, just as we expected and as your letter from Dr. Bernstein said it would."

"What is it?" Frannie asked.

"Eight point nine." Perlman pursed his lips. "But that's largely residual. It will keep coming down the next few months."

"So," Joe asked, "there's nothing to worry about? I'm cured?"

"Cured," Doc Perlman said. "That's not a word we use. Maybe cancer-free, and it's too early to say for sure. But things look good. You look good. We'll do another blood test in three months."

"So that's all?" Frannie asked. "No other tests?"

"Not unless Joe wants another DRE."

Joe remembered exactly what DRE stood for. "I'll pass."

"Good. We'll wait for the radiation to work its magic, and I'll see you in three months. But I did want to ask you something, if you don't mind. Sexual function. No problem with erections since the radiation?"

Frannie answered for him. "No problem at all, at least none I've noticed. Joe?"

Joe shook his head, too embarrassed to answer, at least not with Frannie there. He thanked the little doc and at the front desk, scheduled an appointment for July. Then Joe and Frannie walked out into the bright Sonoma County morning.

Emmy got up early to shower and drive home.

"We have morning classes, and anyway, we hadn't planned to stay over. But things got out of hand."

"And mouth," Jess called after her.

She grinned and disappeared into the bathroom. She'd been too drunk last night to do anything except pass out. She was a nice girl, and he liked her. In fact, he liked her quite a bit, but not in that way, of course. Unlike the first time when she gave him a blow job, which for college girls seemed to be like shaking hands, he thought she might expect him to have sex with her, which was one reason he'd started buying all those margaritas last night. If he was drunk, he could have done it with her if he had to. Back in high school, he had some experience with hetero sex, and it helped if he was wasted. And that way he thought, pulling the blankets over his head, he wouldn't have to feel bad knowing Rah was in the other room maybe having sex with Tiffany. They'd agreed that was okay, though Jess didn't mean it, because it was important no one suspected what he and Rah had going. What he could hope, at least, and through the covers pulled over his head, he heard the shower go off his bathroom, was that Rah hadn't enjoyed it.

Emmy came out of the bathroom, but Jess remained under the covers pretending to sleep. A few minutes later, she sat on the bed beside him, on top of the sheets.

"Jess," she said, and shook his shoulder.

He uncovered and gazed up at her.

"I'm sorry I got so wasted last night." She bent down to kiss him. Her wet hair fell against his face. She moved her lips to his ear and nibbled, then sat up again.

"I really liked Glad and Jack and hope they don't think I'm that kind of girl."

Jess sat up half under the sheet, naked from the waist up. "What kind of girl is that?"

"The kind who gets so drunk, she throws up on the drive home."

"That's probably the kind Jack dated when he was our age."

"That's not who I am."

"Don't worry, Jack liked you fine."

"But what about you, Jess? You pitched so great, all three pitches. Then I got so drunk." Tears were forming in her eyes. "And messed up our night."

"I like you too, don't worry." He put his arms around her shoulders and hugged her. She obviously needed a hug, and the last thing Jess wanted was a crying girl in his bed.

Emmy lay her head on his shoulder. "Thank you." After a moment, she added, "I hope you don't like me in the same way as your grandpa."

"I don't." If she only knew what a horny straight guy Jack was, and he wasn't.

"Next time." Emmy placed her hand on his sheet-covered thigh. "I'll make it up to you for last night."

Oh God, thought Jess.

"But right now, I have to scoot. We're already going to be late for class."

She started towards the bedroom door. She was wearing, he realized, a different outfit from yesterday, a thin white turtleneck and a short skirt that showed off her long legs.

"Emmy," Jess said. "I thought you weren't planning to stay over."

"I wasn't."

"Then why'd you bring a change of clothes?"

"Do you know what the walk of shame is?"

"When you four-pitch in the winning run?"

"No, silly. It's when a girl walks home after a hookup wearing what she wore the night before. Now, don't you get the wrong idea about me, but I always bring a change of clothes, just in case."

Emmy blew a kiss and hurried out the door. Moments later, Jess heard voices in the living room, then the front door of the apartment opened and closed. A few moments after that, Rah knocked on Jess's door then climbed into bed wearing nothing but a smile.

Jack was in the breakfast room drinking coffee and eating a Danish that tasted like toilet paper, having rejected the microwave omelets that may or may not have been made with eggs. In came Jess and Rah, wearing matching blue and white team warm-ups, looking as if they belonged to an entirely different species than the fatsos around the breakfast room.

The guys set their duffle bags beside Jack's table before hustling off to pile their plates with the same crap the fat-asses were gobbling. Not Jack, who treated his body like a temple he didn't want to profane. "So," he said, when the boys returned, "where are the girls?"

"Driving back to school. Where's Glad?"

"Fitness center. She don't eat breakfast."

Two-J's said, "She looks like it."

Jack replied, "I woulda thought Emmy wanted breakfast on account of barfing up dinner."

Two-J's grinned at Rah, who was chowing down one of the so-called omelets. Jess started in on one too, chasing it with a bowl of fresh fruit that looked as if it had not only seen better days, but better weeks. Jess and Rah blazed through their meal. Jack kept looking for an opening to ask a question or two, but Jess and Rah were eating like their pants were on fire. He specifically wanted to question Two-J's in private if there was anything going on between him and Rah beside baseball, because last night and again this morning, Glad had been saying she thought they did. Jack didn't believe it, not with a looker like Emmy around. He kept hoping Rah would get up to re-load his plate, but it was Jess who got up first.

"So, Rah," he asked, man to man, "anything happen with you and Tiffany, or was she too drunk?"

"A little, Grandpa Jack."

Before Jack could follow up, Two-J's returned. "We gotta blow this pop stand. Team meeting. Thanks for coming up."

"I wouldn't miss it. I seen you pitch everywhere you been. Next time, I'm hoping it's Citi Field."

"Me too." Two-J's glanced at Rah, and something passed between them. Jack wondered if Glad was right.

"Jack, I'm sorry I can't drive you to the airport."

"No problem, we'll take an Upper."

Rah and Two-J's wolfed down their second plates of garbage and stood. Jack hugged Two-J's, which always felt funny because his head barely reached his grandson's shoulder.

Rah stuck out his mitt of a hand and shook Jack's. "*Adios,* Grandpa Jack, good to see you again. In Spanish, we say, '*Mucho gusto.*'"

Jack tried it out. "*Mucho gusto.*"

The kid had a great smile, Jack thought. Jess could do worse.

Then Jess and Rah hustled out. Jess turned and put his thumb near his ear, pinkie near his mouth. "Call me! When you're back in Florida."

Then he grinned, and the boys were gone.

CHAPTER SEVENTEEN

Carlie Johannsen was one hell of a golfer, Joe thought. She played from the men's blue tees, same as he did, and although he regularly out-drove her, she was three strokes up at the turn, and five ahead after sixteen holes. Joe picked up a stroke on seventeen, a long par three over water from an elevated tee, sticking a five-iron four feet from the cup, then sinking the birdie putt. On eighteen, Joe striped his drive 280 yards down the middle.

"Great shot, Joe." Carlie smiled and replaced him on the tee box. She wore the same khaki shorts as the day they'd met, and when she bent to place her tee and ball in the ground, they rode up, revealing the top of her very toned thighs. Carlie settled into her stance and addressed the ball, cocking her head slightly right to keep her dominant eye above the ball. She started her backswing, a powerful takeaway Joe had admired all day, reached an apex nearly horizontal, then uncurled rapidly, saving the wrist release until the last possible moment, torqueing her hips and lower body into her follow-through. The ball exploded off her driver following a low whistling trajectory that whooshed into a final parabola, as if propelled by a second stage booster. Her ball landed and skipped past Joe's.

"Wow. Great shot."

"I've been saving it."

"Why?"

"Men don't like to be outdriven by women." She grinned again. *Flirting?* He couldn't figure her out. He followed her off the tee box. Carlie climbed into the driver's side of the cart. She'd driven pretty much the entire round, which was fine, Joe thought; she was the pro, and she'd invited him to play, which made her the host. The thing was, he couldn't understand why she'd invited him.

"You know," she began, "and I probably shouldn't tell you. But when I was sixteen, I had this mad crush on you."

Uh-oh, Joe thought.

"My father was a Swedish banker, and we'd been living in the States for four years, after he took a job in New York. You were such a great pitcher, and I was so sports-mad."

She smiled. She had a nice face, and friendly, light brown eyes, nearly the same color as her short hair.

"I thought you were *so* good-looking. And then, when your marriage broke up, I thought your wife must be so stupid to divorce the great Joe Singer."

Joe remembered his first wife, Sarah, who'd slept with Perez, the first baseman. The first baseman! And the dark days that followed.

"Anyway, when I saw you on the putting green, it all came back. I thought I'd tell you, and we'd have a good laugh."

She looked at him meaningfully. Joe wasn't sure what was funny, but it often took him awhile to ferret out subtext.

Carlie stopped the cart beside their balls. She'd out-driven him by ten yards. "That's the furthest I've seen a woman hit a golf ball."

"Driving was always the strongest part of my game. If I could have done everything so well, I would have made it on the tour."

Joe had 120 yards to the green, Carlie maybe 110. Joe played a sand wedge, but pulled it slightly, leaving himself maybe fifteen feet to the cup. Carlie's pitching wedge landed ten feet past the hole and spun backwards, leaving her a tap in for a birdie.

"Damn," Joe said. "Nice shot. I never could figure out how to spin the ball like that."

"I could teach you."

Not wanting to take advantage of her, or encourage too much intimacy—in part because he found her attractive and it had been a long time since he thought about another woman, and there was all that business about how she used to have a crush on him—Joe said, "How much are lessons?"

She grinned. After they slid their irons into their respective bags, they sat together in the cart.

"Maybe we can work out a trade? Because there's something I very much want from you."

But I'm married. "What's that?"

Carlie stepped hard on the electric cart's accelerator, and the sudden movement nearly knocked them into each other. "We're having a club tournament next month, and I'd like to announce you as a special guest. I think our members would enjoy meeting you."

Joe felt simultaneously relieved and disappointed.

"Why, Joe?" She widened her eyes. "What did you think I wanted?"

He blushed.

"You thought because I told you I had a crush on you when I was sixteen? Men." She laughed. "I thought you knew, because all the regular members know, I've been a lesbian for many years."

"Oh," Joe said.

"So, you thought, I invited you to play a round with me..."

Her eyes sparkled. They really were, he thought, very nice eyes.

"It's okay, then, if I mention, you'll appear at our tournament?"

This was exactly the sort of public appearance he usually turned down. He was naturally shy, and part of him still feared the public. But how could he refuse without it seeming as if she were right about why he'd agreed to play with her?

"Sure," he said, "but I'm not very good in public."

"Then we'll have to work extra hard teaching you to spin a wedge. To make it worth your while."

They arrived at the green. Carlie parked the cart and set the brake. Joe left his putt a foot short, then Carlie tapped hers in for a birdie, finishing five strokes and a personal appearance ahead. He never would have guessed she liked women. But what did he know?

That evening, Joe and Frannie drove to the Village of Sonoma and strolled around the plaza. Sonoma people-watching and window-shopping were among their favorite activities. Although they rarely purchased anything or tasted wine and olive oil, Sonoma charmed them, and they sometimes stopped into the original mission to feel part of its long history.

After they'd circled the plaza, returning to the north side where they'd started, they settled on a bench under the green arching trees. The light was fading. Small birds twittered in the high branches, and swallows, maybe even a few bats, swooped in the gloaming.

Frannie said, "You never did tell me. How old is the golf pro?"

"Maybe forty-five."

"Who won?"

"I lost by five strokes."

The light was nearly gone. "Did you ever figure out why he invited you?"

"Actually," Joe said, feeling guilty, "the pro's a woman, Carlie Johannsen."

Frannie looked at him. "A woman beat you by five strokes?"

"She's really good. She can hit the ball one hell of a long way."

"Is she big and burly?"

"Not really. She's kind of pretty." Joe smiled then remembered he was talking to his wife. "But not as pretty as you."

"Flattery will only get you to first base. So why did she ask you to play a round?"

Joe's eyes did a little flip. "She asked me to appear at the club tournament in a few weeks."

"I assume you said no, like always."

"I said yes."

For the first time in years, really for the first time he could remember, Frannie looked jealous. "She must be prettier than you're letting on."

"I never said she wasn't pretty."

He grinned; Frannie didn't. Everything he said seemed to make things worse. But like the loyal husband he was, Joe pressed on.

"She confessed that when she was sixteen, which means I was, like, thirty, she had this giant crush on me."

"*Really*."

"The thing is," Joe said, "she's a lesbian, so it doesn't mean anything."

"How do you know she's a lesbian?"

"She told me."

"She told you?"

"That's right." He leaned towards her in the dark and kissed her, and not just a little peck. "Love you, Frannie. Now how about dinner? Girl and the Fig, okay?"

"Sure." They ate there probably once a week, and he knew it was her favorite. They stood up, and this time she kissed him, just like in their courting days, really hard on the mouth and grabbed his ass too. Then they crossed Spain Street in Sonoma, California, heading for dinner.

CHAPTER EIGHTEEN

Four days after the game that Glad, Jack, Emmy, and Tiff attended, the Syracuse Mets were settling into a Hampton Inn near the ballpark in Moosic, PA. They were in Moosic to begin a three-game set against the Scranton/Wilkes-Barre RailRiders, the Yankees Triple-A affiliate; Jess had been eager to face them since the season began. Scranton/Wilkes-Barre RailRiders was a stupid name, but last season Jess had pitched for the Binghamton Rumble Ponies, which took the layer cake for stupid. One, there were no ponies in Binghamton, New York; and two, what the hell was a *rumble pony*? All season long, Jess and his teammates had wondered if *rumble* was the sound of too many ballpark franks? Or did *rumble* signify street fighting, *a la West Side Story*, one of Jack's favorite movies, so that *rumble ponies* meant they were bad-tempered miniature horses?

Sitting on one of the queen-sized beds in the room he shared with Rah, Jess decided that although Scranton/Wilkes-Barre RailRiders sounded stupid, they were the *Yankees'* affiliate, and always fielded a good squad. They had three players on MLB's top one hundred prospects list, and someday, Jess thought, he'd face them in a Subway Series in New York. *Yeah, right,* he thought. *And then you wake up.*

In the meantime, he'd been following his day-before-starting regimen. Before the two-and-half-hour bus ride, he'd gotten in his lifting. On the bus, he crunched scouting reports with Rah and watched iPad videos of the RailRiders' best hitters and of his own last two starts. Even though his mechanics were generally good, he was still flying open on four-seamers, especially to right-handed batters, missing high and wide when working the outside corner, and even worse, sometimes splitting the dish when coming inside. He'd been lucky several times against the IronPigs on fastballs middle-middle, but against the number three and four batters on the RailRiders, those pitches would get crushed. *Release point,* he'd thought, watching video on the bus. *Release point,* which Dad had been emphasizing his entire life. *Release point,* he was thinking now, back propped against the headboard, watching his Mini-Me on the iPad. Rotate your hip, drive with your legs. Stay balanced over the rubber. *Release point.*

Jess glanced at Rah, seated on the next bed, bare-chested, playing Fortnite on his Nintendo Switch, wearing boxers. Part of his night-before-starting for his last three starts had involved a different sort of *release.* He still couldn't believe that after being certain Rah was straight, it turned out he'd been sleeping with men since he was fifteen. Nobody in his family knew, of course, and Rah said that if his father found out, he might kill him. Or worse!

Jess glanced at Rah again, lost in Fortnite. How could he bring up sex without being too obvious? Rah loved Fortnite and didn't like to be interrupted. But it was getting late, and another part of the night-before-starting was extra sleep. Maybe propose back rubs, which wouldn't be *too* obvious, because loosening his back and shoulder was another part of night-before-starting. It was key, Jess thought. Yes, key! The Mets, like every other team, were serious about protecting starting pitchers' arms. He remembered Suarez saying after his last start, "Take care of that moneymaker, son!"

Big league clubs employed armies of trainers and massage therapists, and stars often hired private masseuses. Even in Triple-A, tomorrow at the park before warming up, Jess would get a fifteen-minute rubdown from Gus the trainer. But the rub Jess had in mind was different. He shifted to Rah's bed and started stroking his shoulders.

"Doan bother me, Yess, I'm playing."

"Don't you want your shoulders rubbed?"

Jess pressed harder, then moved his lips to the back of Rah's neck.

"*Pendejo!*" Rah shouted, dropping his Switch. "They kill me!"

Rah turned, and Jess kissed his lips. Rah kissed him back so violently it was like getting punched, and they thrashed around as if they were fighting. Then it wasn't fighting, and just as Jess started relaxing into the smooth, pliant feel of Rah's tongue, *knocking* started on their door, softly, then more urgently. Over the next few seconds, Jess grasped the *knocking*, which became a *banging*, wasn't inside his chest. Rah understood at the exact same time, and they jumped away from each other as if scalded, eyes wide with fear.

Jess mouthed, "*Get dressed!*"

Rah grabbed his pants and ran to the bathroom. The door banging intensified. This had been and remained their greatest fear: getting caught in bed. Jess pulled on his Syracuse t-shirt and shorts, shoved his mussed hair off his face, and started towards the door. Halfway there, he glimpsed his eyes in a mirror: stark animal terror.

"One second!"

Jess heard voices in the hall. He looked back to make sure nothing would give them away. *Good, the sheets on both beds were turned down.*

When he unlatched the chain and opened the door, his manager, Ray Suarez, and Tony C., traveling secretary, stood shoulder to shoulder, grinning.

"For a minute," Suarez began, "I thought maybe you and Rah were at a bar trying to get lucky. But Tony said, 'No way, not Jess, night before a start.'"

Remembering Jack's lifelong advice that if you had to lie, be as honest as possible, Jess replied, "We were in bed. I sleep extra before a start."

Suarez said, "Tony, you were right."

Tony C., whose face resembled a slice of meatloaf, nodded. "Okay if we come in?"

Jess backed up, hoping he hadn't missed anything incriminating.

"Where's Rah?" Suarez asked.

"In the crapper." Jess hesitated, then added, "Sir."

Suarez and Tony C grinned. "*Sir*," Suarez said. "That kills me."

Tony C. asked again, "Where's Rah? This is about him too."

Who had ratted them out? Who could possibly know? "I'll get him." Jess stepped around Suarez and knocked on the closed bathroom door, said in a loud stage whisper, "Coach is here to see us."

"*Momentito.*" Rah emerged looking every bit as startled and scared as when he went in.

"Sooooo," Suarez began. "I'm sorry if we woke you guys. But there's bad news about Jess's start."

I'm not starting? Jess thought. *What the fuck?*

"Real bad news," added Tony C.

"Late this afternoon, Randy Vermouth went on the IR with biceps tendinitis. Guess who they're calling up?"

Slowly, like a night-blooming orchid, understanding opened inside Jess. His lips began to tremble, and the next thing Jess knew he was fighting tears. Was he really going to mark the moment he'd been dreaming of his entire life by *crying*! Tom Hanks's iconic line from *A League of their Own* tiptoed through his mind, "*There's no crying in baseball!*" just as Suarez stuck out his hand.

"Congratulations, son! After your last start, I said you wouldn't be here long!"

Next Tony C. pumped Jess's hand. For a moment, it was too much. *Too much!* Jubilation and regret in a single breath: the fear of losing Rah. He stuck out his hand to his catcher, but Rah pushed past it and wrapped him in a bear hug.

"Jess," Rah shouted in his ear. "Yess, Yess, Yess!" Then softer, so the others wouldn't hear, "*Te amo, hombre!*"

Jess stepped out of Rah's embrace, fearful of appearing less than manly.

Suarez said, "They want you on the 6:00-a.m. flight out of Wilkes-Barre."

Tony C. added, "You change planes in DC, then onto La Guardia, landing at ten-thirty. Better start packing, son." He turned to Rah. "For now, you got a single, but soon as they send us another player, you got a roomie, okay?"

Rah nodded and peeked at Jess, who was praying Suarez and Tony C. would leave them alone. Then he thought, *Wait a minute. Wait a minute!*

"Did they say when they plan to pitch me?"

"I was waiting for you to ask." Suarez grinned. "Day after tomorrow, son. You start day after tomorrow at Citi Field."

Those were the last words Jess heard. Eventually, Suarez and Tony C. departed. Jess jumped into Rah's arms and held on.

When the phone rang, Joe was in their bedroom, waiting for the Giants game to start. Mike Krukow, the Giants' color analyst, was finishing his pregame spiel. Joe had pitched several times against Kruk thirty or more years ago and liked him. He muted the volume and answered his phone.

"Dad," Jess said, "could you get Mom? There's something I want to tell you at the same time."

"Everything okay?"

"Everything's great. Get Mom and put me on speaker."

"Sure." Joe switched off the TV and left the bedroom. "You still pitching tomorrow?"

"I've been pushed back a day. Let me know when Mom's there."

Joe found Frannie in the living room, watching this weird British show on which English craftsmen repaired family heirlooms. He'd also caught her watching a docudrama about famous assassins. He wouldn't have thought she'd be interested in either, but she was.

"It's Jess," Joe said. "He wants to tell us something."

Frannie paused her program.

"You're on speaker," Joe said. "Mom's right beside me."

"Guess who's starting Friday night at Citi Field?"

"Oh, Jess!" Frannie shouted and started to cry.

"Son," Joe said, then he was bawling too. "I'm so proud of you."

"Hey, guys," Jess said. "Are you crying?"

Joe looked at Frannie, who answered, "Tears of joy."

Jess said, "When Suarez, the S-Mets' manager gave me the news, my first reaction was to cry too."

"It's only natural," Joe said. "When you dream about something for so long."

Frannie squeezed his hand.

"You call Jack yet?" Joe asked.

"Right after I call you guys. So."

Joe could hear the hesitation in Jess's voice.

"Will you come to the game?"

"You couldn't keep us away," Frannie said. "Soon as we get off, I'll buy tickets."

"That's great, I mean, Dad's okay to travel?"

"I'm cancer-free," Joe said. "Who are the Mets playing Friday?"

"Philadelphia. Nola's pitching." Jess hesitated. "There's one more thing."

"What's that?" Frannie asked.

There was a long pause, then Jess said, "I'll tell you when I see you. Love you, guys."

"Can't you tell us now?"

"In person would be better."

"Love you too," Joe and Frannie said.

There was no danger of Jack crying. One, he hadn't cried in decades. Two, when his phone rang and he saw it was Jess, he turned to Glad, who sat beside him on her couch, and said, "I bet this is the call we been waiting for."

Jess said, "Grandpa—?"

Jack shouted into his iPhone, "They CALLED you up, didn't they?"

"How'd you know?"

Jack bounded off the couch like a spring rooster. "Cause I seen your last start! And because I read that stiff VERMOUTH has a bum shoulder!"

"Can't tell you anything, can I?"

Jack thought maybe Two-J's sounded miffed. "Sorry to steal your thunder!" Then he started shouting again, "I am SO PUMPED! Wait a minute." He bent down and kissed Glad, *bam!* on her red, red mouth. "Start packing, honey, we're going to New York."

"Syracuse?"

"The Big Fucking Apple!"

"Jack," Jess said, "I gotta go, early flight."

"Your parents flying in this time?"

"They said they were. I'm starting Friday."

"Against Nola?" Jack crowed. "Against fucking *Nola?*"

"That's right."

"You'll beat his ass, Two-J's, don't worry." Then a strange thought crossed Jack's mind. "Say hi to Rah for us. What a sweet kid. Me and Glad really like him."

"Me too."

Before Jack could say, *See ya in the City,* the phone went dead.

When his alarm went off at four-fifteen, the room was black and Jess didn't know where he was. It was so early, it didn't feel as if he'd slept yet, and now that he was marginally awake, it felt as if he were still asleep. Then he remembered. *Rah.* They'd broken their rule and slept in the same bed. Rah was beside him, naked except for boxers, his face on the next pillow.

Jess turned off the buzzing cell alarm and raised the phone above Rah's face. The dim light illuminated his closed eye sockets and the hollow between his lips and chin. They'd made love last night after Suarez and Tony C. left, and Jess couldn't remember sex being so tender and loving. And then he thought, *No, it's not that he couldn't remember sex like that. He'd never had sex like that!*

The iPhone switched itself off, and the room plunged into darkness. Jess thought about crawling under the sheet, removing Rah's boxers, and taking Rah in his mouth. Just thinking about that, and he could feel himself getting hard.

But no. They'd said goodbye that way, Rah hated waking up early, and he had a plane to catch. He crept from bed towards the bathroom to shower. With the hot spray streaming over him, the words of a song his mother used to play, "I'm leaving on a jet plane, don't know when I'll be back again," merged with the water, and he sang them over and over, finishing with, "Oh babe, I hate to go."

He nearly made himself cry, which he must have been trying to do. But then it was time to go, and he toweled off, put his Dopp kit in the suitcase he'd brought into the bathroom with him, and dressed in the shirt, pants, Skechers, and Mets windbreaker he'd laid out the night before. Just before leaving the bathroom, he glanced in the mirror and realized he'd forgotten his ballcap, which must be somewhere in the bedroom. He wondered how he was going to find it in the dark, maybe turn on the flashlight on his phone, because he'd decided as a point of pride that he wasn't going to turn on the light and wake up Rah, who had an afternoon game and needed his sleep. And besides, he didn't want to seem too needy; they'd said goodbye the night before.

But when he came out of the bathroom, carrying his suitcase, trying hard not to make any noise, he only made it halfway to the door before Rah sat up and switched on the bedside lamp.

"Weren't you going to say goodbye?" Rah asked.

"Oh, babe," Jess answered, hearing an echo of the song in his head. "I didn't want to wake you."

"You think I can sleep when you leaving?"

Jess put down his suitcase and hurried to Rah's side of the bed. Rah wrapped his strong catcher's arms around Jess's waist and pressed the side of his face against Jess's belly. He held on and held on. After a moment, Jess stepped back.

"I hate to go," he said.

"You're going to do great, Jess."

"I'll call when I land."

"I'll be at the ballpark. Call tonight."

Jess started towards the door, then rushed back to the bed and kissed Rah's mouth. And kissed it some more. When they were out of breath, Rah said, "You doan wanna miss your flight."

Jess started towards the door.

"And Jess—" Jess turned back.

"Doan forget your release point." Rah licked his lips.

"I won't."

Jess smiled and hurried out the door.

CHAPTER NINETEEN

At 10:00 a.m. Thursday, the Mets' PR department announced top pitching prospect Jess Singer, son of all-time team great, Joe Singer, was being promoted from Syracuse and would start Friday against the Phillies. At 7:05 a.m. in Santa Rosa, where Joe was crunching extra shirts into his suitcase, his cell phone began blowing up. How did the New York press get his number? Jess? Mac? The Mets' front office? Joe had disliked interviews even before the scandal twenty-five years ago. He'd never wanted to be a hero, nor did he deserve to be a villain. He couldn't think fast enough on his feet to answer questions, and so for years had been reduced to the classic jock response: *I just want to do my best for the team.*

That became impossible after he was suspended for refusing to defend himself against allegations he tried to throw a game the Mets ultimately won. And though all was supposedly forgiven when the charges were dropped and he was reinstated, the attendant stink, Joe believed, had dishonored his name. That stink, Joe thought, was what people remembered, not his ten years as the ace of a bad team.

He also remembered the way some of his so-called fans had turned on him, especially that joker in New York who'd sent his five-year-old to Joe's table, ostensibly for an autograph, but really to say, in his piping little boy voice, "Say it ain't so, Joe! Say it ain't!"

Joe had never returned to New York for a Mets Old-Timers' game, nor did he supplement his pension appearing at card and memorabilia shows, like Pete Rose, who'd been caught betting on games, or the small army of retired players who'd spent years injecting themselves in the ass with steroids. Joe was shy; he was proud; and, it just wasn't worth it to him.

But this was different, Frannie said. This was about Jess. The Mets' PR department assured him of the same thing, when they called just before he turned off his phone. *The first father-son tandem in team history! Just like Vlad Guerroro, Junior and Senior! Like Fernando Tatis! What a great story, Joe!* And so, completely against his heart's desire, which was to wear the disguise Jack always called the Midnight Jew, *a la* Jon Voight, Joe agreed to do his first press conference since he retired twenty-four years ago.

Because of the time change, they didn't land at JFK until almost 9:00 p.m. A waiting Town Car whisked them to the Bentley, the East Side hotel where they'd stayed when Joe was seen at Sloane Kettering. Jack and Glad were already there. Five minutes after they checked in, there was a knock, and Jack entered, not just grinning ear to ear, but six inches past both sides of his face.

"Hey, Joey." He grabbed Joe's hand. "Hey, Frannie. They gave you one hell of a room, much nicer than ours."

Joe hadn't even noticed, but they'd been installed in a junior suite; one long wall of windows looked across the East River onto Roosevelt Island.

"How was your flight?" Frannie asked.

"Easy." Jack reached up to kiss her cheek. "You know what? Either you're still growing, or I'm shrinking faster than I thought."

"You're shrinking," Joe said.

Jack shot him a look. "We got in early enough, me and Glad had dinner with Two-J's."

"Is he nervous?" Frannie asked.

"I'd be nervous," Joe admitted.

"You," Jack replied, "had me for a parent. But Two-J's had the two of you. He's like a thoroughbred inside the starting gate, waiting for his first race."

Jack grinned. This was his version, Joe realized, of a compliment.

"By the way," Jack continued, "Two-J's said call him when you got in."

Frannie asked, "You don't think it's too late?"

Joe checked his watch. *Ten to eleven.* "Nah, he'll be up. He probably can't sleep, I know I couldn't."

Jack was watching from the back of the press room, by special permission of the Mets, while the beat writers interviewed Joe. How, they wanted to know, did it feel to have his son not only follow him to the majors, but to the very same club he'd pitched for?

"Like a dream," Joe answered.

He was wearing a vintage cap, the same style he'd worn while pitching: blue brim and body, orange NY. He looked like a dream himself, Jack thought. Once again tall, strong, and slender. With gray hair showing at his temples, he almost looked wise. At the very least, Joe looked like an ambassador for baseball as it used to be: before steroids, instant replay, launch angles, the Universal DH, PitchCom, and the pitch clock changed the game. Before sabermetrics. Before openers. Before starting pitchers were lifted after twice through the lineup.

"Joe," called a baldie near the front. "When Jess was growing up, did you give him tips on pitching?"

"Like any son and dad, we played a lot of catch."

"What about his curve?" asked a woman in front of Jack. "Rated the best in the minors. Did you teach him?"

"Actually." Joe grinned. "I spent Jess's high school years cautioning him not to throw it. Shows what I knew."

Damn right, thought Jack.

"Jess's grandfather taught him that curve."

"Your father," asked a white-haired reporter, up front. "The bookie? He's still alive?"

"He was never a bookie," Joe's eyes narrowed. "And yes, still alive and kicking like hell. He's here today to watch the game."

Their eyes met, Joe's and Jack's, and Jack nodded, remembering those terrible days.

"Last question," Joe said, and pointed towards a reporter in the front row.

"Who do you think is better, Joe, you or Jess? I mean at the same age?"

Several reporters laughed. *What a dumbass question,* Jack thought.

"Some of you may know, I struggled my first two years throwing strikes. So, I'd say Jess. Then again, as his dad, I just might be biased."

Joe grinned. He'd looked surprisingly comfortable answering these dumbasses, Jack thought.

"Thank you, fellas." Joe stood, then leaned back towards the mic. "And you women too, of course. You know there weren't any female reporters when I was playing. Some things really do change for the better." He grinned. "Let's go Mets."

Seated behind the Mets' dugout, Joe was jumpy as sixteen cats. Frannie was on his left, Jack and Glad to his right. Joe couldn't remember feeling this nervous, not even for his one post-season start; well, maybe his first All-Star game, when he had to run back to the clubhouse and throw up. Watching Jess complete warm-ups, unable to influence what would happen in a few minutes, was terrifying and humbling. Just like the first day they'd brought Jess to preschool, and he ran off to play, without looking back. There was nothing he or Frannie could do now.

He'd looked so grown up in the clubhouse, dark stubble stippling his cheeks. *You'll do great,* Joe managed. Frannie had hugged him and held on. But Jack, who was incapable of being low-key, had pumped Jess's hand and half-shouted, *You'll fucking kill it, Two-J's, I know you will!*

Jess toed the rubber, peering in for a sign from Furillo, the Mets' veteran catcher. Most likely they'd worked out the first pitch, maybe even the first sequence based on the scouting report and would follow it unless Furillo had picked up during warm-ups that Jess was having trouble executing one pitch or another. Joe hadn't seen anything amiss, however, and hoped that whatever Furillo called, Jess dotted, because you only got one chance to throw your first major league pitch for a strike. He also hoped the Phillies' leadoff batter wasn't sitting dead red if Furillo had called a fastball. Jess bent into his motion. Without realizing he was doing it, Joe held his breath and watched a big breaking first-pitch curve nick the outside corner. Joe turned towards his father, who mouthed, "Fucking A."

It was beautiful. And so was the next pitch, and the one after that.

Jess gave up a solo shot, a no-doubter, to Castellanos in the fourth, then gutted through a two-on, two-out jam in the fifth. When Gallagher sent him out to begin the sixth, he knew he was on the shortest of leashes. If anyone got on, he was gone. But Jess didn't want to be gone. He was having way too much fun. He threw a one-two-three top of the sixth, ending with a slower-than-usual curve that froze the Phillies' left-handed slugger, Bryce Harper. Jess just about danced off the field to the thunder of hometown cheers, reminding himself to *Act like you've been here before.* But he hadn't. The Mets were leading 6-1 in his first major league start. If he could have written the script, it wouldn't have been this good. *Just wait,* he thought, swaddled as if in a blanket by the crowd noise, which only grew louder when his new teammates pushed him up the dugout steps to doff his cap. *Just wait till I tell Rah.*

PART THREE

THE SHOW

CHAPTER TWENTY

Four months later, Jess was preparing for his eighteenth big league start: Oracle Park against the Giants. Although he'd never again been as dominant as in his debut against the Phillies, his record was 8-5, with a 3.41 ERA, and his name came up, Jack loved telling him, on most National League Rookie of the Year lists. To manage his innings, the Mets brass skipped him whenever the Mets had an off-day, and often pulled him after five even when his pitch count was low. Mindful of the Matt Harvey fiasco in 2015, the front office was planning to shut Jess down at 175 innings; counting Triple-A, he was at 135. With the Mets in post-season contention—second in the NL East and leading the second Wild Card—*How to Handle Jess Singer's workload*, was a hot topic on New York sports radio.

The *Post*, *Newsday*, and *Daily News* alternated calling him "Curvy Jess," "Hammer Singer," and "Dr. Hook." He'd been hired as the spokesperson for Summerall Tires, and his agent was working on a sneaker deal. *Bleacher Report* ran a feature referring to Jess as the Boy Wonder and Singer 2.0. He'd rented an apartment on the Upper East Side, and there were social media rumors that he was the Mets' most eligible bachelor. He'd accumulated 200,000 followers on Instagram, 250,000 on Twitter, and on the advice of the Mets' PR office, he'd shut down his public Facebook account.

He and Rah texted every day. Rah favored emojis: four or six smiley faces with sunglasses. They'd promised to talk every night, or every other night, but that had proved impossible because the Mets played so many night games. Jess didn't get back to his apartment or hotel room until after midnight. He could talk then, but Rah had a roommate, both at Applewood and in motels for road games (major leaguers had private rooms on the road). So they ended up speaking once or twice a week, whenever the Mets had an off-day or played in the afternoon. That wasn't enough. Neither of them, Jess realized, knew anything about being in a relationship. They were so frightened of being discovered, they tried never to speak when Rah's roommate was there. No phone sex. No sexting. What if someone found out? Just *Hello, how are you? I miss you.*

He'd managed to see Rah twice since being promoted and not at all since the All-Star Break, which he spent in Syracuse. His major league teammates found it weird he returned to Syracuse instead of going hunting or fishing, or chilling with his family; Jess tried not to talk about it. The visit wasn't all that successful. Rah had a game every day except Monday and Miguel in his room at night, so they had to be incredibly careful. Jess rented his own suite at Applewood. They ate out in large groups two of the three nights, and everyone had questions. What was the postgame spread like? How much was the per diem on the road? What was the best city for hotties? Which Mets were chill, and which were assholes? Did rookies really have to carry vets' suitcases on road trips? And having to dress up in women's clothes, when was that?

Their last night, Jess and Rah went out by themselves to Otro Cuatro, which they thought of as *their place*. They got sloshed on margaritas, then returned to Jess's room and made desperate love in the dark that ended with Jess fighting tears when Rah returned to his room; they wouldn't see each other again for weeks or months. Rah was scuffling at the plate, batting .230 with three home runs, so was unlikely to be called up until September when rosters expanded, and maybe not even then.

The truth was, Jess thought, lying on the trainer's table in the visitors' clubhouse at Oracle Park, waiting for his pregame rubdown, he'd been dying of loneliness. The Mets were a veteran club; the only other young pitchers were relievers. Trey Sparrow had come over in a deadline deal with the Angels, while Big Barnes, who'd made a place for himself in middle relief, was even more of a douchebag than he'd been in the minors.

Pull up your socks! Jess chided himself. *You're in the Show!* And tonight, he reminded himself, his parents were coming to the game. After it was over, they'd all drive to Santa Rosa. He'd only visited once before, and while it wouldn't feel like home, it wasn't a hotel room. Mom had prepared one of his favorite meals: green curry chicken with Thai eggplant. He was looking forward to chowing down around midnight: his first home-cooked meal since he couldn't remember when. But first, Jess thought, feeling the trainer stretching the muscles in his upper back and left shoulder, there was the little matter of the Giants.

After the game, Joe drove them north across the Golden Gate. Frannie sat beside him; Jess stretched out in back. It was later than planned, past midnight; they wouldn't reach home until after one. Jess had pitched okay, good not great. First two innings he couldn't find the plate. To Joe, it looked as if his son was trying to be too fine, a rookie mistake, picking at the corners rather than filling the zone, so his pitch count got up early. He was lifted after five, leading 3-2. In the bottom of the eighth, the Giants tied the game against Big Barnes, a rookie relief pitcher Joe knew Jess didn't like. *Blowhard,* Jess said. *Asshole, and a bully.* Joe knew the type, had played with his own Big Barnes. The game went into extras; the Giants walked it off in the bottom of the eleventh. By the time Jess emerged from the visitors' clubhouse, his dark hair still wet, it was 11:45, and he looked beat.

They drove in silence, and Joe's thoughts drifted. On Monday, he'd been to Doc Perlman for his third follow-up. The little doc wanted to discuss Joe's latest blood test. After falling rapidly the first five months after Portugal, his PSA had leveled off at 0.6. Still a good number, Perlman explained, and probably nothing to worry about, but he'd expected it to reach almost zero.

Joe had glanced at Frannie, beside him in the exam room. In Joe's experience when a doc announced there was *Probably nothing to worry about,* it was time to hunker down.

"Maybe it's a one-time blip." Frannie squeezed his hand. "And it will continue down next month."

"Likely," Perlman said, and Joe relaxed.

"Joe," Frannie said, breaking his reverie. "Don't miss the exit."

Damnit. He shot across three lanes and veered off 101 onto Highway 37. When 37 forked, he followed 121, a twisty country road, not well-lit, that turned north and west towards Sonoma. Another forty minutes, Joe thought. He'd be glad to reach home.

At one-thirty, they were seated around the table, eating green curry. Ruby lurked on the rug, wearing a doggie diaper, her protuberant eyes turned towards Frannie, her moon and sun.

"This is great, Mom." Jess heaped his plate with seconds of rice and the fragrant curry. "Anyone else?"

She shook her head.

Joe asked, "Another beer?"

"If you do," Jess said.

"I'll get them." Frannie stood.

"Mom," Jess asked, "you have your hot sauce, *prik*, what is it?"

"*Prik nam pla.* I'll bring that too." She disappeared into the kitchen.

Joe loved having Jess home. It felt like years, not months, since they'd shared a meal. Frannie returned with two Singhas and the *prik nam pla.* She'd learned to make it and the green curry during the three months they lived in Thailand when Jess was two, the year after he retired. What a sweet time, Joe thought. So different from anything they'd done before, and so good for them as a new family.

"It's awfully late for dinner," Frannie said. "Isn't it?"

"Not really. Ask Dad." Jess looked at him. "It's really hard to relax after a game."

Joe nodded, remembering. "Some nights I could hardly sleep, going over what I could have done differently. Anyway, you can sleep in. You don't have to be at the park till four, right?"

Jess nodded, still shoveling curry.

"I'll drive you," Joe added.

"I'll take an Uber."

"No way," Joe insisted. "Anyway, I'm meeting up with Mac."

"You are?" Frannie sounded a little ticked.

"Boys' night," Joe said. "Hope you don't mind."

"Why would I?" But she sounded as if she did.

"Jess," Joe asked, "you spend much time with Mac? I mean, more than the other coaches?"

"A little." Jess pushed the last of the curry and rice onto his spoon. "He doesn't want the other pitchers to think he's playing favorites."

"Because you're his godson."

"Exactly."

Joe thought about how much he missed Mac, how he wished he'd arranged his life to spend more time with him. Frannie yawned. Joe yawned too. Suddenly, Jess's expression switched from laughing about curry to something more serious.

"There's something I need to tell you."

"Can't it wait till morning?" Frannie asked. "I'm all in."

"I don't think so." Jess faced her. "I should have told you years ago." He turned to Joe. "Please don't be mad."

Joe's stomach flipped. "Why would we be mad?"

"For keeping it secret so long." He gulped his Singha. "And for telling Jack first." His lip curled under his front teeth, a nervous tic since he was little. "I'm gay. That's the truth of me."

"What," Joe replied. "*What?*"

"How long have you known?" Frannie asked.

"Five years." His teeth clamped down on his lip. "Maybe longer."

Oh God, thought Joe.

"Why didn't you tell us?" Frannie asked.

"Are you sure?" asked Joe.

"I'm *sure*," Jess retorted. "Joe Singer's son is a faggot."

"Don't use that ugly word," said Frannie.

No one spoke. If someone lit a match, Joe thought, the room would catch fire. Then, fighting tears, Joe thought, because crying would send a very wrong message, Frannie asked, "Why didn't you tell us? We wouldn't have cared." She glanced towards Joe to make sure it was true. "We love *you.*"

"Because when you're a jock, and not just a jock, but a famous jock's son, you're supposed to be a real man. You're supposed to like girls."

"I don't think you're any less of a man because you like men." Frannie turned towards Joe, eyes imploring. *Say something.*

Joe asked, "When did you tell Jack?"

"In March, at the end of spring training."

March! Almost six months. *And Jack didn't tell us?* He looked at Frannie, who looked as if she was going to cry. Or scream. Or explode. And Joe? More than anything, he felt betrayed Jess told Jack first.

"I made Grandpa promise not to tell. You know how he's always saying he's the Sphinx of Delray? It's the truth."

This hurt, Joe thought. *Really* hurt. A glance at Frannie showed she felt the same way. So, he wasn't surprised she asked the question Joe knew she shouldn't, because it would make this about them, rather than about Jess, who'd just shared his terrible secret. "Why didn't you tell *me?*"

"For a long time, I didn't want it to be true." His eyes bored straight at his mother. "I'm six-five, I throw ninety-five, and I'm gay? I mean, *come on.* Then, later, I didn't want to burden you."

"It wouldn't have been a burden," Frannie said.

"So why tell Jack?" Joe asked.

Now Jess looked like he was going to explode. "When you got sick, and the coaches were saying I might get promoted?"

"They were right," Joe said.

"I had to tell someone."

"Why not *me?*" Frannie asked again.

"I didn't tell you because Dad was sick, and you already had enough to worry about."

She shook her head.

"I'm sorry, Mom. I didn't mean to hurt you."

Jess, apologizing? Joe thought. That was too much! Frannie began to cry and stood up, as if preparing to rocket into motion. But before she could rush out of the room, as Joe knew she wanted to, their beautiful boy rose from his chair and hugged her.

In the morning, that is, later the same morning, Jess and his parents walked the quiet streets of their neighborhood. After brunching at a crepe place, they returned, and Jess jumped in the shower. He felt totally wiped by last night. He'd made Mom cry, and she never cried. As for Dad, Jess didn't know what he thought. Did Dad hate him because he was gay? Dad had said very little and nothing about his feelings, which was just like him. And there was this. Jess hadn't mentioned Rah, which made him feel like a dipshit. It was one thing to admit, in an abstract way, that you were gay. It was quite another, he thought, rinsing conditioner then stepping forward to let the spray strike him flush in the puss, to confess you were sleeping with your catcher.

When he kissed Mom goodbye, he feared she might cry again. But no, that was just his sore conscience. She hugged him, then his larger-than-life, ferocious mother looked him in the eye.

"Never forget. You can tell me anything." He felt a fresh stab of guilt. "Or *do* anything, I'll still love you."

"I know."

She peered at him as if trying to discern who he really was, as if she didn't know anymore, until Jess wanted to say, *I'm still me, you know.* Or maybe that's what she was saying to him.

"See you tonight," he said, having decided to return with Dad after the game.

"Don't," she said. "It's too much driving."

"I want to."

"Then I'll be happy to see you."

Jess climbed into the car with his father, and for twenty minutes, neither spoke. Their silence wasn't unusual. They never said much to each other, and not because they were distant or angry. Dad didn't talk much, unlike Jack, who rarely shut up.

After they passed the Sonoma Raceway and turned onto Highway 37, Joe asked, "Have you told Mac?"

"No."

"Your manager?"

"Are you crazy?"

"What about your teammates?"

"I don't know anyone well enough." He looked towards Dad, whose eyes came to his, long enough for Jess to see he wasn't angry.

"Even if I did," Jess continued. "You know what homophobic ass-holes most players are. All the good old boys and *macho* Latinos. They'd fucking kill me, if they knew."

"I know." Joe removed his right hand from the steering wheel, reached across the front seat, took Jess's hand in his own, and squeezed it. The shock of his father holding his hand—the last time must have been ten or more years ago—nearly unmanned Jess. When Joe released his hand, Jess felt bereft.

After a moment, Joe added, "It must be so lonely for you."

"I'm used to it." *Tell him about Rah.*

"You know, Jess," Dad said, with another sideways glance. "I played with Davey Dean, in the early nineties."

"The A's GM?"

"No, that's Davey Deane, with an e at the end of his name. I'm talking about the special assistant to the commissioner. He came out after he retired, I think it was 1998 or '99."

What? "Why don't I know about this?"

Joe grinned. "You're young and ignorant?"

Jess started to protest, but why bother? "What about it?"

"If things go wrong," Joe said. "Or you just need someone who knows what you're going through, maybe you could reach out to Davey Dean. Or I could for you."

Getting advice from his dad was rare, except about baseball. Best change-up grip. How to sequence pitches to set up batters. He glanced at his father's profile, the slightly hooked nose he'd inherited from Jack and a long line of hook-nosed Singers, the same nose that he had.

"Thanks, Dad. I'll think about it. Really, thanks."

CHAPTER TWENTY-ONE

When Jack read on his computer the Syracuse Mets had been eliminated from Triple-A playoffs and Rah was one of five position players called up for the major league stretch run, he had a bad feeling, pronto. The news was two days old, and Jess hadn't told him. Did that mean Glad was wrong about what kind of roommates they were? Had the boys' relationship changed? Or, most likely, Jess was sandbagging him.

Two weeks ago, when Jess came out to Joe and Frannie on the Mets' West Coast swing, and they called and ripped him a new one, he defended himself by saying he'd given his word.

"I don't want to hear how you're the Sphinx of Delray!" Frannie shouted.

"You should have told us, Dad."

They were both, Jack thought then, in a world of pain. "I told him to tell you. Not my fault he didn't feel comfortable."

That knocked them off their high horse. Later, Jack promised to be more open, and later still, like now, drinking a G & T in his Florida room while waiting for the Mets game to start, he wondered if he should confide Glad's thoughts about Jess and Rah, now that Rah had been promoted.

Tell them, he thought, and pressed the first pre-set on his phone. "Joey?"

"No, Jack, Joe's out for a run. I saw it was you and picked up."

"Ain't Joe watching the game?"

"He will be. Want him to call when he gets back?"

Tell her. "Remember how you wanted me to be, you know, more open?"

"I remember."

"So." Jack pondered how to put it. He slugged his G & T and endeavored to swallow without smacking his lips. "When Glad and I visited Jess in Syracuse, she thought that Jess and Rah, you know, his catcher?"

"We met him in Florida."

"That Rah and Jess, *you know.*"

"What?"

"Roomies with benefits."

From Frannie's end, a long silence. Finally, "You told Glad about Jess, but didn't tell us?"

Vey iz mir. "More like she guessed."

"No, Jack, you told her."

This effing conversation was off the rails. "I had to tell someone, and Jess made it crystal clear it couldn't be you or Joey."

"You know what, Jack? Fuck you."

She hung up. Jack got up to fix another G & T. Then his phone rang: *Joey.* He let it ring four times, to give her the business. When he picked up, Frannie said, "I'm sorry I yelled, 'Fuck you.'"

"You should have said it more normal-like." Frannie laughed, and they were pals again. "Anyway, I'm sorry I didn't tell you."

"How sure are you about Jess and Rah?"

"That they're schtupping? Glad picked up on it, what you might call woman's superstition."

"Intuition?"

"That too. I'm telling you because I bet anything Jess asked Rah to share his apartment."

Frannie muttered something then hung up. Jack made himself that second drink, added a slice of lime, and sat back on the couch, waiting for the game to begin.

On Rah's fourth day in New York, he got his first AB and lined a pinch hit single over the shortstop. Jess was sitting on the dugout bench beside Rick Heynen, the Mets' number one starter and Jess's best friend on the staff; well, more like a big brother. Rah's smile could have lit up Times Square. Rounding first, Rah crossed himself then pointed both hands towards heaven, looking like he was about to levitate.

Heynen said, "Dude looks like he hit a grand slam."

"His first major league hit."

"Friend of yours?"

"You bet." Jess decided not to mention they'd roomed together in the spring, and Rah was staying with him until he found a place. "I threw to Rah the last three years in the minors. He's a really good receiver."

The ball came in from the outfield, and Red Murphy, the Mets' first base coach, called time and asked for the ball, which he rolled to the ball boy, who brought it into the dugout for safekeeping. Heynen, who'd won the Cy Young two years ago and was universally liked and respected around the league, said, "Someone ought to tell him to act like he been here before."

"You can *tell* him," Jess said. "But you'd be wasting your breath."

A couple of pitches later, the Reds' pitcher tried to pick Rah off first and threw wildly. Rah ended up on second, advanced to third on a groundout, and scored the go-ahead run on a medium-deep sac fly.

"Your boy runs pretty good for a catcher."

"Yes, he does," Jess agreed, getting up to join the line of hand-slappers waiting to welcome Rah to the dugout: not only his first hit, but his first major league run scored. Rah approached the dugout's top step, vibrating with excitement, smiling his million-watt smile. Jess caught his eye, careful not to be the first one to congratulate Rah. Jess hated that. But no two ways about it: they'd have something special to celebrate tonight.

Rah's run stood up, and the Mets moved into a tie for first in the NL East. Instead of going out alone with Rah, a bunch of the younger guys, including two of the players who'd been called up with him, and Big Barnes, who'd been cool to Jess all season, but seemed happy to see Rah, headed out to L. Child's Steakhouse on West 54th Street in Midtown.

Jess wasn't sure why Big had cut him dead all season. Maybe he resented how well Jess was doing. Maybe Big was just a nasty asshole. Maybe he was anti-Semitic; he'd made that crack in spring training. Or maybe, just maybe, although he seemed dumb as a doorstop, he'd picked up on Jess being gay when he didn't sleep with Emmy all those months ago in Port St. Lucie. What was certain, Jess thought, walking into Child's in a group of other players, careful not to stand too close to Rah, he didn't like Big any more than Big liked him. What a fucking douche.

Child's stayed open late and catered to ballplayers, reserving a private room at no extra charge on game nights. In addition to filet mignon and twenty-two-ounce cowboy bone-in rib eyes, Child's served slabs of ribs and pricy seafood, including colossal shrimp cocktails. Everything was first-rate and expensive, especially the steaks and drinks. The waitresses, Jess had observed on his previous visits, were what Jack would call top-drawer: young and hot in the way that only New York, L.A., and Atlanta waitresses seemed to be. They were prone to flirt with baseball beefcakes, because, who knew? A pretty girl could snag herself a millionaire beau and never wait tables again.

Jess, however, only had eyes for Rah. Fresh off his hit and game-winning run, Rah was floating on a river of margaritas. Gwen, their red-haired waitress, who had long mascara-ed lashes and breasts barely contained by her bustier, kept brushing against Jess while delivering drinks and jalapeño poppers. She wasn't exactly subtle; in fact, Gwen was the Queen of Anti-Subtle. Jess had noticed Big noticing Gwen's attention to him from his seat directly across the round table.

"Yo, Singer," Big said, "remember spring training, we picked up those college chicks?"

"I remember."

"And this good-looking one, this real hottie, kept hitting on you?"

Not the first time Big had mentioned this publicly. "Sure," Jess said. "Emmy."

"You shitting me? You remember her name?"

"I do."

"Bullshit." Big's eyes had acquired the piggy squint, which meant he was loaded. "Cause as I remember—"

"*You* remember? No way, you were too fucking drunk."

"I remember." Big looked around the table. "Me and Jorge got laid, but despite that hottie hanging all over you, you and Rah went home early."

"What about it?" Jess glared at Big, daring him to say one more thing. "I was pitching the next day."

"Well, I don't know *what* about it, but I sure as hell don't believe you remember her name from March. You're making it up."

Rah, seated closer to Big than Jess, broke in, "Big, me and Jess doan *have to remember* from March. We double-dated Emmy and Tiff, her little friend with the big *tetas*, before Jess got promoted. They go to college near Syracuse."

"Bullshit."

"No bullshit, Big. And Jess, I forget to tell you. Tiff and Emmy came to a game last week in Syracuse. Now, they wanna see one down here."

"Cool." Jess met Rah's eyes. "I have Emmy's number." He glanced from Rah to Big, who looked dazed and pissed off, a frequent combination for the dumb motherfucker.

"I'll call the girls and set it up." Jess grinned at Rah, who always had his back *and* his front. Then he turned to Big. "Maybe Emmy can invite the girls you and Jorge fucked."

"No way!"

Jess followed Big's eyes to sexy Gwen, approaching fast with their second round of drinks.

"Those skanks were totally bush league, and this here—"

Gwen executed a perfect bunny dip, lowered her tray to the stand beside Rah.

"This here," Big repeated, "is the Show."

That night, in Jess's bed, after they'd made love, Jess and Rah sat up, watching the end of *The Late Show With Stephen Colbert.*

"First hit, first run scored." Jess kissed the corner of Rah's mouth. "First steak at Child's"

"Man," Rah said. "It was big."

Jess felt Rah's hand move onto his thigh, under the sheet.

"I was talking about the steak," Rah said, grinning happily. "In case you wonder."

"Are you sure?"

Rah's hand moved onto Jess's penis, which lay flaccid on Jess's thigh, tuckered out from its recent exertions.

"Yes, Jess, I'm sure."

Rah bounded out of bed, naked, and picked up the souvenir ball from his first hit. It lay on the dresser, underneath the wall-mounted big screen. Colbert was talking about tomorrow night's guests, and Jess switched the set off mid-sentence. Rah returned to bed, holding the baseball, then set it on the nightstand.

"You've had a hell of a day," Jess said.

"You make me very happy," Rah said.

"And you make me very horny."

"No way, Jess. I'm gonna sleep." His hand fell on Jess's penis. "Anyway, you're just bragging. You're worn out too."

"I am."

Jess turned off his bedside lamp, and Rah turned his off. In the dark, Rah said, "You know Big's a big stupid *pendejo.*"

"I know."

"We have to be careful."

"I know that too. But I don't want to think about him. I want to think about how you scored the winning run."

"So do I."

Jess could almost *hear* Rah smile. The next thing Jess knew, or didn't know, they were fast asleep.

CHAPTER TWENTY-TWO

Joe and Frannie were flying east to watch Jess's Sunday start against the Braves. Jack, Glad, and her son Dr. Stu were joining them. With fifteen games left in the regular season, the Mets had dropped two behind the Braves for first. But they remained tied with the Nats for the first and second Wild Cards, a game up on the Cards and D-backs, who were tied for the third. Not bad, Joe thought, a puncher's chance. He looked out at the pale sky through his small window; the Mets controlled their own fate. He wished he did.

They were flying on Friday, coming in for a long weekend. They'd reach their hotel after tonight's game started. Saturday, they had tickets for *Hamilton*. Jess's start, the third and final game of the Braves' series, had been moved to Sunday night on ESPN. Joe hoped his son didn't feel too much pressure. If the Mets won the first two, his start would be for the division lead. If they split or, God forbid, the Braves won both, Jess could be pitching to keep the Mets alive in the Wild Card race.

No matter what, Sunday would be the biggest start of Jess's career. Stretch run baseball, Joe mused, still looking out at the endless sky; it's what you lived for. Unfortunately, during Joe's career, the Mets didn't play many meaningful September games, and just for a moment, Joe allowed himself to look back through lenses marked *Regret* and *Sorrow*, imagining how different things might have been if Sarah hadn't slept with Nellie Perez, the first baseman. If Jack hadn't snarled him in the scandal. If he hadn't been suspended for refusing to answer the commissioner's questions. If he hadn't gotten shot and lost the last years of his career.

Then he heard Jack's voice: *If your grandma had balls, Joey, she woulda been your grandpa.*

On the other hand, if he hadn't been suspended, he wouldn't have met Frannie. If he hadn't met Frannie, his life would have been shit, and there'd be no Jess. Without Jess, he wouldn't be flying to New York. If they weren't flying to New York, he wouldn't be seeing Avi Bernstein at Sloan Kettering Monday morning. Three days ago, Doc Perlman ordered another blood test, and instead of resuming its drop towards zero, Joe's PSA had risen from 0.6 to 1.2.

Joe glanced at Frannie, seated on the aisle. They'd upgraded to business after the blood test. When you're six-three and long-limbed, and your wife is almost six-two, extra leg room is worth the money. When, in the words of a song Joe couldn't remember the title of, *everyone knows your name*, and not only that, some people know your face, even though it's changed with age—and their associations with that face and name twenty-five years later combine hero worship and loathing over something they (and you) can't recall the exact details of—the extra privacy afforded by business class was worth the money.

Joe dropped a hand on Frannie's knee. She smiled then returned her gaze to the movie playing on the seat-back screen in front of her: car chase; rocket fire, a solitary woman shooter. Seeking peace in the blue sky outside his window, Joe offered a prayer for all he did not know.

Before starting, Jess liked to sleep in, but Sunday he woke early. *Damn early*, with worry whipsawing his anxious mind. The Braves' first four batters, all tough outs. The pennant race, which was going badly. After splitting the first two games, the Mets remained two back of the Braves, with time running out. That meant the Braves would get the first round bye. Even worse, they'd dropped a game behind the Nats for the first Wild Card; the Nats had won both Friday and Saturday, while the Mets split. The Cards and D-backs had won both of their games, so the Mets were tied with them for the second and third Wild Cards. Because of head-to-head tie-breakers, if the season had ended last night, the Mets' season would be over.

Finally, and this was the stew in which Jess had marinated half-awake the entire night, Furillo, the Mets' regular catcher, had taken a foul tip off his right thumb yesterday. X-rays were negative, but after the game his thumb looked like a hot Italian sausage. After his post-game presser, Gallagher, who'd taken his lumps throughout the season for bonehead player moves, called Jess into his office.

"I don't have to tell you," Gallagher began, not looking Jess in the eye; he never did, "how important tomorrow's game is."

There was a knock at the door.

"Come in," Gallagher said.

Gib, the pitching coach, and Dad's best friend, Mac, entered and stood beside Gallagher. *The brain trust,* Jess thought, though he wasn't sure how brainy any of them were, except Mac.

"So, here's the thing," Gallagher continued, "with Fur out, you wanna throw to Fitz, or your buddy Rah? Mac says he's ready." The manager glanced at Mac, who nodded his approval. "I know you worked together in the minors. You might feel, I don't know—" Gallagher looked straight at Jess for the first time since the meeting began "—more comfortable with him."

In the gray light of dawn, Jess glanced at Rah sleeping peacefully on the next pillow. Of course, he'd picked Rah. It was Rah's big chance. But all night Jess had fretted and sweated. What if Rah called a bad game? Threw the ball away in a big spot? Took a golden sombrero? What if he fucked up pitching to Rah, and everyone blamed Rah?

Jess rolled onto his side, scooched his naked back into Rah's front, snuggling deeper into his feather pillow. He needed more sleep. More sleep! Release, he thought. Release point. *Release.*

The next thing Jess knew Rah was bent over him, shaking his shoulder.

"Sleeping Beauty." Rah grinned. "*Despiertate!*"

"What time?"

"Past ten."

Jess remembered not sleeping half the night. *Past ten?*

Rah lightly kissed his lips. "I wanna get early to the park, watch video."

Jess reached for Rah's hand, tried to pull him back to bed.

"No way, Jess." Rah pushed his hand away. "We gonna eat and go to Citi."

Rah started towards the bathroom. Two steps from the door, he pulled his boxers down, wiggled his ass, and directed his million-watt smile over his shoulder at Jess. Then he disappeared behind the door and the shower started.

Jess, or maybe Mac, had left them great seats. If it were Mac, he must not have known Jack, Glad, and Stu were occupying three of the seats, because Mac hadn't forgiven Jack for what had happened back in the day. He never would. Jack had endured twenty-six years of the Stink Eye, so on second thought, these seats must have come from Jess. Or the front office, which would prove what he'd been saying to Joey since they arrived at the ballpark. *The brass is finally waking up to what they got in Two-J's. Rookie of the Year, even if he don't take home the hardware.*

As for Mac, Jack thought. *Fuck him.* Jack hadn't forgiven himself either. But lately, it burned less, his guilt balmed by Two-J's success and Joey's pleasure in his son's career.

"You ready?" Jack tapped Joey's knee. They sat four rows behind home, Joey on his left, Frannie past Joe, Glad on his right, Stu, past her.

"Ready as I'm gonna be."

Jess blew in a heater, followed by a hook.

"He looks great, don't he?"

Joey nodded. "I hope he's holding something back."

Jess delivered his last warm-up, then Rah, his friend and, Jack thought, likely his fuckbuddy—why was Rah starting today? Gallagher was an idiot—pegged a rope to second.

"Here we go," Jack said to Glad, rigid with anticipation, ready for the first pitch.

Jess was perfect through four. Not only no hits or walks, not even a loud foul. The Braves' starter, Strider, was nearly as good, but the Mets scratched out an unearned run in the third, so at the end of four, the good guys were up 1-0. Joe hadn't seen Jess pitch so dominantly since Little League, when he was so much bigger and better than the other kids, Joe would find himself silently rooting someone, anyone, on the opposing team would manage a hit to keep the entire team from being humiliated. Not today. Today their little group, and all the fans in the surrounding section, were thrilled Jess had no-hit stuff, although no one was saying anything, of course, so as not to jinx him.

What Joe and Jack were saying, to avoid mentioning the no-hitter, was that Jess seemed really focused and relaxed, effortless, right? and that he hadn't shaken off his catcher even once.

"He did too," Joe insisted. "The change-up in the first to Olson."

"I don't think so," Jack said, never willing to admit, Joe thought, that he was right about anything. Jack wanted Jess to succeed, no ifs, ands, or buts, and he supposed his father was proud of what he'd accomplished, yet somehow, Jack made him feel like shit about himself at least half the time.

Joe looked past Jack and Glad and discovered that Glad's son, Stu the doctor, seemed focused on Frannie and not the game. This wasn't the first time Joe had caught him looking her way. What was that about? Then Stu directed his attention to the diamond and so did Joe, just as Jess painted the corner. *Strike one.*

"Two-J's on fire," Jack announced.

Jess struck out the first batter, induced a weak grounder to short from the second, then seemed to lose focus. He fell behind Rosario, the Braves' veteran left-swinging outfielder, three balls, one strike.

"This guy's a tough out," Jack muttered.

"Bust him in," Joe said.

Jess did, a fastball up, fouled straight back.

"Now, the Two, Jess," Joe whispered, "outside black."

Jess rocked into his wind-up, glove covering everything except his eyes. Their seats were so good, Joe thought, it felt like being on the field. The pitch started its journey home from far to the first base side of Rosario's front shoulder, then broke sharply down and away, tumbling towards the outside corner. Rosario froze, and Jess's curve sliced the black, just like his father ordered.

"Stri—riiike three!" bellowed the ump, pointing his right hand at the sky.

"Pitching 101!" Jack jumped to his feet. "High and tight, low and away."

On the field, Jess pumped his left fist and smiled at his catcher. The Mets jogged off, Jess jumped the foul line as he always did, and the hometown crowd chanted, "Jess, Jess, Jess!"

Five perfect innings.

In the bottom of the fifth, the Mets scored three runs, so when Jess went out to pitch the sixth, he carried a four-nothing lead. Most of the season, and every start since August, he'd been pulled after five, to keep his innings down. But his pitch count was super low, sixty-two through five, and though no one had said a word in the dugout, he knew he had a perfect game going. After Pete launched a three-run bomb to the back of the second deck, and home run trotted around the bases then returned to the dugout to bump forearms with his mates, it was like, *Let's go, Jess! Get that perfecto.*

He cruised through the sixth, completing his second turn through the lineup, striking out Harris on three pitches. Eighteen up, eighteen batters set aside. His pitch count rested at seventy-four; he'd struck out seven, induced six ground balls from righties, mostly off his change. He walked towards the dugout re-seeing the strikeout, Harris swinging under high heat, six inches, at least, out of the zone, up near his eyes, which was where Rah had called for it. Jess emerged briefly from the mind-forged tunnel in which he was striding alone, glanced briefly at Rah, who was walking from his position behind the plate towards the dugout. Rah was calling a great game, out-thinking the opposing batters. Their eyes met; Rah nodded. Then Jess looked down, re-entering the tunnel in which he walked alone and saw one thing only: the next pitch, the next, the sequence, then the batter after that.

Seated in the right corner of the dugout, keeping his left arm warm in his jacket, though it wasn't cold, a few feet away from everyone, Jess wondered how long GG and Gib would leave him in. He hadn't pitched the seventh inning in more than two months. After today, twelve games remained in the regular season; he had two more starts, and then the post-season, if they made it. But would GG really take him out, pitching a perfecto, to keep his innings down? Jess glanced to his left down the bench. Gallagher stood on the top dugout step shouting encouragement to Collins, the Mets' right fielder, who had a sweet lefty swing. Jess didn't believe they'd remove him if he stayed perfect. But what if he walked a batter, so he still had a no-no, but not a perfect game? As a team, the Mets had only produced one no-hitter by a starter in sixty years—Johann Santana on June 1, 2012—and Santana was never the same after throwing 134 pitches.

What was more important, individual glory or helping the team make the post-season? Dad had never thrown a no-no; the closest he came were two complete game one-hitters. On the field, Collins hit a can of corn to right. Jess removed his jacket, picked up his glove from the bench beside him, and mounted the dugout steps seeing nothing, not even the mound, just the sides of the tunnel through which he strode: the next pitch, the next, then the one after that.

Watching Jess warm up for the seventh, Joe remembered his first one-hitter. He was twenty-six, at the top of his game, and perfect through eight. Twelve strikeouts. The leadoff batter in the ninth, Winston "Winnie" Hopkins, a lifetime .240 banjo hitter, swung at an 0-2 fastball that was supposed to be two inches outside but wasn't, and rolled it towards the hole between first and second. Benning, the slow-footed second baseman, laid out, while Perez, the first baseman who had yet to reveal himself as the backstabbing motherfucker he turned out to be, dove too, but the ball bled into right. Bye-bye no-hitter, bye-bye perfecto. All these years later, Joe could remember knowing—as the ball left his hand—that he'd missed his spot. Afterwards, while he stood behind the mound, rubbing up a new ball, the Shea Stadium crowd rose and cheered and cheered while Joe tried not to weep, not knowing then that this was the closest he'd come to perfection. Three batters later, the crowd cheered again when Joe walked off the mound, the one-hit shutout complete. But it was the first cheer, bittersweet, adoring and spontaneous, when he *failed*, that Joe would never forget.

He hoped Jess would do him one better and get the last nine outs. The first two batters went down quickly, but Olson, the Braves' power-hitting first baseman, kept fouling off 3-2 pitches and finally worked out an eight-pitch walk.

"There goes the perfect game," Jack said. "I hate that fucking Olson."

"Great hitter," Joe said, and watched Jess, who stood alone while the crowd cheered, just off the mound, rubbing up a new ball, just as he'd done thirty-one years ago. *Don't lose focus*, Joe thought. *Keep your release point, Jess. Release point. Release.* And just when Joe was starting to worry about Jess, Rah quick-stepped to the mound, hid his mouth behind his catcher's mitt, said just a few words, then patted Jess on the shoulder and returned to his spot behind the plate. Two fastballs later, Riley skied out to Collins in right.

In between innings, as the fans were being led through "Take Me Out to the Ballgame" by the organist, the Mets' on-field reporter, Cassie Hayes, appeared in the aisle beside Frannie's seat with a mic in her hand. Cassie Hayes: flaxen-haired, blue-eyed, button-nosed.

"Joe." She waved her mic. "Could I ask you and Jess's mom"—she turned the considerable brilliance of her smile towards Frannie—"a few questions?"

"On camera?" Joe hated being interviewed.

Cassie smiled. "Of course, we can get you from the camera in the—"

"Cassie," Jack broke in. "You don't mind if I call you Cassie, do you?"

"Not at all. Who are you?"

"Jess's grandpa."

Joe looked past Jack to Glad, who clamped her hand on Jack's knee, as if holding him back.

"You know what Two-J's is trying to do here, dontcha? What he's in the middle of?"

"You mean the—"

Jack jumped up as if he was going to push past Joe and Frannie and beat Cassie Hayes over the head with her own mic. "Not another fucking word!"

"Maybe after the game," Cassie said, edging away.

"That would be better," Joe said, as Cassie fled up the aisle. He turned towards his father. "Thanks, Jack."

"What a fucking idjit!" Jack rolled his shoulders like a boxer trying to get loose before a fight. "In the middle of you-know-what, she wants to bug Joe, '*How does it feel? Yadda, yadda, yadda.*' Fucking idjit."

"Enough, Jack," Glad said.

Just then, the final strains of the seventh-inning-stretch song broke in on Joe's consciousness. "One, two, three strikes, you're out, at the old ball game!"

He glanced at Frannie who smiled, and everything was right as rain.

When Jess advanced through the tunnel-vision tunnel from his corner seat in the dugout to the top of the mound to commence the eighth, he had a new mantra: pitch to contact. He'd already thrown eighty-eight pitches and didn't know which he feared more: losing the no-hitter, or not being sent out for the ninth, even if he still had the no-no going because his count was too high. Then he got lucky. Ozuna scorched a first-pitch liner to the warning track in center that Nimms ran down. Jones grounded out on the second pitch, and Menendez struck out on three pitches. The crowd cheered; it must have. But Jess was so locked in and locked down, he heard and saw nothing except the tunnel to his corner of the dugout.

The Mets' first two batters singled. Just before going out to the on-deck circle, Rah approached Jess's Fortress of Solitude at the dug-out corner and entered his Cone of Silence. Jess surfaced from the very deep pool in which he'd been throwing pea-sized four-seamers. Rah leaned so close Jess could feel his breath. "You can do this, *cariño*, I know you can."

Rah walked the length of the dugout, mounted the steps, and knelt in the on-deck circle. After Mauricio popped out, Rah strode to the plate, hit a grounder to short on the first pitch, and the Braves turned two. Inning over.

"You think Rah did that on purpose?" Frannie asked.

"Maybe," Joe said. "I'm sure Jess is chomping at the bit to get back out there."

"Rah didn't run very hard, did he?"

"No," Joe said. "He didn't."

"Pretty smart," Jack said, joining their conversation. "I like that kid."

"Me too," Glad called, from the far side of Jack.

So do I, Joe thought, thinking *You can do it, son.*

A moment later, Jess emerged from the dugout, head down, and walked towards the mound. Half the large crowd stood and applauded.

"Sit down," Jack growled at everyone and no one. "Sit the fuck down!"

Joe was thinking with his son. Number eight batter, probably the Braves pinch hit. Nine, another pinch hitter, then the top of the lineup. *Go hard after the first two,* Joe thought, *pinch hitters coming off the bench cold, trying to be heroes.*

On the field, Jess threw his final warm-up over Rah's head.

"Shit," Jack said, "he's too amped up."

"He'll be fine," Joe said, remembering his own almost perfect game. "Just don't make the first pitch too good."

Frannie squeezed his hand. They weren't together back then, but she knew the story. Jess spun a curve that split the plate for strike one. Then he doubled up and threw a second Charlie. Strike two.

"Rah's calling one hell of a game," Jack observed.

Yes, he is, Joe thought.

Jess's next pitch was high heat, which the batter swung through. *Perfect,* Joe thought, squeezing Frannie's hand. *One down.*

Pillar, batting for Harris, popped up the second pitch, a change-up low and away. When the ball settled in Pete's mitt, the crowd roared and got up on its feet. One out to go for the second no-hitter in Mets' history, and everyone in the park was standing except Jack.

"You wanna fucking jinx him?" Jack shouted. "You wanna fucking jinx him?"

On the field, in the ocean of light that turned night into day, little Ozzie Albies dug into the right-handed batter's box. Good hitter, thought Joe, and better from the right side, over .350 last year. Power to all fields, but you can get him to chase. Joe smiled at Frannie. The entire crowd was standing except for Jack, whose fists were clenched, whose eyes were closed, chanting, "Don't fucking jinx him, don't fucking jinx him."

Jess hid his face behind his glove, like Jack had taught him. He found his sign, rocked into motion, and threw what looked to Joe like the hardest pitch he'd thrown all night. Albies fouled it straight back. Jess rubbed up a new ball, settled on the rubber, nodded at Rah, and threw a four-seamer that caught too much of the plate. Cell phone cameras flashed all around Citi Field. Albies strode, uncurled, and launched a high drive down the left field line, parabola-ing towards the upper deck. Every Mets fan held his or her breath while Joe prayed to the God of Pitchers and Catchers. *Foul. FOUL! GO FOUL!* The scorched shot hooked just left of the pole, crashing into the facing of the upper deck, 450 feet from home. All around Citi Field held breath exploded like forty-three thousand popped balloons.

"Motherfucker!" shouted Jack, up on his feet like everyone else.

No more heat, Joe thought. *You know what to do.*

Jess stood behind the mound, facing the Home Run Apple in dead center, rubbing up a new ball, the 32 on his back shining for everyone to see. *My number,* Joe thought. *Sandy's number too.* Jess climbed back on the bump, peered towards home, and delivered: heater high and tight, knocking Albies off the dish. Rah pegged the rock to Jess, who stared in again, face hidden by his glove.

"The hammer," Jack growled. "Drop the hammer."

On the mound, Jess rocked forward then back. The pitch started high and outside, above Albies' head, but ten feet from home fell off the celestial table, plummeting towards the outside corner. Albies saw too late it would be called a strike and swung awkwardly, without hope, after the pitch was behind him. Rah caught the ball, and after he'd squeezed it, hurled the ball still inside his mitt thirty feet straight up, then raced towards the mound. Jess leapt into Rah's arms, and Rah, who'd managed to toss his mask aside during his sprint towards Jess, wrapped his arms around Jess's waist and lifted him skyward, staring up at Jess with his million-watt smile, relief and love, yes, love, in his eyes.

Hundreds of cameras went off, capturing the image that would come back to bite them. Then the Mets' infielders reached the mound, followed by the bench players, the outfielders, and the coaches. And one of the players, probably Pete, the first baseman, who'd started the tradition several seasons ago, ripped off Jess's jersey, and there he stood, bare-chested, in the arms of his teammates, just a boy, really, Joe's son, with nary a hair on his chest.

Joe hugged Frannie. Then he hugged Jack, who shouted, "They better not lose his jersey, it's worth a fortune."

The crowd cheered, roared, and cheered. Jess waved, bare-chested. Sometime later, a field reporter led Jess to home plate, and while he was being interviewed, a teammate doused him with a cooler of Gatorade.

Joe's cheeks hurt from smiling so much, such happy pain. Later, as they were gathering their things, Joe glanced past Frannie and spied Cassie Hayes advancing down the aisle, trailed by a cameraman. In her hand, a mic. In her blue eyes, the glint of purpose. This time, Joe knew, he'd have to talk to her.

CHAPTER TWENTY-THREE

Early Monday morning, Joe and Frannie started up York Avenue. Joe's appointment wasn't for an hour, and it was only fifteen minutes to MSK, but it wouldn't hurt, Frannie had convinced him, to arrive early. There were, no doubt, multiple appointments at the same time, but if they arrived first, he might be seen first. Anything to make the morning more bearable. Or maybe they'd stop for coffee, although Joe didn't remember passing a Starbucks the last time.

The last time. He glanced towards Frannie, walking on his right under the trees fronting Rockefeller University. He knew she wished he'd just had the surgery in March, then they wouldn't have to be terrified all over again. It was strange to think of her rooting for the surgery, which Avi had said would *change him as a person*, which Joe knew meant they wouldn't have sex anymore. At least not that way.

Years ago, Joe remembered, just after they married, they adopted a gray tomcat off the streets in Hermosa Beach, where they were living. Actually, Tough Guy, TG, for short, adopted them. He showed up in their backyard, scarred and chewed up, and began throwing himself at their feet, rolling around on his back, trying to convince them to let him inside. When they did, he'd spray the walls, marking his turf. They took him to a vet, who said they should neuter him. Joe didn't like that idea. After all, the cat's name was *Tough Guy.*

"Look at it this way," the vet replied. "He's starting to lose more fights than he's winning. After he's neutered, instead of being the barroom brawler, he'll be the guy at the end of the bar telling stories and drinking a beer."

Joe wondered if that's what his future held, and that's if he were lucky. He didn't understand how the cancer could have returned already, not when he'd had the fancy procedure in Portugal. Was this one of those nightmares in which the operation was a success, but the patient died anyway?

Last night, after the celebratory press conference—which turned into a mini-coronation of Jess as not only the second coming of his father, or maybe Sandy K., but the greatest thing in American Jewish culture since lox and bagels—he and Frannie had returned to their hotel room and made love before falling asleep. There was nothing especially memorable about the sex. They'd always enjoyed each other's bodies. But it wasn't only the sex, which remained surprisingly fulfilling after all these years, but as Frannie said, the exquisite press of flesh on flesh. His on hers, Frannie's on his. And if the sex disappeared because of a new cancer treatment, could he live with that, sipping a beer at the end of the bar?

Minutes after arriving in the MSK waiting room, they were led inside: the ongoing privilege conferred by knowing Stu. In the sterile exam room, Joe reclined on a paper-lined steel table; Frannie took a seat. Five then ten minutes passed; Joe's brain powered down. Then came a knock, and before he or Frannie could answer, Dr. Bernstein entered, followed by Stu Goldberg and a third doctor, a slim Asian woman who looked no more than thirty or thirty-five. Joe was surprised to see Stu; in the hospital, should he call him *Dr. Goldberg*? And he certainly hadn't expected a strange, attractive woman in the room while they discussed his *prostate* and the side effects of different treatment options.

"Joe," Avi began. "A pleasure to see you, although I *vish* this visit *vasn't* necessary."

Joe nodded, still fretting about the woman doctor.

"Thank you, Avi," Frannie said.

"Of course," Avi continued, "you know Dr. Goldberg."

Stu said, "We were at Citi Field together yesterday, watching Joe and Frannie's son throw a no-hitter."

"Yes, yes," Avi replied, in such a way Joe doubted he'd heard of Citi Field or a no-hitter. "This is Doctor Tran, a fellow in radiation oncology."

She didn't look like a *fellow*, Joe thought. Long black hair, feline cheekbones. Should he shake her hand? *No.* "Pleased to meet you, Doctor Tran."

She nodded, all business.

"So," Avi continued, "we reviewed your California tests. I suppose"—he looked directly at Joe, then Frannie—"you're wondering *vhat* the hell happened?"

"That's right," Frannie replied.

Too loudly, Joe thought, and louder than she'd probably intended, because she added, gently, "I thought the treatment in Lisbon was a success?"

"Complete success." Avi pursed his lips, and just for a moment he looked his age. Then the customary brilliance returned to his eyes. "Joe's PSA going up so soon after the single-dose likely means"—he hesitated, the way, Joe thought, managers did before sending you down—"the cancer has metastasized, and there's a lesion, most likely on one of Joe's lymph—"

"But," Frannie broke in, eyes darting from Avi to Stu, and even to Dr. Tran, as she sought a revision of that ugly word, *metastasize.*

"But," Frannie continued, "Joe's PET-CT, that's what it's called, right?"

Avi nodded.

"And the bone scan in March, didn't show cancer anywhere else, or Joe wouldn't have had that goddamn single dose, he would have chosen surgery."

"Frannie." Stu stepped towards her, eyes full of concern, and Joe wondered, not for the first time, why he was here? "The lesion would have been too small to detect in March. Or maybe there was no lesion yet, just a single prostate cancer cell loose in the blood. Avi?"

Avi nodded. "Even if Joe's prostate had been removed, he would still have developed this lesion, *and* suffered the side effects of a prostatectomy. Leakage, loss of sexual function."

Joe avoided looking anywhere near Dr. Tran.

With her eyes popping and telltale red blotches blooming on her cheeks, Frannie asked, "You're not just saying that because what you recommended didn't work?"

Holy shit, Joe thought. It looked as if Stu Goldberg was about to defend his famous friend, but Avi raised his hand. "That's a fair question, one I'd ask myself. There's no doubt the single dose destroyed the cancer in the gland." He turned towards Joe. "It's just bad luck. What I think you call a curveball. I'm sorry. We always knew this cancer was aggressive."

Joe thought about the months he'd delayed last winter, yet somehow his thoughts remained on the great man's use of *curveball*, and what a great one Jess had commanded yesterday, including the final pitch to Albies. He glanced at Frannie, who was wiping her eyes.

"So now what?" Joe asked.

"There's a new imaging test we want you to have, a PSMA PET-CT," Avi answered. "It's still experimental in the US, but best practice in Europe and Australia. It can pinpoint minute amounts of prostate cancer outside the gland. Once it's been located, we'll irradiate the lesion, three doses in five days, a process known as SABR."

"What about surgery?" Frannie asked.

"To remove the lymph node?" Avi asked.

"His prostate."

Avi glanced meaningfully at Stu. "I've already explained, there's no cancer in Joe's prostate, so *vhy vould* we remove it?"

Frannie's eyes flashed. "Let me ask something else. Joe's urologist in Santa Rosa, Dr. Perlman, recommended hormone therapy. He would have injected Joe last week, but Joe wanted to ask you first."

"Hormone therapy," Avi said slowly, as if explaining to a child, "will not cure Joe's cancer, since it no longer exists in his prostate. I don't know why your Doctor Perlman would advocate for this."

Frannie glanced Joe's way, then all at once she seemed to explode. "Because he wants to save Joe's life!"

Stu said, "We all do."

"Frannie," Avi added gently, "in twenty-four hours, we'll know exactly where the lesion is hiding, and you and Joe can choose whatever treatment you *vhant*. But removing Joe's prostate or starting hormone therapy will not cure Joe's cancer, that I assure you. All it *vill* do, is unnecessarily end sexual function and change Joe's life."

Joe glanced at Frannie just as Stu turned towards her too, concerned, solicitous, and all at once, he realized Stu had a crush on her. Who could blame him? Not Joe, although it did piss him off.

"Do you mind," he asked, "if we talk about the sex part some other time?"

The physicians nodded, even Dr. Tran, and the next thing Joe knew, they were arranging for a PSMA PET-CT. Whatever the hell that was.

After all the postgame interviews Sunday night, followed by a Monday morning appearance on ESPN radio, the Mets' PR department called to ask if he'd be willing to appear on *The Late Show With Stephen Colbert* to discuss what it felt like to be only the second pitcher in the history of the franchise to throw a no-hitter, something not even his famous father had accomplished? After that, the publicist said, he'd be expected to limit his personal appearances until after the season.

Jess said yes to Colbert and the subsequent ban on appearances. It made sense. The Mets were one game back now with twelve to go. After an off-day Monday, they'd play twelve out of the next thirteen days. Jess was scheduled to start twice, and if the team needed him, he could come back on three days' rest and pitch a couple of innings on the final day of the regular season. Or maybe start one of the first playoff games if they got in. It all depended on how the next twelve games played out.

But Jess's phone kept ringing. Everyone, it seemed, wanted a piece of him. Jess kept refusing. He had his orders and didn't need the distraction. But then the Colbert scheduler called to announce their researcher had discovered that in the entire history of baseball there had never been a no-hitter in which BOTH the pitcher and catcher were rookies. If Jess agreed to come on—and he could pick any night this week—they wanted Rah Ramirez too. Sources had informed them he and Mr. Ramirez were good friends and roommates, was that true?

"Hold on a minute," Jess said.

He knew how much Rah loved television; hell, he'd learned English from TV. He knew how much Rah admired Stephen Colbert— they watched his show most nights—and that he'd jump at the chance to appear on his show. And he knew how much he loved Rah.

"Okay," he said. "But you'll have to clear it with the club. And I'll have to clear it with Rah. I'll call you back."

Then he walked towards the living room, where Rah was playing Fortnite on the Xbox. *Just wait till I tell him,* Jess thought. "Rah," he said, and placed his hands on Rah's shoulders.

"Doan distract me, Jess."

"You're not gonna believe this."

Then he nibbled Rah's ear, until Rah stopped playing that silly game.

Monday afternoon, after Jess called to announce that he and Rah were appearing on *The Colbert Show* Wednesday night, Jack and Glad changed their flight to remain in New York until Thursday to be part of the studio audience. Jack purchased an expensive bottle of West County Sonoma pinot noir—Glad's favorite—and they made love at four in the afternoon with the lights out and the black-out shades drawn. Even so,

Jack could see Glad's lithe flanks and petite rump. When he rolled her over and entered her from behind, because at his age this was the easiest position for him to finish, and Glad seemed to like it too, he couldn't see her face, just her platinum poof of hair. He sure as hell could hear her because Glad was making a racket. Jack had always admired a woman who wasn't too prim to get loud. Glad yowled like a banshee until Jack went off too, collapsing against her, making all sorts of sounds he didn't know he had in him. Then he held on, palms cupping her tiny breasts, thinking, *Ain't life grand.*

After they cleaned up and opened the curtains and poured second glasses of pinot, Jack and Glad sat at the little table in front of the big view over the East River. Glad still looked flushed. Fluttering her lashes, she said, "You're really good at sex, Jack. I give you that." She grinned. "It's like your thing."

Jack sipped the wine. He preferred scotch, but this pinot wasn't bad. "Thank you, Glad."

"I mean, it's not like you're a brain surgeon, or own a house in Provence."

"Or the Jersey Shore."

Glad smiled, her eyes ocean-blue under a purple cloud of eye goop, her hair a color never seen in nature, while judging by what was left down below, was likely brunette, who knew when, fifty years ago? In Jack's considerable experience, few Jewesses combined blue eyes and dark hair, and he sometimes wondered if Glad wore colored contacts.

She continued, "But it's not nothing, Jackie." She widened those blue eyes. "And now that I'm so old." She hesitated, then burst out, "I mean, *really!* I haven't been fucked like that in thirty years."

"Who you kidding, Glad? You never been fucked like that."

"And modest too. Just once, by the original Mister Goldberg."

"Stu's father?"

She wrinkled her nose. "Or maybe it was the next one."

"How many were there?"

"If you can't remember, I'm not telling you."

It was three, and he knew it.

"Besides, I don't ask about your women."

"You could if you wanted."

"You know what? You're not half as smart as you think you are."

Yes, I am, he thought. *And that's why I ain't saying nothing else.*

Somehow, Avi arranged for Joe's PSMA PET-CT that very afternoon. To be honest, Joe knew there was no *SOMEHOW* about it. Stu had explained Avi was a member of the National Academy of Medicine, which for a doctor was like being in the Hall of Fame, except docs could be inducted while they were still working, instead of having to wait five years after retirement.

Scheduled for the last time slot of the day, or maybe an extra one added especially for him, the procedure required drinking a liquid that would light up like a Christmas tree in one of his lymph nodes, or God forbid, his spine. That freaked Joe out more than anything, realizing a toddler cancer cell had hopped on a Big Wheel and pedaled away from his prostate, then raised its pseudopod: *Can You See Me Now?*

Later, while they walked back to their hotel in the semi-dusk, Frannie's cell phone rang. Without knowing who it was, Joe *knew* who it was. *Jess.* Her eyes softened, and she couldn't stop smiling. And then there was the sound of her voice, as if she didn't have a care in the world.

Joe wondered, although he could never know, if she emitted the same unconditional love-light when she spoke to him? He'd never experienced that with his own parents, not after his mom went crazy, and Jack, well, Jack was Jack. And just for a moment, strolling down York in the half-dark, Joe felt stabbed by jealousy. Not because Jess had thrown the no-hitter he never did, but because Frannie loved him best. But then, in a blazing moment of self-knowledge, Joe realized he wasn't jealous of Jess, but of Stu Goldberg, and the way he'd looked at Frannie in the examination room. *Wait a goddamn minute*, he'd thought then, and again now. *I'm still here!*

Then Joe returned to the moment, walking beside Frannie, who exclaimed, "*The Colbert Show*! That's amazing!"

After a quick dinner, they returned to their room. Joe felt as if he were carrying a four-hundred-pound monkey on each shoulder. What if he was *really* sick? He'd see Avi on Wednesday, get his results, and agree to a treatment plan. If it was in his lymph node, that was bad. If it was in his bones, that was worse, but Avi had said not to worry because he wasn't feeling any pain.

Meanwhile, the chimp bouncing on his left shoulder kept nattering, *What if Frannie's hot for Stu, like he is for her, that motherfucker?*

"Joe," Frannie asked later, when he emerged from their hotel room bathroom. "You want to watch the Mets?"

"They're not playing tonight."

"Some other game?"

"You know," he said. "You don't have to come with me Wednesday morning."

"Of course, I'm coming with you. How could you possibly think I wouldn't?"

"You were so upset and rude to Avi this morning."

"I sometimes think he's more interested in promoting his new treatment and preserving your sex life than saving your life."

"I don't think so."

"I already told you, I'm more concerned about keeping you alive than about our sex life. It's not that big a deal."

Maybe it's not that big a deal for you. And Joe knew he should keep his mouth shut, but somehow it popped open. "Maybe it's not that big a deal for you, because you've got Stu waiting in the wings."

"What the hell does that mean?"

"I saw how he looked at you."

"What about how you were looking at Doctor Tran?"

"I wasn't looking," Joe said angrily. "I only have eyes for you."

"I wasn't looking at Stu."

"Well, he was sure as hell looking at you."

"I noticed." She took a deep, steadying breath. "At the game last night too. I don't know what the hell that was about."

"It's about how gorgeous you are."

"Oh, Joe. I'm so scared."

He didn't know if he moved towards her or she moved towards him, but suddenly they were kissing, and he tasted tears. Then he took her blouse off, and she knelt in front of him, unzipping his jeans. And after they'd made love as wildly, sweetly, and violently as any time he remembered, he lay beside her in their king-size bed, pressed against her from head to toe.

"That's why," he whispered, "I'd like to hold onto our sex life."

"And if that were our last time?" She pressed more tightly against him. "We'd still have flesh on flesh."

"I want you to know. If something happens to me, and you end up with Stu, that's all right."

"Nothing's going to happen to you. Anyway, Stu's too short for me."

"But if you ended up with Stu, you'd have a smart Jew the second time around."

She moved her lips to his ear. "You're plenty smart for me, Joe." Then she bit him. *Hard.*

"Ow!"

"That's what you get for talking crap."

They lay in silence, flesh pressing flesh, lost in their own thoughts.

CHAPTER TWENTY-FOUR

L ate Wednesday morning, three days after his no-hitter, Jess threw his normal bullpen in preparation for his Friday start. Rah caught him; the team now considered Rah his designated catcher. Mac and Gib watched. Despite throwing twenty-five more pitches than usual to finish the no-hitter, Jess felt great. When he finished, Mac explained he'd be on a short leash his next two starts. No more than seventy pitches, no more than five innings, whichever came first.

"We can't have your goddamn golden arm falling off, now can we?"

Unfortunately, the Mets' post-season chances had taken a hit Tuesday night, when they lost to the Marlins, dropping them two games behind the Nats for the first Wild Card, and into a tie with the Cards and D-backs for the final two. They had another home game against the Fish, today's Businessman's Special, before heading to Philly for four games starting Thursday.

The noon start facilitated Jess and Rah's appearance on *The Colbert Show*. They needed to arrive no later than five, and hopefully 4:30, at the Ed Sullivan Theater on Broadway and 53rd to tape their segment. Because he was starting Friday and, therefore, 100 percent certain not to pitch in today's game, Jess had permission to leave Citi Field by three, even if the game went into extra innings. Rah needed to stay, however, in case the team needed him. Although there should be plenty of time, Jess and Rah had brought their going-on-Colbert clothes to Citi and arranged for a car service to wait outside the players' entrance to whisk them away as soon as they were showered and changed.

Rah was a nervous wreck. Last night, he'd laid out four possible outfits and tried them on for Jess. In the end, he picked the same gray slacks, gray silk shirt, and humongous gold chain he wore the first time he'd met Joe and Frannie.

In the end, there was no need to worry. The Mets scored six in the second, four more in the fourth, and at the end of five innings, they led 12-1. During the seventh-inning stretch, when the fans were being led by the scoreboard through a boisterous rendition of "Take Me Out to the Ballgame," Gallagher walked the length of the dugout to where Jess sat with a couple of the other starting pitchers, shooting the shit, and waiting for the game to end.

"So," said Gallagher. "I hear you and Rah are going be on TV tonight."

Jess hadn't said anything to the older pitchers, who'd made him carry their bags when he first came up.

"What the fuck, Jess?" asked Burbank, whose straight blond hair flowed down from under his ballcap and over his shoulders. "You been holding out."

"What show?" asked Rick Heynen.

"Colbert. Turns out there's never been a no-hitter thrown by a rookie pitcher to a rookie catcher."

"The blind leading the blind," said Rick.

"So why you been holding out?" Burbank demanded.

"I don't like blowing my own horn."

"Man," said Wetherby, the team's only Black starting pitcher. "If you don't, who the fuck gonna blow it?"

"When you throw a no-no." Burbank grinned. "Lotsa people wanna blow your horn."

Burbank often appeared on *Page Six* of the *Post*, photographed with models and starlets.

"Jess," Gallagher said, dropping a palm on his shoulder, "if you want to leave now and beat traffic into the City, that's okay."

"I can't leave without Rah, sir."

Outside the dugout, in the crowded stadium, the crowd was singing, "Buy me some peanuts and Cracker Jacks."

As he did every day at this time, Wetherby said, "I don't see no cracker named Jack."

Gallagher said, "Tell you what, I'll call the pen and have Mac send Rah to the clubhouse. Fifteen to two, we're not gonna need the third string catcher."

"Thank you, sir," Jess said, and meant it.

"You earned it." Gallagher grinned. "No-No Singer."

Gallagher walked away, as the crowd bellowed, "To the Oooooold Baaaaaawl Game."

"Thank you, *sir*. Give me a fucking break," Wetherby said. "Dude's eyes are messed up."

Rick said, "Get me Colbert's autograph, okay?"

Jess started down the steps to the clubhouse tunnel, not knowing if Rick Heynen really wanted Colbert's autograph or not. Then he heard the older guys laughing.

Joe's scan revealed a metastatic lesion in a lymph node in his lower abdomen. Understanding medical shit was like driving in the fog with high beams. Everything bounced back blinding him while this wind in his ears drowned out everything Avi said except *metastatic*. And maybe he heard *Stage Four* too. Good thing he had Frannie to listen. Now he wished, jealousy be damned, Stu Goldberg was there to translate.

"Joe?" Frannie asked.

He peered at her through the fog.

"Avi asked you something."

"Sorry, I missed it."

Avi raised his eyebrows.

"Avi wants to know if you agree to start the three-dose radiotherapy?"

Suddenly Joe knew what he needed to hear. "Am I dying?"

"Someday." The old man allowed himself a smile. "But if we ablate this lesion, which I'm convinced we can do,"—he waved his hand to demonstrate his contempt for the puny lesion—"and you don't develop another, which I can't guarantee, then the five-year survival rate is nearly ninety percent."

Frannie said, "But you said Joe is Stage Four."

So she'd heard it too.

"Stage Four means the cancer has moved outside his prostate, and we can't cure it. But it doesn't mean he's dying anytime soon."

"I'll do it." Joe glanced at Frannie. "What about side effects?"

"There shouldn't be any from the radiation. Maybe fatigue. But as I've explained, if you begin anti-hormonal therapy either before or after radiation, you'll lose sexual function."

"So should I?"

Avi's eyes flitted towards Frannie then returned. "That's not for me to say. But studies show anti-hormonal therapy won't affect long-term outcomes."

"Then why," Frannie asked, "did Doctor Perlman suggest it?"

"In my opinion, just like Rick in *Casablanca*, Dr. Perlman is misinformed." Avi started towards the door. "My scheduler will be in touch."

"Thank you," Joe called after him. They followed Avi out of the examination room, passed the front desk, and rode an elevator then an escalator to the ground floor, emerging moments later into the startling fall sunshine.

Jack and Glad arrived early at the Ed Sullivan Theater and took seats reserved for them in the third row of the studio audience. Jess and Rah were the first scheduled guests, right after the monologue and before the musical act, a band Jack not only hadn't heard play but hadn't even heard of: Zelda and the Head Knockers.

As the crowd flowed into the theater filling every seat, Jack grew more and more nervous. Then the lights dimmed, and the band began to play. Jack glanced at Glad who was staring at the stage, presenting her small heart-shaped face to him in profile: poufy platinum hair and one heavily made-up blue eye. He'd really fallen for this mouthy old broad. How wonderful was that: romance blooming at a time of life when it was just as likely everything would wither.

The music finished with a flourish, and Colbert strode onto the stage in a natty gray suit. The thing about Colbert—and this was true for all the celebrities Jack had met, mostly in sports through Joey—was that famous people looked exactly like themselves. Jack didn't know who he expected them to look like, maybe some dressed up version, but it always tickled him stars looked just like he thought they would. This Colbert was really a wiseass, cracking wise about the pres and majority leader, who Colbert said looked like a turtle in mating season. And this and that, that and this, with the audience, who were his fans, shrieking with laughter.

Then the monologue ended, and after a short pause, which Jack knew when the show aired would be filled with commercials, Colbert said, "And now, a special athletic treat. As some of you may know, on Sunday night, in the heat of a pennant race, Jess Singer, a rookie pitcher for the Mets, and son of former team great, Joe Singer, threw a no-hitter, only the second no-no in the often hapless history of the Mets."

The audience cheered.

"What makes this no-hitter even more special, and in fact, one of a kind, was that Jess's catcher, Rah Ramirez, is also a rookie. In fact, it was Rah's first major league start. How great is that!" Colbert looked around, with light rebounding off the lenses of his signature specs. "So all right, even you Yankee fans—"

Half the room cheered, meaning, Jack concluded, they rooted for the fucking Yankees.

"Please give Singer and Ramirez a *Colbert Show* hot welcome!"

Jess and Rah emerged from the corner of the stage, looking like two million bucks. Jess wore a narrow-lapeled black suit over an open purple shirt and looked, Jack thought, like a movie star. Rah wore so much gold around his neck he looked like a jewelry store on 47th Street.

The audience stomped and whistled. Jess and Rah raised their hands and waved, looking, Jack thought, exactly like what they were: two handsome young athletes at the top of the world.

Glad moved her mouth to Jack's ear. "They look great together, don't they?"

Jack nodded, trying not to think about all the things Glad might mean.

"So how old are you guys?" Colbert asked, after Two-J's and Rah settled on his couch.

"Twenty-two," Jess said. "Both of us."

"And how long have you known each other?"

"I've known Jess"—Rah was grinning so widely Jack didn't know how he could speak—"since we are eighteen, and I first come to the US."

"Rah hardly spoke English back then. He learned watching *Friends* re-runs."

"Why didn't you watch my show?"

"You talk too fast." Rah displayed his perfect teeth. "And too many big words."

"And Jennifer Aniston and the other *Friends* actresses are better looking," Jess said.

"You know how to hurt a guy." Colbert mugged for the audience. "My sources tell me you guys are not only best friends, you're roommates."

Uh-oh, Jack thought.

"When Rah got called up a month ago, he didn't have a place to live, so I let him sleep on my couch."

"Amazing. Did you guys know you were the first rookie pitcher and catcher to combine on a no-hitter?"

Jess said, "Not until your show called."

"Even more amazing." Colbert feigned surprise. "My research team are such smart young people."

"You know, Mister Colbert," Rah began. "Now that I unnerstan more English, yours is my favorite show."

"Smart man," Colbert quipped.

"And thass why," Rah said, "Jess and I, we bring you a present."

"*Our* sources tell us." Jess mugged for the camera. "You wear a seven and a half."

"That's right."

"You have a quite a big head."

"I try not to."

"You have a right to be a big head," Rah said.

"Why, thank you, Rah."

Rah handed Colbert a blue-and-orange-logo-ed Mets cap. Jess asked, "Aren't you going to put it on?"

Colbert eyed the hat with suspicion. "You're not wearing your caps."

"Mister Colbert," Rah said. "We wear caps when we're working, and you're working now."

Colbert laughed. "Okay, but I'm gonna look dorky." He put the cap on his head, where it looked like the topmost pancake in a wobbly stack. "How do I look?"

Jess and Rah looked at each other. Jess said, "Dorky."

"Watch it," Colbert said.

"How about?" Rah said. "We sign it for you."

Colbert reached for the Sharpie that just happened to be out on his desk, which was when Jack realized the whole cap business was a set-up. Colbert passed the cap and Sharpie to Jess, who passed it to Rah, who signed the brim. Then Jess signed and returned the cap to Colbert, who set it on his head. The crowd cheered.

"Can I ask a favor, sir?" Jess asked.

"I'm already doing you a favor wearing this hat."

"It look fah-bulous," Rah said.

"My friend and the ace of the Mets' staff, Rick Heynen, asked me to get your autograph."

Colbert mugged for the camera. "Are you sure it's not for you?"

Rah said, "I'd like your autograph."

"I thought so," said Colbert.

Colbert signed three photographs that also just happened to be on his desk. Rah's, they'd learn later, read, *For Rah Ramirez, Great Smile!*

Stephen Colbert. He passed the signed photos to Two-J's. "And now, Jess, I'd like to ask *you* a question."

"Sure."

"Answer the question I'm sure you've been asked a million times. Please tell us what it's like to have a famous father, who also pitched for the Mets?"

"My dad," Jess said, "is a really great guy who taught me almost everything I know about pitching, except for what my grandfather, Jack, taught me."

"And if I'm not mistaken, your grandfather is in the audience tonight?"

"That's right," Jess said.

"Jack Singer," Stephen Colbert said, "please stand up and take a bow."

Knees wobbly, Jack stood and waved to the studio audience, which applauded as if he'd done something extraordinary, when all along, it was Joey, and now Two-J's, who'd brought honor to the Singer name.

Later that night, Jess and Rah were sitting up in bed in their room at the Mets' hotel in Philly watching *The Colbert Show* when Jess's Twitter account began blowing up: *Not Just Roommates—Baseball Fags!* Soon, it was the top trending item in the Twitter-verse. By the time Colbert went off, someone named Flushing Fred had attached the photo of Jess leaping into Rah's arms after the last out of his no-hitter: Rah's arms around his waist; Rah's face inches from his belt buckle; Rah's eyes, burning with love and admiration, locked on Jess's face, *#More Than Batterymates #What Else is Rah Catching?*

Jess couldn't sleep. Even Rah, who typically passed out when his head hit the pillow, then didn't move for nine hours, tossed and turned all night, getting up to use the bathroom every hour or two, while Jess feigned sleep so they wouldn't have to talk because what could they say in the middle of the night that wouldn't make things worse?

By 5:00 a.m., when Jess moved to the other bed because he really needed sleep and Rah's flipping, groaning, and moaning made that impossible, there were half a million retweets, although the original had been taken down. Jess hadn't recognized the hashtag of the original tweeter—Flushing Fred?—and wondered who it could be and what he and Rah should do. Ignore it? Deny it? Rah worried and he'd said so many times, that if the other Latin players found out, they'd totally kick his ass.

And what a nice ass it was, Jess had thought but didn't say, because this wasn't a time for joking. Rah feared that if his father heard in Cuernavaca, he'd never talk to him again. *This is no laughing matter, Jess,* he could hear Rah saying, and Jess agreed. Just like the end of a pennant race was no time for distractions, and this was the King Kong of distractions. If the Mets didn't make the playoffs, everyone would blame him! *Oh God,* Jess thought, offering a prayer to his father's God of Pitchers and Catchers. Philly fans had the well-earned reputation of being the rudest, crudest, most potty-mouthed fan base in the league. He could already hear them, when he was on the mound. *Hey faggot, hey faggot! Swish pitcher! Swish!*

Jess decided if he didn't get at least a few hours of sleep, he'd never make it through his start tomorrow. He switched off his cell, took the room phone off the hook, and though it was already past five in the morning, found the Ambien he kept in his ditty bag for emergencies. Returning to bed, walking on tiptoes to avoid making noise, he glanced at Rah in the bed, face buried in his pillow.

Oh God, Jess thought, *I love him so much.* And despite the troubles they were facing, the tiniest part of him, an infinitesimally small and hidden part, thought maybe this wasn't the worst thing. Gay marriage was the law of the land, except in the land of baseball. Climbing into the spare bed, he hoped he wasn't so upset the Ambien wouldn't work. And then, like the young man he was, Jess told himself when he woke at nine or ten and turned on his phone, the first thing he'd do, even before checking Twitter, was call Mom. She'd know what to do; she always did. And thinking that, Jess fell asleep.

When Joe woke, the rumors about Jess and Rah were all over the internet. He checked ESPN to see if the morning sports shows were discussing it, but no. He tried Jess's cell, which went straight to voicemail. He dialed a second time and left a message, asking Jess to call back. He didn't know what else to do. Frannie was walking. He'd decided to allow her to enjoy the river walk in peace before all sorts of troubles, none of them of her making, fell on her head. They were supposed to hear from Avi's office to schedule the first radiation, and last night before falling asleep, Frannie had been saying she should fly back to California for a few days because she didn't want to leave Ruby in the kennel for so long. Joe said maybe he'd fly back too, and do the radiation there, but Frannie insisted he do it in New York. They fell asleep, plans unsettled and unknown, until they heard from Avi's office. Joe wasn't sure, and Frannie wasn't either, if he could begin radiation in New York and finish in California, but they suspected the answer was no. And so, she'd gone walking to ease her mind, which was when Joe had checked sports sites and discovered what was going on. The jubilant photo of Jess in Rah's arms in the flush of his no-hitter sure looked different above the caption: *More Than Battery Mates?*

Joe suspected it might be true and toted both sides of the ledger. 1) Jess was gay. 2) Joe and Rah roomed together. 3) He knew how much Jess liked Rah, and how much Rah seemed to like Jess. And on the other side? *Nada.*

Why hadn't he figured it out before? If there was ever a two plus two equaling four, this was it. Why did it matter? It just did. The Mets were in the middle of a pennant race; after last night's victory, they were tied for the final two Wild Cards, with momentum on their side. There were unwritten rules in baseball. No stealing bases when your team was ten runs ahead. No bunting to break up a no-hitter. No sleeping with your teammate's wife. And of course, no sleeping with your teammates. Now, here was one he hadn't thought of: no outing teammates on social media.

Of course, no one knew who'd first tweeted about Jess and Rah, but someone would figure that out. Eventually, everything got figured out. Sitting up in bed, Joe just *knew* it had to be a player. And likely a teammate: Who else would know?

Boy, Joe thought. *When shit hits the fan, it sure makes a mess.* Then his phone rang, and he answered, hoping it would be Jess, but suspecting it was his father.

"Joey," Jack said, "you seen the news?"

"Yeah."

"Talk to Jess?"

"His phone's off."

"Yeah, I tried too."

Then neither of them spoke for what felt like a really long time. Finally, Jack said, "Maybe you could reach out to Mac."

"I will." Then Joe realized what else they could do. "We should be in Philly when Jess pitches tomorrow. You know what assholes those Philly fans are."

"Fucking-A right."

"If you hear from Jess, have him call me. Frannie's going to be out of her mind."

"Like I ain't," Jack said.

Jess woke after ten, foggy from Ambien. For a confused instant, he was in Redondo Beach, late for first period. Then he remembered who and where he was. *Jess Singer, outed Major League pitcher. Streets of Philadelphia.* He glanced at Rah's empty bed and dread broke over him, spinning the breath out of him and replacing it with fear. Was Rah gone? Where was he? Then, coming fully awake, Jess heard water running in the bathroom; Rah showered first thing after waking. So, he wasn't gone, not yet, though Jess had realized while he slept that they were going to have to stop sleeping together. Rah would have to start sleeping in his own room on the road. And Rah should get his own place in New York. Or would the Mets ship Rah back to Syracuse, to tamp down the scandal? No, the Triple-A season was over.

Jess sat up, wondering who he should call in the Mets front office? Should he and Rah deny the Twitter allegations? He remembered Dad had suggested he get in touch with that guy, Davey Dean, in the commissioner's office. What if he just announced at a press conference, *Hey, this is who I am!* Would MLB support him? And what about Rah? If Jess came out, it would be impossible for Rah to say none of this was true, and he didn't want to put Rah on the spot. Rah, who was petrified his father would find out.

And while he was thinking about the allegations, he wondered, as he'd been trying not to, who had outed him? Who was calling himself Flushing Fred? Who would know? And even if someone knew, who would want to fuck him over this way? A teammate? Jess didn't want to think about that part. He didn't want to think about any of this. What he really wanted was to take another Ambien and go back to sleep. Because as soon as he turned on his cell and replaced the room phone in its cradle, the day would turn six shades of crazy. He'd be right back in the ugly, fucked-up world, and he wasn't ready. Jess walked to the bathroom, praying Rah hadn't locked it from inside.

The handle turned. Jess entered without knocking and approached the walk-in shower. Through the steamy glass, he could see Rah under the spray. Jess removed his boxers, opened the shower, and Rah turned towards him. His eyes looked swollen. Had he been crying? Or was it lack of sleep, or shampoo in his eyes? Water streamed off Rah's face and beautiful body. Jess stepped partway into the stall, and for a moment, feared Rah would say, *Don't come in*, though they'd showered together ten or twenty times before. Rah nodded, ever so slightly, and Jess stepped into the stall, into Rah's arms, then closed the swinging door behind him. He held on, and the hot water washed over them. He'd hold on, he told himself, until they were ready to face the day.

CHAPTER TWENTY-FIVE

Joe's first SABR session was Friday morning. Pain? *No.* Fear? *Plenty.* Worry? *Off the charts.* With Joe's encouragement, Frannie was returning to California on an afternoon flight, and he wanted to say goodbye in person. But step one of SABR was mapping the lesion—paralleling what happened in Portugal for the primary tumor—and it was taking forever.

Joe had been cautioned to keep completely still during mapping. If not, SABR might irradiate the wrong goddamn part, and he'd never walk or piss straight again. Could that be true?

When the mapping was finished, the lesion still had to be zapped. When at last it was over, Joe rode the elevator to the first floor, hurried past the security guards, boarded the escalator to the ground floor, exited onto York Avenue, and set out, jogging, towards their hotel.

Avi had assured him he'd feel fine after the procedure, which he did. Maybe later he'd feel tired. Or nauseous. But now, jogging south, he felt nothing. *Nothing* was good. But would *nothing* prevent the cancer from spreading and save his life? Unbelievable. It was all unbelievable. First, that he had a cancer he couldn't see or feel; second, that it had *metasto, whatever*; and, third, that SABR, which he also couldn't see or feel, might save him.

Joe ran faster. He was still three blocks away, and Frannie should have gotten into a cab five minutes ago. This whole cancer crap, going back to January, Joe thought, as he skirted an old lady on a walker, a uniformed aide at her elbow, felt as if it were happening to some other Joe. When he was most famous, he'd come to think of Jewish Joe Singer as someone outside of himself, much like Rickey Henderson, the greatest leadoff batter in history and the stolen base king, who famously spoke about himself in the third person. *Rickey does this, Rickey says that.*

So was Joe Singer, Frannie's husband, Jess's dad, in fact, sick? Joe guessed he was. Right now, what really mattered was kissing his wife goodbye. Yesterday, when she'd phoned the kennel, she learned Ruby wasn't eating. Dropping weight. Peeing everywhere. In other words, a dying dog, and no one, Joe felt, should die alone. He insisted over and over that Frannie should fly out to say goodbye, and when she protested, he said simply, "I've got this. Just come back soon."

Poor Frannie, Joe thought, running in place at a red light as cars poured off the Queensborough Bridge. Dying dog in California, sick husband in New York, while in the City of Brotherly Love, Jess bore the weight of the gay and straight worlds on his shoulders.

When the light changed, Joe shot forward. He would have flown with Frannie, but as they'd suspected, all three SABR treatments needed to be done in the same facility. The next was Monday; the third and final one was Wednesday. Joe veered left off York and pulled up, panting, in front of their hotel. Goddamnit, he'd missed her. Missed her! Joe bent over, hands on his knees, biting great gulps of air. When he looked up, Frannie was exiting the revolving door, pulling a roller bag. Joe kissed his wife goodbye.

A minute later, her cab sped away. Joe rode the elevator to the tenth floor and headed to their room. Maybe he'd nap. Maybe he did feel a tad fatigued. Or maybe he was dreading the rest of the day, especially the train ride with Jack. He hadn't been confined in a small space with his father in years. To be honest, he was dreading all of it. Jack. The train ride. The public scrutiny. But he'd be there for Jess, no matter what.

Jess was trying to maintain his normal starting routine. Sleep in. *Check.* Large breakfast. *Check.* Arrive early. *Double check.* Quality time with

Rah the night before? *Checkless.* He'd hardly seen Rah since yesterday morning. Later, at Citizens Bank where the Mets lost 6-2, Jess had sat near the other starters in the dugout, charting pitches, while Rah spent the game in the bullpen. In the locker room, before and after, with everyone watching, or so they feared, Jess and Rah barely glanced in each other's direction. The dispiriting loss dropped them a game behind the Cards, who'd won six in a row, for the second Wild Card, with nine left to play. They remained tied with the D-backs, who'd also lost, for the final spot.

After the game, Gallagher had called Jess into his office and asked him to close the door. Eighteen hours later, face-down on the trainer's table, having the long muscles of his back and left shoulder massaged and stretched, Jess remembered the uncomfortable silence. Finally, with his eyes characteristically directed elsewhere, Gallagher said, "I guess you know why I asked for this sit-down."

"Not really."

"You're kidding."

"Yeah," Jess admitted. "I'm kidding."

After a second silence, Gallagher asked, "You think I give a good fuck who you sleep with?"

"I don't know, sir." Jess hesitated, then added, "Do you?"

"I don't. I don't even know if that shit on Twitter is true."

If the skipper expected Jess to confirm or deny, he was nuts. Jess and Rah had decided to say nothing and wait for the mess to blow over. Maybe it would. The original tweets from Flushing Fred had been taken down almost immediately.

Suddenly, Gallagher's eyes sought contact. "You know what I *do* care about?"

Jess shook his head.

"If you can block this out and pitch like yourself tomorrow."

"Yes, sir. I can."

"Good." The manager's eyes resumed their gaze at a spot two inches past Jess's head. "Fur's going to catch. I know Rah called a great game last time." Gallagher looked straight at him again. *Amazing.* "But with all this shit about him being your *personal catcher?* No way."

Jess said nothing.

"All right, Jess, get a good night's sleep."

Eighteen hours and ten minutes later, with the assistant trainer's thumbs digging into his shoulder, Jess remembered exactly what Gallagher had said next.

"Any idea who tweeted that shit?"

"No, sir."

"If you did, would you tell me?"

"No, sir, I wouldn't."

Eighteen hours, ten minutes, and twenty seconds later, he wondered if he should have said more to Gallagher, or called that guy in the commissioner's office, like Dad had suggested. Or called back Emmy, who'd left two voice mails and several texts on his phone. Eighteen hours and eleven minutes later, he was wishing the assistant trainer's thumbs could reach inside his skull and massage his brain. But mostly, he was wishing the assistant trainer's thumbs were Rah's.

From the jump, Two-J's wasn't right. He walked Schwarber, the leadoff batter, on four pitches, his normally smooth delivery unraveling like a cheap suit. Then he went two and oh, and three and one on Santos, everything high and glove side to both batters. Forced to come in, he gave up a laser to right-center that one-hopped the wall and scored Boyer from first.

Jack glanced at Joey, slouched behind his Midnight Jew disguise, like that ever fooled anyone. Black felt hat, white feather in the band, dopey dark glasses. Singer, *père et fils*, sat on the aisle in Section 122, maybe twenty rows behind the visitors' dugout. Half the nearby fans wore Mets gear, hats or uni tops going back to Darling and Gooden, who'd pitched even before Joey's day.

Joey shook his head, nervous, as if he had the same grievous feeling Jack did. Jess's first pitch to Bohm, the third baseman, bounced five feet in front of the dish, skipped past Furillo, and all the way to the backstop, allowing Santos to advance to third. *Vey iz mir,* Jack thought, as an anxious buzz rose from nearby Mets fans. Jack focused on Jess, whose next pitch sailed so high and outside, Furillo had to jump up to catch it.

"Shit," Joey muttered.

"Double shit," Jack answered.

"Hey, fruitcake. Hey, pansy," yelled some Philly fans a few rows forward.

Jack pretended he hadn't heard it. He hoped Two-J's didn't either. But maybe he did, because his next pitch split the plate, and Bohm socked it so high and deep, deep, deep to center Jack thought it was gone, but at the last minute, Nimms the Mets' center fielder jumped and hauled it in against the fence. Santos trotted in from third, doubling the Phillies' lead, 2-0.

"At least," Jack said, behind his hand, "with the bases empty, maybe Two-J's can relax."

Joey didn't answer. Jack didn't believe it either. On Jess's third pitch to Bryce Harper, he hung a curve Harper launched maybe four miles into the upper deck in right. Harper, the conceited prick, admired his blast for what felt like twenty seconds, then flipped his bat head high—what an ass!—and slow-trotted while the Philly fans rose up on their hind legs and barked, "Bryce, Bryce, Bryce!"

Just when Jack thought things couldn't get any worse, the schmuck right in front of him, wearing a Mets cap, no less, and a vintage Beltran jersey, shouted loud enough for everyone to hear, "What's wrong with that goddamn faggot?"

Jack counted in his head, *One, two, three* to keep from mouthing off. *Four, five, six* followed, but no amount of counting was going to stem Jack's anger. He knocked off the schmuck's cap and poured his twelve-dollar beer on the putz's noggin and down the back of his goddamn Beltran jersey.

"Hey!" The schmuck stood and turned around. Fifty, brown-haired, and pasty-faced, with a big, wet bald spot. "What the hell's wrong with you?"

"Excuse *me*," Jack said, "my hand slipped."

"*Dad*," Joey said.

"Slipped?" asked the schmuck, wiping beer off his face.

On the field, Two-J's' catcher and Gib, the pitching coach, converged on the mound.

"Musta been the shock of hearing Jess Singer, who just threw a no-hitter, called what you called him."

"I didn't call him anything."

"So now," Jack said, "on top of everything, you're a lying sack of shit?"

The schmuck, with his wet head and soaked jersey, glared at Jack, then, seeing how insane he looked, backed off and sat down, like Jack knew he would. He wouldn't have minded taking a poke at the douche, even if it had gotten them kicked out of the park. It was already a crap night. On the field, the pitching coach patted Two-J's on the butt and returned to the dugout.

Jack scowled at Joey, who looked like a dope in his Midnight Jew get-up. It was going to be a long goddamn night. Jack sat and said a little prayer, promising this and that if Two-J's pulled himself together. But he didn't believe it. Some nights, and this felt like one of them, it was better to cut your losses and go home early.

Jess lasted just three innings, threw fifty pitches, and gave up five runs, all earned. *Effing disaster*. He watched his team bat in the top of the fourth, then beat it to the locker room, iced his arm, rode the stationary bike for twenty minutes, then showered, fighting tears of humiliation as the hot water poured over him. He hadn't pitched like this all year. Hadn't pitched this shitty maybe ever. His most important start of the year, and he'd pitched like a scared little bitch. He'd let the team down, let Rah down, and he couldn't blame it on the Philly fans. Once he walked the leadoff batter, he couldn't hear what they were shouting because his internal critic started screaming, *Bitch, bitch, bitch, scared little bitch!* at the top of its weird little lungs, and that was all Jess could hear, especially after the Harper moonshot. *Bitch, bitch, bitch, scared little bitch!*

Jess stepped out of the shower. The final score was 8-5 Phils, and the loss dropped the Mets two games out of the first and second Wild Cards with eight to play; the Cards had won their seventh in a row that afternoon, beating the Reds. If there was any bright spot, and in his current frame of mind it was hard for Jess to see one, the Nats also lost. The Nats had been sitting comfortably alone in the first Wild Card spot ten days ago, but with their third loss in a row and the Cards victory, the Nats and Cards were tied, with the Mets two games behind them, and a game behind the D-backs, for the third and final Wild Card. If the season had ended today, they'd be going home.

Jess dressed and sat in front of his locker, waiting to see if Gallagher was going to call a team meeting. While he waited, his friends among the other starting pitchers trooped by on their way back from the shower and told him not to worry. The last was Rick Heynen, the staff ace.

"Hell, Jess," Heynen said, "you can't throw a no-no every time."

Heynen, who was starting Sunday, sat down beside him wearing a towel.

"I know you feel like shit, but remember, don't get too high or low."

"I really fucked up."

Heynen, an inch taller than Jess, six-six with impossibly long arms and legs, said, "Sure, but the pen gave up three runs, and anyway, pitching right after a no-no? It's like the first hole after an eagle. Nine times out of ten, you're gonna hook your drive into the woods."

Heynen, Jess thought, was a really good guy. Kind-hearted, down-to-earth, though he'd won the Cy Young two years ago and nearly won it again last year.

"Thanks, Rick."

"You're what, twenty-two?"

Jess nodded.

"When I was your age"—he grinned—"I was throwing A-ball. And here you are, middle of a pennant race." He gazed at Jess with what Jess had never quite realized, perhaps because he'd never sat this close to Heynen before, were exceptionally kind brown eyes. "You got that Twitter shit to deal with. That's a ton to put out of your mind."

Jess didn't know what to say. It was all too much! Then he remembered the signed photo. "Hey, I've got something for you." He reached into his locker for the autographed glossy. *To Rick Heynen, from your biggest fan, Stephen Colbert.*

Heynen read the inscription and smiled. "I bet he never watched a game in his life."

Heynen stood and walked off still wearing just his towel. Jess watched him go. When he turned back towards his locker, from the corner of his eye, he glimpsed Big Barnes at the far end of the locker row, where Heynen had just disappeared, grinning malevolently.

"Yo, Singer." Big's pig eyes narrowed. "Nice job today."

"You too."

Big had given up one of the three bullpen runs.

"You know what, pussy?" Big grinned. "Wait, I forgot, pussy's what you don't know about."

"Fuck you."

"Don't you wish. So tell me, you think Colbert's going to invite you and *your Rah-Rah boy* back on his show?"

"One thing's for sure, he's never going to invite your fat ass."

Big stepped down the locker row towards Jess, who advanced to meet him, their jaws six inches apart.

"You know what, fudge-packer?" Big's spittle landed on Jess's cheek. "Fuck you!"

He shoved Jess hard, two-handed. Jess stumbled back against the wall, then launched himself into Big's chest, as if he were back at Redondo High playing safety, careful to lead with his right, not his left shoulder. Big toppled like an oak, and Jess landed on top of him. The next thing Jess knew they were rolling around the locker room floor, throwing punches without much effect. Then multiple hands were pulling them apart.

"Stop it! Stop the fucking fighting."

Jess and Big scrambled apart and stood, arms restraining them from behind. Suddenly, Big pulled away from whoever was holding him and swung from the heels. Jess's teeth snapped together. His neck snapped back, and Jess learned, once and forever, that seeing stars after being punched in the face wasn't a metaphor.

Stars, stars, everywhere, stars, was all he could see. If Jess had been able to see smaller celestial bodies, he would have seen Rah rush up and step into a punch as if pegging a throw to second, and then there weren't only *stars,* but spurting blood everywhere when Rah's fist broke Big's nose.

Joe and Jack arrived at the door to the Mets' locker room after the game, but it was closed to visitors. Twenty minutes later they were still outside, and the mood among the waiting sportswriters was grim. One of the *Post* columnists, whose face Joe recognized from the grainy thumbnail above his columns, tried to pigeonhole him, not once but several times, about the Twitter posts. When Joe produced the *No comment* comment he kept in his back pocket, the reporter, whose name Joe now recalled was *Steve* something, got pissy, tempting Joe to push back and tell him to back the fuck off. But he didn't because that had never been his style.

Instead, he repeated, "No comment."

The reporter, whose wavy silver hair made him look like a fox terrier, wouldn't let it go. "Do you agree the gay Twitter storm accounted for Jess's terrible outing?"

Joe snapped, "What do you think?"

"No, Joe," the reporter fired back. "This is about what you think."

"Listen, buddy." Jack stepped between them. "You got kids?"

"Two boys."

Jack moved closer. "If it was one of your boys, and a reporter who wouldn't accept a respectful *No comment,* kept shoving his fucking puss in your grill, what would you do?"

Edging away, the reporter answered, "I'm just doing my job."

"Is your job being a dick?" Jack squared his shoulders. "We're just people here, and no comment is no fucking comment."

The reporter found somewhere else to stand. Another five minutes crawled by, then the clubhouse attendant unlocked the door and the crowd steamed in, Joe and Jack among them. The reporters headed towards the interview room to nab front row seats. Joe and Jack looked around, wondering where to go, then Joe spied Mac across the locker room and walked towards him.

"I was hoping y'all would show up; Jess said you might."

Mac, who still walked much like he'd run in his playing days, which, given the girth and breadth of his thighs, was faster than anyone expected, hustled up one row of lockers, down the next, then turned hard right without knocking through the closed but unlocked door into a trainer's room where Jess lay on a massage table, head elevated, pressing an ice pack to the left side of his face, which was swollen and purple.

"What happened?" Joe asked.

Mac said, "Big Barnes sucker-punched him. They'd been tussling, and when we broke 'em apart and someone was pinning Jess's arms, Big hauled off and cold-cocked him."

"What were you fighting about?" Joe asked.

Jess removed the ice pack from his cheek. "Big's an ath-hole." He grinned. "Thorry, my tongue's thwollen."

Jack asked, "You get your licks in?"

"No." Jess glanced towards Mac, still grinning, though Joe didn't see what was funny.

Mac said, "Two shakes of a tail after Big slugged Jess, Rah busted Big's nose. Man." He grinned at Jess. "Blood was flying everywhere, and they closed the locker room to mop it up and get Big the hell out of here so the back page of every New York rag ain't got a picture of his busted proboscis."

"What was the fight about?" Joe asked again.

"Big hates me." Jess said.

"He's a jealous fucker," Mac said. "Gallagher held a closed door, told everyone to keep their mouths shut. Now he's doing his presser; I guess we'll find out if they do."

Joe looked at his son, wondering how much the fight had to do with the Twitter business. "You okay?"

Before Jess could answer, Mac replied, "X-rays of his jaw come back negative. But he's going be eating a lot of soup the next few days, aintcha Jess?"

Joe looked from Jess to Mac, unsure why, given that the Mets lost and Jess pitched piss-poor, it felt like the day was ending well.

"Lotsa thoup," Jess agreed.

Jack asked, "So how're we going get Two-J's outta here without anyone seeing his face?"

Slowly, everyone's eyes turned towards the black slouch hat in Joe's right hand.

Mac asked, "That the same piece of garbage you was using twenty-five years ago?"

"New one." Joe turned towards Jess. "What size you wear?"

"Theven and a half."

"Me too." Joe passed the mantle of the Midnight Jew to his son.

When at long last Jess lay down in bed that night, he was not only battered but blue and lonely. He longed to call Rah, but knew he shouldn't, so he'd turned off his phone. He ached to sneak down the hall and knock on Rah's door, but accepted he shouldn't do that either. They'd agreed not to be seen alone together, agreed not even to talk much until this blew over—if it ever did!—but every time Jess reviewed what had happened, or closed his eyes, he didn't see his fight with Big, or the beginning, end, or any other part of his pitching performance, but Rah, Rah, Rah! Punching the living shit out of Big's nose.

My prince has come, Jess thought, grinning, though it hurt to grin. And not only *My prince has come,* but, *Rah must really love me.* Such a public declaration, so that lying in bed, Jess felt a rush of feeling. Everyone who'd seen it, coaches and teammates, Jess thought, would understand: broken nose = true love.

So, of course Jess couldn't sleep. He tossed and turned, a lovesick twenty-two-year-old, contemplating what might happen next, when he heard a gentle knock at his door. Or thought he did. But it was past midnight, in fact closer to one than twelve, so waking logic announced there was no knock, yet it grew louder. Who could it be? Jess climbed out of bed, starting towards the door. Rah, only Rah.

"I'm coming!" he whisper-shouted. "I'm coming!"

His mind flipped to high school.

Are you coming?

No, but I'm breathing hard.

Jess un-slid the chain, counter-clockwise-d the thumbscrew below the handle, and opened the door.

"Hey, Jess!" Emmy smiled from under a Mets cap, blonde hair drawn in a pony through the back of her cap.

What the?????

"I've been calling and texting. I drove down for the game."

He couldn't form a thought.

"My God, what happened to your face?"

As if he'd pricked his finger in a fairy tale, Jess couldn't speak.

"Let me in." She glanced right and left. "There's people staring."

That broke the spell. Jess stepped back, and Emmy followed him in. She wore a lightweight bubble parka over sneakers and tight jeans. She looked great, as she always did. And under her parka? A replica Mets jersey with his number, 32.

"Where's Tiff?" he asked, wondering if she was knocking on Rah's door.

"At school." Emmy shrugged her Pretty Girl shrug. "I'm not a stalker, you know."

"Let's thee, you knock on my door in the middle of the night, wearing my jersey." Jess suddenly realized all he was wearing was boxers.

"After those tweets about you and Rah? And then you pitched so badly? I had to see you."

Jess retreated to the sofa; Emmy followed. Jess put on his pants; Emmy removed her jacket. They sat on opposite corners of the sofa.

"Is it true, about you and Rah?"

She was so pretty. If Jess were a girl, he'd want to look just like her. And he hadn't grasped this until just now—how had he missed it?—but her hair was the same color as Robert Redford's.

"No comment." Then he thought, *What the hell?* And nodded.

"I *knew* it! Why didn't you tell me?"

So many reasons. Then it was Jess's turn to shrug. "How'd you find my room? They're not supposed to tell anyone."

"I have my ways."

"Tell me."

"I told the desk clerk I was your wife, here to surprise you."

"And he believed you?"

"People believe what they want."

"And if you believed that tweet, why'd you want to see me?"

Emmy took a deep breath. "Of course, I was a teensy bit hurt, but then I thought, 'So *that's why* I had to make the first move. And the second.'"

She sighed, which to Jess, sounded more than a teensy bit hurt.

"Did I ever tell you," she asked, "that my brother's gay?"

"No way!"

"So it's not that weird to me."

Jess found himself wondering—he couldn't help it—if her brother had the same blond hair.

"I almost decided not to come, but I'd spent all that money on my ticket, and I really wanted to see you. And then, when you pitched like shit, so I knew your mind wasn't in the game, I was really glad I'd come."

"Why?"

"You're going to think I'm crazy."

"I already think you're crazy."

"I thought, at least until the season's over, if it would get everyone off your back, I could, like…" She shrugged. "Pretend to be your girlfriend. Maybe sit with the team wives. Maybe go out after a game and be seen at a club or restaurant."

Jess thought, *This girl is crazy.* "Why would you want to do that?"

"I want the Mets to make the playoffs, and if you don't pitch better, there's no way in hell that's going to happen." She inched closer on the couch. "And just because you're gay, which I always suspected—I mean, because of my brother, Bobby, I have some serious gaydar—doesn't mean I don't still like you."

"Whoa," he said. "I'm in love with Rah."

There, he'd said it aloud to someone besides Rah, and that made it real.

"I meant." She shrugged. "As a friend."

For a second. he thought she might cry. And then a tear or two did slide down her cheeks. "I'm fine," she said, wiping her cheeks. "Really."

Oh Christ. Jess slid the rest of the way across the couch and hugged her. Emmy sighed and sagged in his arms.

"If I liked girls"—he drew back so he could see her face and she could see his—"I'd like *you.*"

"That's the nicest thing any boy ever said to me." Her eyes narrowed. "Who hit you?"

She touched his cheek gently, and he drew back in pain.

"I got in a fight with Big in the locker room after the game, and when they were pulling us apart, Big slugged me."

"He's such a pig." She looked enraged. "I never told you what my girlfriend Taylor said, the one who slept with him?"

Jess shook his head.

"He's *such* a pig. Did it hurt?"

Jess nodded.

"Do you want ice?"

"I've been icing for hours. But hey." He grinned, and it still hurt. "It's all good. Right after Big punched me, in front of half the team, Rah broke his nose."

"Really?" She laughed. "Serves the fucker right." Then her look turned somber. "Is it going to be in the news? I haven't seen anything on Twitter."

"Because Big threw the first punch, the club has warned him to keep his mouth shut, or else."

"And because he's such a piece of shit and you're so great." She touched his hand. "I've already watched your no-hitter twice, beginning to end."

"You *sure* you're not a stalker?"

She smiled. "Someone will talk, you'll see. And when that happens, you'll be really glad to have me as your pretend girlfriend."

He grinned, then winced; it hurt to grin. "You're probably right. I wish I could ask Rah. But we agreed not to talk and to keep this on the down-low."

"So," Emmy said. "Just let me know. I should get going."

"Where?"

"Back to school."

"Isn't that, like, five hours?"

She nodded.

"Sleep here. You can have the bed."

"Where will you sleep?"

He patted the couch.

"You can have the other side of the bed." She smiled sadly, if such a beautiful smile could ever be sad. "If you think you can keep your hands off me."

He thought, *This is really crazy.* But he also felt how grateful he was to have company. And all of a sudden, Jess felt so tired he could barely keep his eyes open long enough to cross to the bed and fall into it.

CHAPTER TWENTY-SIX

After the tumult at Citizen Bank, a postgame train to Penn Station, followed by a 1:00-a.m. cab to their hotel, Jack had trouble negotiating sleep. At two-thirty, he downed two bolts of scotch and two of them little blue pills; not the kind that leadened his pencil, the one that sealed his eyes and kept them shut. He woke at eleven, the latest he'd slept in years, feeling as if his mind had been dragged through the mud and put away dirty. What was that kids' movie, *Cloudy With a Chance of Mothballs?* That's how his head felt, so fuzzed it took some time to realize the buzz was a phone, not a fly, which stopped before he reached it. Then, while he stood above the pot waiting for his eighty-two-year-old bladder to finish its business, and Lord knows he wasn't going to muck with that since once it got going it was safer not to stop, his cell phone, abandoned on the nightstand, began playing "Yankee Doodle Dandy". He let it.

Finally, head clear, bladder empty, he shaved, did his push-ups and crunches, dressed and called Joey, then arranged to meet in the lobby and walk up to the Celestial on First, a greasy spoon of the sort he favored: familiar food, no sushi, breakfast served twenty-four seven.

Striding uphill from York towards First, leaning into a brisk wind—it was nearly October, his birthday in two months—Jack peered up at his son's face in profile. Crow's feet walked around his eye; wrinkles creased his cheek; salt and pepper seasoned the hair above his ear. *He ain't a kid no more.* Inside the Celestial, Jack ordered eggs over easy, home fries, and sausage, same as Joey.

"I didn't know you ate eggs over with sausage."

"My whole life," Joe answered. "I learned it from you."

"Why didn't I know that?"

Joey grinned. "Don't get me started."

What the hell does that mean? But Jack said nothing because he took Joe's meaning. After an awkward silence he asked, "You heard from Jess this morning?"

Joe shook his head.

"What about Frannie?"

"She had to put her dog down."

"That funny-looking mutt?"

Joey nodded. The waitress arrived with their chow. She was tough-looking, sixty if she were six, dye job gone bad, wearing white nurse shoes and support hose. She slapped their plates on the Formica, set the Heinz in front of Jack.

"Anything else?"

"We're good."

She deposited the check beside his water and slipped away. Jack watched his son cut into his eggs, then salt-and-peppered his own. For a minute or three, they chewed in silence. When he'd cleaned his plate except for a smear of yolk and a hillock of hash browns, Jack napkin-ed his lips and asked, "When you flying to Cali?"

Joe met his eyes. "I'm not."

"Don't you think Frannie wants you there, since she had to kill her dog?"

"She's flying back tomorrow."

Jack almost asked, *Why the hell not?* Then he knew. "There something you ain't telling me."

Joey nodded.

"The cancer's back."

Joey nodded again.

He was about to demand, *Why didn't you tell me?* Instead, he asked, "You tell Two-J's?"

"He's got enough on his plate."

"For damn sure." He forked half the paprika-ed potatoes to his lips, chased them with the dregs of his coffee. "How bad?"

"Bad enough."

"What's that mean?"

"It's metastasized."

Joey smiled, though Jack didn't see what was funny.

"I finally said it right," Joey said.

"Where's it moved to?"

Joey shrugged.

"Someplace they can cut it out?"

Joey shook his head. Jack mouthed the last clump of potatoes and waved his coffee cup at the waitress.

"I had the first dose of radiation yesterday. Next one's Monday, then Wednesday."

"They gonna remove your prostate?"

Again Joey shook his head. The waitress arrived with a fresh pot and filled their cups. When she took off, Jack asked, "What happens next?"

"Maybe it comes back, maybe it doesn't."

"Don't take a genius to know that. Doc give you the odds?"

"More likely it does. But he didn't say when."

Jack sipped his coffee, which was hot and black, but not too strong, like the Chock full o'Nuts he cut his taste buds on. "Don't fucking die on me, Joey."

He grabbed the check and walked to the register, though he usually counted on Joey settling up. He threw the old waitress 20 percent, then Jack and his son emerged onto First, headed downhill towards the river.

Jess arranged with Ray Mattis, the Mets' traveling secretary, for Emmy to sit with the Mets' wives and girlfriends at Saturday night's game. He also arranged for her to sit in the smaller wives' section on Wednesday in Miami, when he was pitching next. Then Jess and Emmy went down for a late breakfast in the hotel restaurant where he was counting on some of the other players seeing her. Sure enough, not only players, but Gallagher, Gib, and Mac were finishing up when he and Emmy walked through the dining room, and Jess made a point of stopping at their table. He finished intros to the manager and pitching coach, but before he could introduce Mac, Emmy broke in.

"Mister Davis, you're like a god in my house." She turned to Jess. "He's my dad's favorite player ever."

Jess said, "My dad's too."

"Why, hell!" Mac grinned. "Your fathers are a mighty fine judge of character."

"If it's not too much trouble"—Emmy shrugged—"could I get your autograph for my dad? He'd just die!"

Jess watched Mac's cheeks blossom in a smile. "Emmy's a big fan. She came in from college for last night's game, and she's staying around for tonight's game too."

Gib, the hard-ass of the coaching staff, said, "She's probably hoping to see better pitching than last night."

"That's for sure," Emmy said.

The coaches laughed.

"I'll sign a picture," Mac said, "and get it to Jess before the game. What's your dad's name?"

"Frank Williams."

Jess glanced at Gallagher, who was staring at him with a *What the hell is going on?* expression because he no doubt remembered asking Jess two days ago if the Twitter posts about him and Rah were true. Now here was Emmy hanging on his arm.

Baffle them with bullshit, Jess thought.

Rah and a couple of the other younger Latin players walked past, following the hostess, headed for a table. Rah did not look surprised to see Emmy; he looked hurt, and maybe even jealous, his eyes momentarily latching onto Jess's before skittering away.

Jess and Emmy continued to their table and sat, a few places from Gallagher and the coaches on one side, a few tables from Rah on the other. When the brain trust departed, they smiled and waved at Emmy.

As for Rah, Jess didn't know if he was just following the plan they'd agreed to by ignoring him, or if he was actually pissed. Probably both.

The Mets won Saturday, 7-2, behind Wetherby's six hitter. Rah caught, called his usual excellent game, and doubled in a run. Even better, the Cardinals finally lost. The Nats and D-backs lost too, and just like that, with seven to go, the Mets were one game out of the first and second Wild Cards and tied for the third. Since Rick was starting the series finale, everyone was feeling optimistic about getting onto tomorrow night's Miami flight tied for at least one of the Wild Cards entering the final week of the season.

The mood in the locker room couldn't have been more different than twenty-four hours earlier. Salsa blasted from the Latin corner, hip hop from the African American guys, while the white players clustered around Rick's locker, listened to twang. (Unsurprisingly, there was no gay Jewish locker row pumping out *Hava Nagila*). Big, who'd sported a white gauze pad over his nose in the bullpen, which made him look like Jack Nicholson in *Chinatown*, had approached Jess in the locker room after the game. In earshot of several veterans, he apologized. Jess didn't believe a word, but shook Big's hand, anyway. According to Mac, Gallagher had ripped Big a new one during a private sit-down, telling him if he had any hope of making the post-season roster, he better clean up his shit and pronto.

Whatever. Big was the same asshole he'd always been. Nothing would change that, except now he had a gauze pad on his nose that everyone could see. Jess wondered if Big *was* Flushing Fred. Or if Big had tipped off a friend named Fred? On the advice of the Mets' PR department, Jess had shut down his Twitter and Insta accounts, resolving never to think about Big again.

Jess was more worried about Rah, who was still cutting him dead in the locker room and in the dugout. It's what they'd agreed to—no contact until this blew over—but Jess regretted the decision. He missed Rah, and what if their relationship really was over? He also regretted letting Emmy stay a second night and flying her down to Miami when he pitched on Wednesday. It had seemed like a good idea last night, but now, after getting the cold shoulder and cold eyes all day from Rah, he was worried all the time.

He hadn't even been able to thank Rah for punching Big in the face, and Lord knows, he deserved more than a simple thank you. Returning from the shower wearing just a towel, he peered down the row of lockers where Rah was halfway dressed, naked from the waist up, his muscular chest hairless except for little black whorls around his nipples. Jess knew them well. Rah looked up. Their eyes met briefly, then Rah turned away.

Emmy was outside the players' exit when Jess emerged, his curls wet and slicked back. She crossed to his side, kissed his sore cheek, said, "Whoops," when he winced, and slipped her arm under his. Moving her lips to his ear, she whispered, "How's my pretend boyfriend?"

"Pretending." He kissed the corner of her mouth as one flash after another went off.

They walked to her car, which was parked in the VIP section just outside the players' entrance. Driving back to the Marriott, she chattered happily about how welcoming all the other girls had been, especially Rick Heynen's wife, Sherry.

"She invited me out to lunch after you guys go to the ballpark tomorrow. If you think that's okay."

Jess, who was driving Emmy's car, took his eyes off the road to glance at her. "Why wouldn't it be okay? Sherry's great."

"You know."

Jess looked straight ahead to make sure they were safe, then turned again towards Emmy as the lights from an approaching car washed over her.

"It's weird, Jess, isn't it?"

"That's for sure."

They drove in silence, then almost in unison they said, "How about going out for a cheesesteak?"

And broke up laughing.

CHAPTER TWENTY-SEVEN

Jack didn't like it, not one damn bit. The whole trip back to West Palm he kept thinking he shoulda stayed with Joey, even if Frannie was coming back tomorrow. He'd seen it a million times. When cancer metastasized, you were a goner. If not now, then sooner than later you were a dead man shuffling towards the River Styx. It wasn't right, he kept thinking, drinking Chivas on the plane. It wasn't right, he thought, still drinking when he got home, and not calling Glad like he'd promised.

It wasn't right to outlive your son, when you still had so many things to make right. They were a burr in each other's saddle. He shoulda stayed in New York, even for just one night, but he woulda had to pay to change his flight and pay for a hotel room. But it wasn't right. He shoulda stayed.

Sunday morning, Jack was roused by a pounding on his door, which morphed into a pulsing bladder. The real estate above his neck was pounding too. For a second, he looked around, too *farblondjet* to move. Where was he? He'd sucked down too much hooch, more than he'd drunk in years, musta passed out in the den. Christ on a popsicle, he had to pee, a condumbdrum worsened by the pounding in his head and nether parts.

"Hold your horses," he shouted, and un-reclined the recliner.

Jack barefooted it towards the door, calculating odds he'd have time both to open it and reach the john before his bladder let go. He really wanted to see Glad, that's who it must be, he was supposed to call last night, and anyway, he had a few choice words for her. He ripped the door open, and sure enough: Glad, all dolled up.

"Wow." She peered over her sunglasses. "You stink."

"Hold that thought," he called over his shoulder, really booking because don't look now, it was trickling down his leg. He slammed the guest bathroom door, extricated his poor wet pointer. It wasn't right!

When Jack emerged with only a towel around his middle, he was hoping Glad would be gone, but also hoping she wasn't.

"Why didn't you call last night?" she asked, getting up from the couch. "And why didn't you answer this morning?"

"Don't you be asking questions. I'm the one with questions."

"What happened to your pants, Jack?"

"Why didn't you tell me about Joey? And don't tell me Stu didn't tell you."

She opened her mouth, then her lips sealed. They gazed at each other. "It wasn't my place."

He nodded. Of course, it wasn't.

The Mets won Sunday's game behind Heynen's seven shutout innings. Watching from his seat in the starting pitchers' corner of the dugout, Jess was not only filled with admiration, it was hard not to feel jealous. Rick's stuff was so dominating, his stride so long and effortless, his pitches flew past the batter. And Rick not only overpowered; he out-thought batters. They couldn't have hit his pitches if they knew what was coming, but at least half the time, they looked as if they were swinging swords not bats, just like in *The Benchwarmers*.

It wasn't only Rick's pitching that triggered Jess's jealousy. His wife, Sherry, was not just pretty and kind, she clearly loved him. They had three kids, two boys and a girl, four, six, and seven. Watching Rick stride off the mound at the end of the seventh, with the game in the bag, to the cheers of Mets fans who'd made the trip from New York, Jess thought, *I'll never have that.* Not the cheering fans, which he had plenty of, but the grace and assurance, the sense that everything fit together, no faking or pretending. Rick just *was.*

Afterward, on the team bus to the airport, Jess called Emmy, who was driving back to school. She really knew a lot about baseball, more than any girl he'd ever met. She'd loved eating with Sherry who said Rick thought of him as a kid brother. Wasn't that great? Emmy couldn't wait to see him in Miami. And had he heard? The Cards and Nats lost so the Mets were tied for all three Wild Cards!

She'd make a perfect baseball wife, Jess thought, hanging up. *Just not for me.*

He texted Rah, *How are you?* But Rah's phone must have been turned off because he didn't respond.

Joe received his second blast of radiation Monday morning. Afterwards, he and Frannie walked to Sables, a delicatessen on Second Avenue run by Chinese brothers that served, in Joe's humble opinion, the best lox and lobster salad anywhere. He couldn't remember if Sables had opened during his playing days, or after he retired. What he did know was that the brothers, or maybe only one of them, had worked for Zabar's, and that they had aged tremendously in the twenty or twenty-five years he'd been a customer, their hair changing from black to gray to almost white. They remembered his name though he only came in once or twice a year, singing out, "Hey, Joe!" when he approached the counter. Sables was one of the few New York restaurants he'd given a signed eight by ten; it had hung on the wall behind the appetizing case for as long as Joe could remember. The funny thing was that it was in Sables, a deli run by Chinese brothers, ordering a toasted everything with Irish smoked salmon, veggie cream cheese, capers, red onion, and tomato, that Joe felt most Jewish.

Frannie had arrived last night after spending less than forty-eight hours in Santa Rosa, just long enough to pick up Ruby from the kennel, see how sick she was, and arrange for the vet to put her down.

"It was awful, Joe. Ruby was so sick, yet so glad to see me, her big weird eyes lit up. But the whole time I was there, I kept thinking I should have been here with you."

"No," he'd assured her. "You did the right thing. I was fine."

But now, starting lunch, he didn't feel fine. Looking closely at Frannie, he saw that she looked as exhausted as he felt. He returned their plates to the counter, asked to have Frannie's lobster salad and his bagel and a shmear boxed to go. Kenny, one of the brothers, asked, "Hey, Joe, you okay?"

"Just tired." And because how tired he felt frightened him, Joe added, "I'm having radiation."

Kenny's eyebrows lifted. "You take care, Joe."

Instead of walking, they cabbed to the hotel and passed out for the afternoon.

Tuesday afternoon, Jess jogged and stretched, shagged flies during BP, then threw a short bullpen to Rah under the watchful eyes of Mac, Gib, and Gallagher. This was the first time he'd worked with Rah since the Twitter storm, and Jess didn't know if the coaches believed the whole mess had blown over, or if Fur Furillo, thirty-one and built like a barrel, needed to baby his balky knee. What Jess did know was that throwing to Rah felt plenty weird. Actively pretending that he and Rah hadn't spent the last five and a half months sharing a bed and everything else, was mentally exhausting—in large part because Rah was so completely shut down, no smiles, no banter, as if around Jess, Rah was a different person.

Which he was.

Throwing at 50 percent, just getting the kinks out while getting his mind right for tomorrow's start against the Marlins' young lineup, focusing on getting them to chase by staying just off the plate, Jess kept thinking surely the coaches could see Rah wasn't Rah, which was a giveaway that everything Flushing Fred had tweeted was true.

Whatever the coaches had or had not noticed, it was killing Jess to throw to Rah not-Rah. Over the years, he'd received countless pep talks—from Jack, Dad, and coaches—on the importance of staying mentally strong. Baseball, the speech went, more than any other sport, was a game of failure. The best hitters failed two-thirds of the time. To succeed as a pitcher, you had to amnesia the last pitch, the last batter, the homer you'd just served up, and execute the *next* pitch as if the previous one hadn't happened. But throwing to Rah was different; Jess had to block out so much only to see Rah's mitt and not Rah, that he was hoping he wouldn't have to throw to Rah ever again! Certainly not this season.

At last, the ten-minute bullpen ended. Rah rose from his crouch, removed his mask, and approached Jess on the bullpen mound. The coaches joined them.

"Ball was coming out great, Jess," Rah said, avoiding eye contact.

Gib agreed. "I thought so too. How'd it feel to you, Jess?"

"Hell of a lot better than last time."

The coaches grinned. Rah didn't.

"Easy to beat," said Mac.

Gallagher said, "You won't go more than five tomorrow, in case we need you Saturday, or Sunday, if we still need to get in." Gallagher's off-kilter eyes shifted towards Rah. "You guys are going to find out, in a pennant race anything goes."

Jess glanced furtively at Rah. *Well, almost anything.* "I'm ready."

The coaches nodded, then exited through the bullpen gate back onto the field.

"Rah, did you get my texts last night?"

On Rah's lip, sweat pearls sparkled. "We said no contact. Let's do that."

Jess nodded, and Rah followed the coaches out of the bullpen. After a moment Jess started towards the clubhouse door, wondering how he was going to get through the next twenty-four hours.

CHAPTER TWENTY-EIGHT

Gallagher sent for Jess as soon as he arrived at Marlins Park. The Mets had won last night behind Burbank, remaining tied for the first Wild Card with the Cards, who also won, while pulling a game ahead of the Nats and D-backs, who both lost. Jess assumed Gallagher wanted to talk strategy or remind him he wouldn't throw more than five. This was the first time Gallagher had called him in before a start. Usually, it was Gib who wanted to go over opposing batters, so this felt weird. Then he found the manager's door closed: weirder. Gallagher bragged about his open-door policy. Jess knocked, and from inside the manager's voice called, "That you, Jess?"

"Yes sir."

Gallagher had company: a fit, middle-aged guy, dressed in a sports coat, dark slacks, blue shirt, and striped tie.

"Special Agent Tom Nelson." He handed Jess a card, which confirmed his name and title: *Special Agent, Federal Bureau of Investigation.*

"The Mets," Gallagher said, "have received death threats for you."

Jess's heart: *Rat-a-tat-tat. Rat-a-tat-tat.* "Death threats?"

"They're credible enough we're taking them seriously." Nelson, whose eyes sat somewhere on the road between blue and gray, glanced at Gallagher, then back at Jess. "If Singer pitches tomorrow, he's one dead faggot."

Faggot, Jess thought. *The Twitter storm.* "Any idea who it is?"

"We were hoping you could tell us."

"How should I know?"

"Weren't there tweets about you and your catcher?"

"We were on TV together after my no-hitter."

"I know." Nelson permitted himself a smile. "I saw the game and *The Colbert Show*. Are the tweets true?"

Jess's heart: *Rat-a-tat-tat. Rat-a-tat-tat.*

Gallagher said, "You don't have to answer that."

Nelson said, "It could be relevant."

Suddenly Jess felt furious. Blame the fucking victim. "It's probably some gay-bashing fan of the Nats or Cards who doesn't want me to pitch."

"If you don't want to," Gallagher said, "you don't have to."

All Jess could think was that if he didn't pitch, and word got out about the death threat, everyone would *know* he was queer, and not just queer, but a sissy.

"Not pitch, Skip? Are you kidding?"

Gallagher said, "This is no time to be a hero."

"But it's the last week of the season!" Jess turned towards Nelson. "What makes you think the threat is credible, and not just some drunk?"

"Because there was more than one call. When it's a crank call, there's only one."

Jess thought about all the cop shows he'd watched growing up. "Did you get his phone number or was it a burner?"

Nelson shook his head. "The answering machine doesn't do that."

For a moment everyone was silent, and Jess wondered if somehow Big was behind this too.

Gallagher asked, "Wouldn't it be hard to sneak a gun into the stadium?"

Nelson replied, "There are metal detectors, if that's what you mean."

Jess said, "I don't know anything about guns, but I've seen a lot of television. Even if someone had a gun, wouldn't it be too far to shoot someone on the field?"

Nelson nodded. "Hard, but not impossible."

"Then I'm pitching." Jess faced Gallagher. "Okay?"

Gallagher turned towards Nelson, but because his eyes didn't always follow, Jess couldn't tell exactly where the manager was looking. Agent Nelson said, "They say the season's last week is sudden death, right?"

Gallagher said, "That's a shitty thing to say."

"I'm joking. We'll meet with stadium security to make sure they're on their toes." Nelson turned towards Jess. "Good luck out there."

Jess met the agent's eyes. *What was he saying?* Then Nelson smiled. "I meant with the pitching. The rest? We're doing due diligence."

Jess thought, *This guy doesn't like me. Or he doesn't like gay guys. Or he's in the closet and doesn't want anyone to know.*

Jess turned towards his manager. "I'm going to get ready."

Gallagher nodded. "Two times through the lineup, max, so don't hold back."

Jess shook Special Agent Nelson's hand and headed for his locker.

After his third radiation session Wednesday afternoon, Joe felt wiped as a blackboard. He crawled back to his hotel and decided to take a short nap, which turned into a long and longer nap, ending only when Frannie shook his shoulder.

"Wake up."

He couldn't understand why no light streamed through the wall of windows.

"What time is it?"

"Eight-thirty."

He remembered lying down and a dream about falling out of the sky. Frannie leaned over to kiss him, and blood returned to his brain. She smelled good, and Joe realized that if it was dark outside, it must be 8:30 p.m., not morning. If it was night, the game had started. And then he saw the television playing, with the sound muted.

"Turn it on, please," he said.

Frannie fiddled with the remote, and Gary Cohen's voice came on. After a few moments, Joe put together the score was 4-2 Mets, bottom of the fifth. Jess was still pitching, one out, runners on first and second.

"Why'd you let me sleep so long?"

"You needed it." She sat on the bed beside him and gripped his hand. On the screen, Jess looked out of sync, missing inside then outside, to fall behind Brinson, two and oh. On the screen, Jess stepped off and bounced the rosin bag on the front and back of his hand.

"I really, really missed you, Joe, when I was away."

Her voice, which tailed off as if there was something else she wanted to say, got his attention. "Are you okay?" he asked.

She nodded *Yes*, but her face said *No*. Then there was a roar from the television, and Brinson was home run-trotting, celebrating a three-run dinger. Jess stood behind the mound, back to the plate, rubbing up a new ball. Gallagher emerged from the dugout and waved his right hand to the bullpen. Joe remembered how much he'd hated being lifted after giving up a home run. Jess handed the ball to Gallagher and walked off the mound, beginning the lonely trek to the dugout.

The loss to the Marlins dropped the Mets back into a tie with the Nats for the final Wild Card spot, with four games left in the season. The Cards had won again, moving one game up on the Mets and Nats, two up on the D-backs. Afterwards, icing his arm and riding the stationary bike, Jess couldn't stop thinking about how he'd let the team down. Coughed up the lead like a flounder. Let the bullshit with Agent Nelson mess up his head. The whole time, he'd struggled to focus. This pitch, next pitch, next batter; he couldn't do it. After answering questions in the interview room, then waiting for Gallagher's presser to finish, Jess waited at his locker for a chance to talk to the manager. Emmy would have to wait. He wasn't looking forward to seeing her, not the way he'd pitched. He felt stressed about the whole deception thing and stressed about Rah. He wanted to apologize to everyone. To Rah, to Emmy, the fans, his teammates. He felt like the biggest loser. He also wanted to tell

Gallagher that because he hadn't thrown many pitches, he could come back for a few innings on Saturday or Sunday if the team needed him. Gallagher looked beat when Jess sat down in his office. Jess had showered and changed, but Gallagher still wore his uni.

Jess said, "I'm sorry I fucked up."

Gallagher's misdirected eyes looked past Jess's shoulder. "I shouldn't have let you pitch, not with that threat and everything."

"It was bullshit," Jess said.

"That FBI guy didn't think so."

"I could pitch this weekend. What did I throw, sixty, sixty-five pitches?"

"We'll see." Gallagher hesitated. "After the game started, I heard from MLB's VP for diversity, Davey Dean. He wants to see you Friday morning, when we're back in the City."

If I agree, Jess thought, *wouldn't that be the same as admitting I'm gay?*

"I'm not sure I want to."

"That's your choice, but why?"

What could he say, he didn't want anyone to get the right idea?

"Well, think about it."

Jess nodded, and Gallagher added, "I notice you've been avoiding Rah."

Oh, Jesus. Jess said, "After all those tweets? We didn't..." He looked at Gallagher but couldn't find his eyes. "It's easier."

"As for pitching this weekend?"

Jess nodded again.

"Like I told you, if things are still undecided Sunday? it's all-hands-on-deck."

Jess returned to his locker and texted Emmy to meet him at the hotel. Then he called Rah, who didn't answer.

Jack was watching, of course, when Jess gave up the three-run bomb. He'd had a bad feeling all day, thinking he should have driven to Miami to see the game in person, but he didn't like driving back that far at night, and anyway, Jess hadn't invited him. The kid had a lot on his mind. Too much. For reasons Jack didn't understand, Jess had confided when they spoke that morning that Emmy was flying in for the game. He wanted to ask, what the hell are you doing? Is her last name *Beard*? Instead, he gnawed his own tongue, figured Two-J's had his reasons. But as the game played out to its dispiriting conclusion, Jack couldn't help thinking that if he'd been in the stands, the outcome would have been different. Okay, that was magical thinking, but didn't he and Two-J's have a magical connection? Who had he told first about being gay? He should have been there.

When the game ended, he phoned Glad, who said, no, it wasn't too late to visit.

"Are you sure?"

"You want to come over or not?"

"I wouldn't want you to say yes, if it's no."

"If I didn't want you to see you, wouldn't I say so?"

He was there in five minutes.

"What," Glad asked, "you were already outside when you called?"

He followed Glad to the living room; she ventured to the kitchen to fix him a drink. His eyes found, as they did every visit, the picture of a much younger Glad with her first husband, her son Stu and the girl she never mentioned. Jack approached the bookshelf and lifted the gilded frame. The girl looked thirteen or fourteen, Stu sixteen or seventeen. Same hair, same nose. The girl had Glad's blue eyes.

Glad returned with his drink, saw what he was looking at, set his drink on the coffee table, and fled to the kitchen. A cork popped. When Glad didn't return, he followed her to the kitchen, carrying the picture.

"I been wondering about her since I first seen it months ago."

"Why didn't you ask?"

"I figured when you wanted to tell me, you would."

"Maybe I don't want to."

"Maybe you do."

Glad placed her left hand on her hip like a ballerina, raised the stem to her lips, and threw it back. Then she refilled her glass, corked the bottle, returned it to the fridge, and set out for the living room, where they sat together on the couch, Glad with her wine, Jack with the scotch she'd fixed.

"We named her Jane; don't ask me why. Whoever heard of a Jewish girl named Jane? Maybe it was all those Tarzan movies with Johnny Weissmuller?" She smiled. "The original Mister Goldberg thought the sun rose and set with her. But me and Jane, we were too much alike, strong-willed, pigheaded. We fought a lot.

"When she turned sixteen, she went off the rails. Maybe it was the times. Maybe it was Jane. Boys, drugs; you name it, she was into it. She stopped paying attention in school. She stopped paying attention to anything I said. Sometimes I think she just went crazy. We couldn't control her, and my husband, he couldn't say no to her. So it was up to me, Jack. I grounded her and took away her car keys."

Oy, he thought.

"The night it happened, she snuck out and starting thumbing to a friend's house, which she wouldn't have done if I hadn't taken her keys." Glad looked at him with her big blue eyes. "The boy driving ran a light, and a pickup hit the passenger side where Jane was sitting. Both drivers walked away, but Jane never walked again or said another word. It took her three weeks to die, and only when we pulled the plug."

"Oh my God, I'm so sorry."

"It's been forty-six years, but not a day goes by I don't think about what might have been."

He waited for her to say more. And waited. When she didn't, Jack asked, "Do you want me to go?"

"No, you big dummy." She set down her wine and opened her arms. "I want you to stay."

He hugged her and held on, and damn, if tough-as-nails Glad Goldberg didn't start sobbing. Holding her, he did the math. Forty-six years ago, plus sixteen when Jane died. Sixty-two. If Glad was twenty-one when she gave birth, that would make her eighty-three, Jack's true age his next birthday. Or maybe a few years more.

"Glad," he said, talking into her hair, which was stiff as cotton candy. "When I think about Joey dying before me, on account of that cancer, I don't see how I can stand it."

She nodded, her head on his shoulder.

"But now that I know about Jane, and I think about what it must have been like losing her so young?"

She lifted her head and peered at him, mini rivers of mascara running on her cheeks.

"Where are you going with this, Jack?"

"I'm thinking, what a tough old broad you are. And how well you came through that terrible thing."

"Not really, Jack." She shed a few more tears, then wiped them away.

"Trust me. Way better than I did losing my wife."

"Thanks for the compliment."

"There's more. I'm really glad I know you. We may be old, but we're lucky."

She kissed him. He kissed her back.

"There's one more thing."

"Maybe you should quit while you're ahead."

"No, this is something no one else knows." He peered into her baby blue, heavily made-up, still young-looking eyes. "I'm going to be eighty-three next month, not eighty. I've been lying about my age for a long time."

She laughed. He almost asked, *What about you?* But Jack was no dummy.

Glad said, "Enough talk." And led him off to bed.

CHAPTER TWENTY-NINE

Thursday morning, so early zero light pierced the curtains, Jess lay in bed, worrying. He worried all the time. About his last two outings. About the Mets making the post-season. About Dad. Rah. About the whole charade with Emmy. He wasn't worried about the so-called threats because they were just that, *threats*, from some gay-bashing chicken-shit bastard. But his worrying had been waking him at three and 4:00 a.m., for nights on end. He'd be twenty-three in a few months, and he'd never had trouble sleeping. Until recently, his head touched the pillow, and that was it, lights out till morning. And now? He was turning into Grandpa Jack, getting up to pee every few hours, his mind alert to every sound.

Worrying, Jess heard a knock, or did he? He'd been hearing knocks and whispers for hours, then un-hearing them. He glanced at the far end of the king bed where Emmy slumbered, blonde hair spread like a golden fan. *She* hadn't heard anything. But there it was. Again. *Knock-knocking.* Jess crept from bed, turned on the light near the door, and opened. Rah stepped quickly into the room.

It felt like years since he'd seen Rah in the flesh.

"Jess, why you call last night?"

"I wanted to see you."

"Here I am."

Rah kissed his lips. They hugged and held on. From the bed, still in the dark, Emmy asked, sleepily, "Jess, is that you?"

Rah looked shocked. "Yess, you fucking kidding me?"

Emmy asked, louder this time, "Rah, is that *you?*"

Rah reached for the door. Jess pushed him away and set his back against it. "You don't understand."

"I unnerstan."

Emmy bounded from bed and leaned against the door beside Jess. She wore a green satin nightgown, not especially revealing, but it *was* green satin. Rah looked like his head was going to pop off and even in the dim light, just the overhead near the door, Rah's face was turning the same green as Emmy's nightgown.

"*Pendejo!*" Rah screamed. "You betray me, man!"

"Rah," Emmy said. "This is pretend, for the cameras."

"No cameras here."

"At the games," Emmy said. "I sit with the wives and girlfriends."

"I doan believe you."

"Jess loves you."

Rah looked shocked. "Who says so?"

"I told her."

"You did?"

Jess nodded. For a moment, Rah seemed calmer. Then he looked across the room and saw the king bed.

"If you love *me*, why she sleeping in your bed?"

"If she's pretending to be my girlfriend, where else would she sleep?"

"Yess, this is too fucked up."

Emmy said, "I have an early flight. Give me two minutes, and you guys can be alone."

"No," Rah answered. "I never should have knocked."

Jess tried to take Rah's hand, but he pulled away.

"No, Yess. If someone see me coming out of your room, we really fucked."

He's right, Jess thought.

Emmy said, "It's nice to see you, Rah. Tiff said to say hi."

Rah shook his head, as if to say, *What the hell?* Then he smiled. *Ah, Rah's smile.*

"Say hi for me too."

He left. It was five-forty-five, and Jess was wide awake staring at his pretend girlfriend, but very real friend. Rah was right. This was nuts. And that's when Jess realized he had to call Davey Dean as soon as the commissioner's office opened in New York.

The Mets won Thursday afternoon in Miami and flew home; the Nats and the D-backs also won Thursday, while the Cards lost. Entering the final weekend, the Mets, Nats, and Cards were tied for all three Wild Card spots, with the D-backs one game out. The Cards finished the season against the Cubs, who'd been terrible all year. Everyone around the Mets expected the Cards to win out, or at least take two of three, and punch their ticket to the post-season. No matter. With their final three against Washington, the Mets controlled their own fate. Win two out of three, and at the very worst, they'd be the second Wild Card. If they won all three, and the Cards only won two, the Mets would be the number two seed in the Wild Card round and host a game on Tuesday against the number three seed. The Brewers, champs of the NL Central and the number one seed, would host the number four seed.

It was enough to make your head spin, Joe thought. But here was what really mattered. Because the Mets and Nats were tied and playing each other, they couldn't end the season deadlocked. If one of them swept, that would open the door for the D-backs. Otherwise, assuming the Cards didn't choke big-time, the Wild Card teams would likely be the Mets, Nats, and Cardinals, with the D-backs outside looking in. This weekend's games would not only determine who made the playoffs, but who played who. Having home field advantage mattered. Not playing the Brewers also mattered; they were damn good. As a competitor, Joe thought, you couldn't ask for more. Win two out of three against the Nats and move on. Get swept and go home. In his thirteen big-league seasons, Joe had only reached the post-season once, and here was Jess, with a good chance in his very first season.

Jess had called last night after the team returned to New York. After talking to Frannie, he asked to speak to Joe.

"Dad," he began. "I took your advice."

Joe didn't know which advice Jess was talking about and said so.

"I called Davey Dean. We're meeting at ten tomorrow morning."

"That's good, son."

"I hope you'll come with me."

Just after nine, Joe started walking towards the new MLB offices in 1271 Avenue of the Americas, in what used to be known as the Time & Life Building. Several lifetimes ago, Joe had been interviewed there for a feature in *Sports Illustrated*, long before the gambling scandal Jack dragged him into had darkened his legacy, back when he was simply the best pitcher in New York and the Great Semitic Hope: Jewish Joe. During the scandal—he'd been suspended for refusing to discuss Jack's alleged role—he'd met with the commissioner in his toney East Side headquarters. All the historic black and white photos, the carved desk decorated with bats instead of columns, wood and horsehide every-where, and the former commissioner, high tone himself, a university president. Joe remembered it like yesterday.

A more recent yesterday, in fact, twenty-four hours ago, was equally upsetting. Something seemed wrong with Frannie. It wasn't anything she'd said, more what she hadn't. She didn't want to talk about Ruby or having to put her down. She didn't want to talk about any-thing else she'd done while away. And she didn't want to make love, not the first night she returned late and woke him, and not last night. She seemed distracted and remote, although last night after they'd turned the lights out, she hugged him with all her might, which was really quite a lot of might, then whispered, fiercely, "You know I really, really love you, don't you, Joe?"

"I do."

He waited for her to say something more and when she didn't, wondered if he should have said, *I really, really, love you too.*

But she already knew that.

Joe was walking west on East 62nd, and he'd been so lost in thought he'd lost track of where he was. He looked up and saw he was stopped at a red light at the corner of Park. He was out of breath. He still didn't feel quite himself and wondered if he ever would. There was no northbound traffic, and he crossed against the light to the center median where he waited, stranded, as if on an island, by cars streaming south.

In addition to everything else worrying him, Joe had realized this morning that the Days of Awe started Sunday night. The High Holidays were incredibly late this year. Erev Rosh Hashanah was October 2, the final day of the season. Sometimes Rosh Hashanah came in early September. Joe knew the confusion had to do with Jews still using a lunar calendar; instead of a leap day every four years, there was a leap month, which threw everything out of whack.

Fortunately, the Mets' final regular season game, like games all around the majors, started no later than 3:00 p.m., so Wild Card teams, if they needed to, could travel on Sunday night. For Joe, the afternoon start meant the Mets would finish before Rosh Hashanah started and the Book of Life opened. Eight days later, at the end of Yom Kippur, the Book of Life would close, and everyone—Jess, Frannie, the Mets, and Joe himself, he hoped—would be inscribed for a good year. A healthy year for Joe and his family, a long playoff run for the Mets.

Joe had never worried about being inscribed in the Book of Life. He'd just assumed he had a lot of years left; multiple Books of Life in which his name would be written. Of course, not knowing, he hadn't worried about Jess being gay and outed, or what some lunatic fan might do about it. Now he was. He tried not to worry. In Days of Awe, Joe thought, miraculous, *awesome* things still happened. Repentance, prayer, and charity, he remembered, could avert the evil decree.

Put it in the Book! Joe prayed, modifying Howie Rose's game-ending call on Mets' radio. *Put it in the Book!*

The light changed, and southbound traffic stopped. Joe crossed to the west side of Park, headed towards Madison then Fifth, where he'd turn south along Central Park, headed for the meeting with his old teammate, Davey Dean, and his son, Jess.

Jess sat beside his father outside Davey Dean's office. Their meeting should have started twenty minutes ago. Mr. Dean's assistant was a good-looking African American, a few years older than Jess, with a Bluetooth earpiece in his left ear, above a diamond stud. He had short hair, wore a blue dress shirt and narrow tie. He'd offered tea or coffee. Both Singers had declined, but now Jess was wishing he'd accepted. How cool, he thought, that Mr. Dean's assistant was a good-looking guy, that Mr. Dean was so secure he didn't care about appearances.

"Davey will see you now."

Before they could stand, the office door opened, and Davey Dean, whose image across the ages Jess had researched online—young and uniformed, a dark-haired Adonis; late twenties, when he retired; then mid-forties, when he joined the commissioner's office—came towards them, hand extended, a welcoming smile on his face.

"Sorry to keep you waiting."

Dean was several inches shorter than Jess or Joe. Well-trimmed hair, flecked with gray; dark eyes, softened by laugh lines. For an old guy, Jess thought, Dad's age, he was quite handsome.

"Good to see you, Joe. God, it's been a few years."

Dad nodded, typically tongue-tied. Or maybe he didn't have much to say.

"Glad to meet you too, Jess."

Mr. Dean extended his hand, and Jess squeezed hard, but nothing crazy. He didn't want to come off as limp-wristed, but didn't want to be a macho jerk either.

"Glad to meet *you*, Mister Dean."

Davey Dean smiled. "Call me Davey," he said. "Everyone does."

Father and son followed MLB's vice president of diversity into his office. Comfortable chairs had been arranged in front of his desk. Mr. Dean settled in a black leather chair behind it. Framed eight by tens decorated the wall behind him. Davey Dean with Frank Robinson. With Joe Torre. Tommy Lasorda. Sandy Koufax. With the last three commissioners and quite a few players Jess didn't recognize. And there was one of Davey Dean standing beside Sir Elton John.

Jess said, "Thanks for taking the meeting on such short notice."

"I'd been waiting for you to get in touch since that nasty business on Twitter. I almost reached out, but decided you needed to call me." He glanced towards Joe. "I hope I'm not speaking out of turn, but your dad said you might call."

Jess turned, thinking, *Dad, are you kidding me?*

Joe nodded.

"Me and your dad go way back." He glanced at Joe again. "Back in the day, I had a real crush on him."

Jess's head was whirling. *Dad?*

"Of course, Joe didn't know about it. Although I had boyfriends while playing, I was so deep in the closet around other players, I couldn't see the door. Eventually, my fear of being discovered was just too stressful, and I had to get out."

Dad said, "One of Davey's managers, whenever he saw Davey coming, used to say, 'Davey Dean, Davey Dean, every girl's dream.'"

Jess had read that online—it was old news—but when he glanced at Mr. Dean, behind the gracious smile he saw a world of pain.

"So tell me," Mr. Dean began, "and of course this entire conversation is confidential, why did you call?"

"Flushing Fred was right." Jess could hear his voice tremble. "I *am* gay."

Mr. Dean turned towards Dad. "You have a very brave son."

"I know."

Jess had told himself that no matter what, he wasn't going to get emotional. But after hearing Dad? *No.*

Mr. Dean asked, "What about Rah Ramirez?"

"What about him?"

"Again, this is just between us. Regarding the insinuations about you and Rah."

"I can't speak for Rah."

"Did you tell him you were coming to see me?"

Jess shook his head. For the first time since they'd entered his office, Mr. Dean stopped smiling.

"Why not?"

"We agreed." Jess hesitated. "Until this blows over."

"Trust me, Jess. This is never going to blow over."

In the awful silence, Jess glanced at his father, who was staring at his folded hands.

"What about…" Mr. Dean checked the notepad in front of him. "This young woman you've being photographed with."

"Emmy's a friend. She *knows*."

"Beautiful girl," Joe offered. "Really knows baseball."

"How very 1950s of you," Mr. Dean said, with a bit of snark in his voice. "A beard," Mr. Dean continued. "How quaint."

A *beard*? Jess glanced at his father.

"It's an expression," Joe said. "Before your time."

"What about the threats, Jess? You think it's right to involve her in those?"

"What threats?" Joe asked.

"Just some asshole," Jess muttered.

"So why *did* you come in to see me, Jess? Because it seems like you have an answer for everything."

"Not really." Jess couldn't meet Dad's eyes, and now he couldn't look at Mr. Dean either. "I'm not sure what to do. I just know I can't go on as things are."

"Do you want to come out publicly?"

"I guess I do." Jess couldn't believe he was saying this.

Joe asked, "If he does, what will the commissioner's office do?"

"We'll arrange the press conference, although maybe his team should. And we'll support him publicly."

Joe asked, "Jess can count on that?"

"Absolutely. I know you had issues with the commissioner back in our day, but times have changed, or I wouldn't be here. If you don't believe me, Joe, just remember how they moved the 2021 All-Star Game from Georgia to Colorado."

No one spoke. Jess knew Mr. Dean was waiting for him to say something. Finally, he asked, "What about timing?"

"The sooner the better."

Jess looked at his dad. He was really glad he'd asked him to come along. "What do you think?"

"It's the last weekend of the season, and you're tied for the Wild Card."

"So," Jess asked, "you think I should wait?"

Dad nodded. "You don't want to be the lead story all weekend."

Mr. Dean cleared his throat. "How about a Monday press conference? The day after the regular season, the day before the post-season."

Jess looked into his father's kind eyes, and both Singers nodded at precisely the same moment, despite the flashing Jumbotron only Jess could see. If the Mets reached the post-season, he'd likely be pitching Tuesday.

"Good." Mr. Dean smiled. "Waiting till Monday will give you time to square things with your front office. And now I'm going to give you an old queer's advice. If possible, have Rah at the press conference. This affects him too."

Mr. Dean stood and extended his hand. Jess and Joe stood, and this time Jess squeezed as hard as he could, smiling when Mr. Dean winced.

"Let Malcom know when you've spoken to the Mets brass, and we'll arrange the presser for Monday."

Jess and Joe thanked him then exited, heading for the seventeenth-floor lobby, and the strange sparkling day spread before them. Alone with his father in the elevator descending towards the street, Jess said, "I didn't know you knew Davey Dean."

"You don't know everything." Joe grinned. "Thanks for inviting me along."

"I should be thanking you."

"Thank me after we tell your mother."

Jess wasn't sure what Dad meant, but he was saved from asking when the elevator stopped on the seventh floor and three strangers climbed in.

CHAPTER THIRTY

The Mets won Friday, but lost Saturday afternoon, so as the final day of the regular season dawned, they were tied with the Nats for the first Wild Card. The Cardinals, Joe thought, had choked big time, not only losing Friday and Saturday, but getting pummeled by the last-place Cubs. The D-backs had also choked, losing Friday and Saturday, so they were a game behind the Cardinals for the third Wild Card. Or maybe, Joe conceded, neither team had choked, and losing both games demonstrated how difficult baseball could be. Because the Mets had been bad for so many years, Joe knew what it was like to play September games for the dubious distinction of ruining someone else's dreams. One of the best games he ever pitched was on the final day of the season against the Phillies, a complete game shutout that knocked them out of the playoffs.

Joe sat at the desk in their hotel room sipping coffee, waiting for Frannie to wake up. He'd been out of bed since five-thirty reading sports on his cell, and it came to this. If the Mets won, they'd be the second seed and host a Wild Card series starting Tuesday. If the Cards won, they'd tie the Nats, but because they beat the Nats in head-to-head play this season, they'd take the second Wild Card and play the Mets on Tuesday. If the Cards lost, the Nats would be the second Wild Card, and the Mets and Nats would play again on Tuesday. However, if the Mets lost today, the Nats would be the second seed and host the first Wild Card game. If that's what happened, and the Cards lost, no real problem. The Mets would be the third seed and play the Nats in Washington, where they'd had a winning record for the past three years. However, if the Mets lost and the Cards won, 911; the Cards had won the season series, which gave them the tiebreaker, and the Mets would start against the Brewers in Milwaukee, where they'd been swept in the regular season.

Post-season possibilities hurt Joe's head. It was like imagining a future in which he didn't exist. He swiveled and gazed at his sleeping wife. Something was clearly wrong. In twenty-five years of marriage, there had never been anything wrong with Frannie so, naturally enough, Joe wondered what *he'd* done wrong. Other than getting cancer, he couldn't say. He guessed getting cancer was enough.

Joe returned to bed, slipped under the sheets, pressing against Frannie from behind. He didn't mean anything sexual; he was just being friendly. But then he felt his body stir, and by body, he meant his penis, which was encouraging because after cancer and radiation, who knew? Frannie woke, or maybe she'd been sandbagging the whole time. Suddenly, they were making love, their first go round since she'd returned. And maybe because it had been so long, and he was so damn anxious, he came in a New York minute. The next thing Joe knew, Frannie started to cry.

Omigod, he thought, *was it that bad?*

"I'm sorry, Joe."

She climbed out of bed and returned, face washed, hair brushed, mouth smelling of toothpaste.

"Joe," she began. "There's something I have to tell you."

He looked into her beloved face in the gray light of morning. Across her fluid features, emotions swam like salmon struggling upstream.

Omigod.

"It's something that happened in Santa Rosa." She shook her head. "No, it's something I *did*."

Joe felt like he was driving towards a wall. Frannie's remoteness. Not wanting to make love. Crying. It all made sense. And Joe perceived quickly, in a way that was unusual for him, that unless he acted, Frannie was going to confess something he didn't want to hear.

"Whatever it was." He touched her wrist. "I'm sure you had your reasons."

"No, Joe. No reason."

"My cancer came back. Jess has been outed. You had to put Ruby down."

She cried harder.

"You had reasons, Frannie. Whatever it was, I don't want to know."

"Please, Joe."

"Whatever it was," he repeated. "Won't change how much I love you."

"I don't deserve you, Joe."

"No, Frannie." Of this, he was certain. "I've never deserved you. Without you…" He spoke into her hair. "I'd just be a dumb jock."

"You're so much more than a dumb jock."

"You only say that because you love me."

"I say that"—she gave him a salty kiss—"because it's true."

Ten blocks away, Jess was waking up. He stretched and glanced at Rah's empty pillow. *Damn.* He'd decided to wait until after today's game to tell Rah about the press conference. Rah had been playing more, entering most games as a late inning defensive replacement, and he'd started yesterday, singling and scoring. Jess hadn't wanted to divide his focus from baseball, but he also didn't want Rah to learn about the press conference from anyone else. He didn't expect Rah to appear, but he'd promised Mr. Dean he'd ask, and so he would. Jess told himself he wouldn't blame Rah for staying away. He was less established, and Latin. Besides, even after filling in Gallagher, Mac, and Gib on Friday, Jess couldn't believe he was going to hold a press conference to tell the whole world he was gay, when he'd spent every day until now trying to hide it. But somehow having Dad present when he spoke to Mr. Dean not only made it seem real but the right thing to do.

Jess rolled onto his right side—he never slept on his left side to protect his pitching arm—trying to get back to sleep. A minute later, he flipped onto his belly, slipped his hands under his thighs, and burrowed into the sheets. Gallagher hadn't seemed surprised, while Gib, whose entire universe revolved around arm slots, BAFIPs, velo, and spin rates, was like, *What? You're what?* As for Mac, Jess believed Dad had tipped him off.

"Why now?" Gib demanded. "Why not wait until after the World Series?"

Before Jess could answer, Gallagher said, "I haven't told you guys, the team's been getting death threats for Jess."

Gib started to speak, then stopped. After silence, he said, "You think the threats are going to stop if Jess rubs everyone's noses in it?"

"I'm not trying to rub anyone's nose in anything." Jess glanced between the three older, not necessarily wiser, heads: Gallagher's wrong-way eyes; Mac's weathered cheeks; and Gib, who looked like a red balloon about to pop. "Mr. Dean asked me to hold the press conference Monday, and I said I would."

Jess snuggled into his pillow, trying to lure himself back to sleep. When that failed, he headed for the bathroom, wondering what Rah was doing. Probably, he thought, stepping into the shower, Rah was still in bed, sleeping.

Jack woke Sunday, knowing he'd be flying to New York for Two-J's press conference. He still didn't think the presser was a good idea, but he'd always have his grandson's back. The only question was fly tonight after the game, or crack of dawn tomorrow. There was also Glad. Last-minute tickets cost two arms and a foot, especially Sunday night when New Yorkers flew home to work Monday. Glad had made it clear that if he invited her on a trip, he had to cover her ticket. What with Two-J's in the Show, he'd been flying extra, and while he *knew* he could afford it, decades of squeezing every nickel made Jack loathe to open his billfold. He heaved himself out of bed, did his push-ups and crunches, and decided halfway through to book Sunday night or Monday morning, whichever was cheaper, then tell Glad. Maybe she'd offer to pay her own way.

Jack started a pot in his ancient Mr. Coffee, then checked the fridge calendar held on with a Joe Singer magnet. *Holy shit!* Tonight was Erev Rosh Hashanah. Shaking his head, Jack felt pummeled by a mob of emotions. 1) What a bad Jew he was, not knowing when New Year's started. 2) What was wrong with Joey and Glad, not telling him? 3) Jess was holding a press conference on Rosh Hashanah to announce he was a homosexual. 4) Assuming the Mets made the post-season, and further assuming Jess's announcement didn't change the Mets' plans to start him Tuesday, Jess would throw his first pitch just as Rosh Hashanah was ending, and the Book of Life was open, with every Jew's soul hanging in the balance.

Jack hadn't believed that malarkey in a long time, not since his first wife lost her mind. What was God to him, after that? What Jack believed was: make that first pitch a strike and don't take shit off no one. And maybe, just maybe, he owed Joey an apology, twenty-seven years late.

Mr. Coffee steamed and gurgled, while Jack pondered which was worse. Flying Erev Rosh Hashanah, or the first day? No real Jew would fly either time, so he should just pick the cheaper ticket. Wait, Jack thought, as the pot filled with Chock full o'Nuts, the ticket could be cheaper because no Jews would be flying. And maybe Glad wouldn't want to fly on the holiday, so he wouldn't have to worry about her ticket. Of course, he'd forfeit the considerable pleasure of her company.

Mr. Coffee hissed and beeped. Jack carried a hot cup towards the spare bedroom to book a flight.

Jess watched Rick's warm-ups from the right corner of the dugout where he sat with Burbank and Wetherby, as he often did. Jess was charting pitches since Gallagher had confirmed he'd start the Wild Card game on Tuesday, whether it was in Washington or New York.

Having tomorrow's starting pitcher record today's pitches was sort of an anachronism since the same information would be available after the game on the team's data base. But Jess liked doing it, in part because Dad and generations of pitchers before him had charted pitches. But he also liked charting because it sharpened his attention and kept him in the game, even though he wasn't playing.

He finished his preliminary setup just as the PA announcer boomed, "And now, please rise and give President Hart a warm Citi Field welcome, as he prepares to throw out the first pitch."

The door to the Mets' bullpen opened; three golf carts emerged and started down the first base foul line. When the phalanx of blue and orange carts neared first base, Jess could see that the first and third carts were filled with Secret Service agents: muscular guys in blue suits. The president rode in the middle cart, which stopped in front of the Mets' dugout. Hart climbed out, wearing a blue suit like the Secret Service guys, but instead of a shirt and tie, underneath his suit coat, he sported a Nationals jersey. *What a dick*, thought Jess.

Hart walked towards the mound, flanked by Secret Servicemen, waving towards the crowd with both hands. The crowd rose, applauding. When Hart reached the mound, he removed his suit jacket and handed it to one of the Secret Service agents, exchanging it for a glove. When the crowd saw that Hart wore a replica jersey of Stephen Strasburg, a retired Nats pitcher, boos mixed with cheers.

"What a douche," Jess said to Wetherby, who was seated beside him.

"Got that right," Wetherby replied, as they watched Heynen, who at six foot six towered over the president, shake his hand, then pass him the ball.

The president moved four feet in front of the mound. Furillo squatted. Jess glanced down the dugout and caught Rah's eye. They smiled, then looked away. He wondered what Rah would have felt preparing to catch the ceremonial pitch from the American president, who wound up and lobbed the ball towards home. Furillo caught the pitch on the fly, maybe a foot outside: better than most ceremonial pitches, which tended to bounce. Hart raised his right hand, calling his own pitch a strike, though it was clearly a ball, and the crowd cheered.

Burbank said, "I wish I got to call my own balls and strikes."

"Me too," Jess said.

Furillo trotted out to the mound, shook the president's hand, and handed him the ball. Hart raised it overhead, cheering for himself, then returned to his golf cart, surrounded by Secret Service agents, including the poor schlub carrying his jacket. Jess glanced down the dugout and met Rah's gaze directed his way. *God*, he thought, *I miss him.*

The caravan of carts disappeared inside the Mets' bullpen. On the mound, Rick finished his warm-ups, then peered towards the plate. He fired a first pitch fastball, and the ump's right hand shot up, this time reflecting reality.

Joe and Frannie were seated in the Mets' team box with: several friends of the owner from the world of high finance; their wives, two of whom definitely checked the trophy box; the team president and the director of analytics; and two other retired Mets who'd played for the 1969 championship club. Joe hadn't met the ex-players, who were white-haired and elderly, nor the lords of finance and their young women. He knew Bill Abbott, the team president, very slightly. Abbott, who'd worked for the Mets a decade ago had returned when the new owner bought the team. Most people liked Abbott and the new owner, who was not only a billionaire, but a hometown fan. He'd announced when he took over, that he was going to erect a statue of Tom Seaver and resurrect Old-Timers' Day. The statue now graced the promenade in front of Citi Field, but so far, Old-Timers' Day was a mirage. Joe had never participated in an Old-Timers' Day, and now he wasn't sure he'd get the chance. The first decade after he retired, the Mets invited him, but he said no; for years, he nixed everything that would take him out in public. Then the Mets stopped sponsoring the event. Apparently, it lost money.

Joe looked down at the field, where the game remained scoreless, bottom of the third. The owner's friends and their wives had been hitting the complimentary food and drink at the back of the suite. But they'd also been fan-chatting Joe and the other retired Mets, one of whom, the right fielder on the '69 team, seemed to be having trouble following what was happening on the field. Poor guy, Joe thought. Younger than Jack, but losing his marbles.

"Joe." Frannie kissed his cheek. "You want anything?"

He moved his lips near her ear. "Just you."

She smiled.

"Come back soon," he added. "You don't want to miss anything."

He watched her walk towards the bar, trying not to wonder what she'd tried to confess to him that morning. It didn't matter. Except for Jess, she was the best thing that ever happened to him, and anyway, although he would never say anything to her, he was beginning to fear he wouldn't be around that long. So what did it matter? He knew she loved him. Everything else was gravy.

Halfway to the bar, while Joe was still watching, Bill Abbott, the Mets' team president, took her elbow. He said something to her Joe couldn't hear. When she answered him, Joe returned his attention to the field. A minute or two later, just after Heynen retired the Nats in order, Abbott and Frannie were at his side. Joe stood up. Abbott was nearly as tall as Frannie, lean and gray-haired with an unlined face.

"Joe," Abbott said. "Can I talk to you for a moment?" He lowered his voice. "*In private?*"

Joe glanced at Frannie, whose face gave away nothing. "Sure."

He followed Frannie, who followed Abbott. In a quiet spot, near the end of the buffet table, Abbott said, "As an organization, we're very proud of Jess."

"As his father," Joe replied, "so am I."

"Will you be at the press conference?"

Oh, Joe thought. *That's what he meant.* He glanced at Frannie, who was smiling, then back at Abbott. "Do you think we should be?"

"That's up to you and Jess. He's very brave. And one hell of a pitcher, Joe. Just like you."

"Thanks." He wondered where this was going.

"There's one more thing," Abbott said. "We haven't announced it yet, and you're the first ex-player I'm telling. There's definitely going to be an Old-Timers' Day next year, late July or August. And with Jess on the team, we won't take no for an answer."

"You won't have to." Joe reached out and shook Abbott's hand. "You can count on me."

Abbott grinned. "That was easier than I thought."

"It's the new me," Joe said, thinking, *Make hay while the sun shines.*

"And now, if you'll excuse me, I'm going to watch the game."

Abbott started back to his seat. When he was out of earshot, Joe asked, "Who said you can't teach this old dog new tricks?"

She met his eyes and smiled, as if reading his thoughts. She always could. Joe kissed her, then said, "I'm going to watch the game too."

He headed for his seat. Frannie headed back to the bar.

Heynen and Kline, the Nats' starter, kept putting up zeros. Jess kept charting, looking for tendencies in the Nats' batters. First pitch swinging. Did they chase? Only problem was, he and Rick were so different. Rick threw one hundred right-handed, relying on a wipeout slider for swings and misses. He threw lefty, topped out at ninety-five, his curve was his out pitch. Of course, Rick was married to a woman and had three kids, while Jess was in love with his catcher. But he was trying not to think about *that* right now, although at eleven tomorrow morning, he'd be at MLB headquarters in front of television cameras. He'd decided not to mention Rah or answer questions about him. He wasn't sure how that would work, if a series of *No comments* would equal announcing *I'm in love with Rah Ramirez.* He'd try to talk to Rah after the game, but for now he'd chart.

In the top of the seventh, the Nats scratched out a run on two singles, a sac fly and a passed ball. In the pitchers' corner of the dugout, there was bitching about Furillo's knees, how if he moved the way he used to, he would have blocked the slider that skipped under his glove and let in the run.

Wetherby, who said what he thought and didn't care who heard, said loudly, "Damn, your boy Rah ought to be catching close games."

Burbank, blond ponytail threaded through his ballcap just like Emmy, answered, "They're all close this time of year."

Wetherby added, "For damn sure, Rah better be catching you Tuesday."

Jess glanced down the bench towards where Rah had been sitting, but he must have been sent to the bullpen to warm up potential relief pitchers. On the field, Heynen snapped off a backdoor slider, K-ing the Nats' left-handed pinch hitter, limiting the damage to one run. The Mets started towards the dugout. Suddenly, the sellout crowd booed, or groaned, some collective expression of distress. Jess looked up at the scoreboard; the Cards had scored four runs and gone up on the Cubs, four to two, in the eighth. *Holy shit. We might be headed to Milwaukee.*

In Delray Beach, Jack was losing what little mind he had left. He'd been packing between innings. Halfway through the seventh, he was up or down to, depending on which end you looked from, underwear and socks. Heynen had been charged with an unearned run, and unless the score changed in Chicago or Flushing, the Mets would be starting the post-season in Milwaukee, and he had a ticket to New York!

Jack decided not to think and focused on packing. Three pairs of socks and three boxers. If he was breaking every goddamn rule by flying on Rosh Hashanah, he sure as hell needed clean boxers. Watching, packing, worrying, Jack felt so *verklempt* he didn't know which end was up. Glad had declined to accompany him. "No way," she'd announced. "I'm not flying on the holiday. What kind of Jew are you?"

"A better grandfather than a Jew."

"That's for sure."

Jack regretted she wasn't coming. And what she'd said about being a bad Jew stung more than he let on. It was one thing for him to think it, something else for Glad to say it. What, she thought he didn't have feelings?

On his big screen, the Mets were attempting to rally: no outs, a runner on first. In the old days, that is, before the pinheads took over and half-ruined the game, the Mets would have been bunting to move the tying run to second base with only one out. These days? Who the hell knew?

Jack watched with growing anger when the Mets' seven hitter swung away and struck out. Gallagher couldn't manage his way out of a sack with both hands! Then Furillo, whose bum knee and fat ass had led to the unearned run, banged into a 6-4-3 double play—and just like that, the Mets were six outs from cooked.

Vey iz mir, thought Jack. But to demonstrate to any higher power watching that he was a true believer, if not in Yahweh, then in the Jewish God of Pitching, Jack tossed another pair of socks into his suitcase.

Gallagher sent Heynen out to start the eighth, and he walked the leadoff batter on four pitches. He looked gassed. The pitching coach came out to the mound to discuss the weather and stall. When he returned to the dugout, Gallagher emerged and headed for home plate, indicating he planned a double switch. Gallagher continued on from the home plate umpire to the mound and took the ball from Heynen, who started, head down, towards the dugout.

No need to hang your head, Jack thought, *you pitched great.*

Furillo also headed for the dugout, and Jack saw that there was a catcher walking in from the bullpen with the relief pitcher, Big Barnes. Even before Gary Cohen, the TV voice of the Mets, announced the name of the new catcher, Jack could see it was Rah Ramirez.

What was wrong with Gallagher? Didn't he know Rah broke Big's nose and they hated each other? Who knew what Gallagher knew, the dumbass. Jack settled in to watch, fearing the worst. But Big induced a pop-up, then a strikeout, and got ahead, one ball, two strikes on

Abrams, the Nats' shortstop. Jack watched Big shake off one sign after another from Rah. Finally, he nodded, and instead of wasting a fastball high and wide, or a slider, low and out of the zone, Big fired a fastball, middle-middle. *Putz!* Abrams deposited the ball 410 feet away over the center field fence and slow trotted the bases, while the Mets fans in the stands made not a single fricking sound. In Delray Beach, Jack tossed another pair of boxers in his suitcase, thinking, *Oh shit, Nats up three-zip, this is bad.*

In the luxury box, the mood was grimmer than grim. The owner's friends announced they had to leave and cleared out with their wives. *Good riddance,* thought Joe. He considered a drink, but he hadn't touched alcohol since the cancer returned. Maybe it made no difference, maybe it did. Anyway, Frannie was drinking for both of them. He'd been watching her knock back scotch for several innings. Maybe, he thought, as she returned from the bar with a fresh one, he should have let her confess since whatever it was seemed to be eating her up. Or maybe it was the Old-Timers' Day conversation with Abbott.

She sat down wearing a pixilated grin, while down on the field, Rah approached the plate, batting helmet on his head, lumber in his hand.

"Looks bad, doesn't it?"

Joe nodded.

"Maybe it's better," she added, "if Jess doesn't pitch in New York the day after the press conference."

Joe shook his head. "I'm sure he was counting on pitching great Tuesday to take everyone's mind off tomorrow."

Rah dug in. The Nats' reliever tried to sneak a first pitch fastball across the plate, which Rah roped into left center. The ball found grass, rolled to the track, and Rah, who ran well for a catcher, cruised into second. Frannie squeezed his hand, which Joe understood to mean she was focusing on the game.

After giving up the two-run bomb in the top of the eighth, Big had come off the mound looking so pissed off and upset, Jess almost felt sorry for him. They hadn't said a word to each other in days, but with Big seated ten feet away looking like the top of his head was on fire, it was hard to ignore him. Instead of going over to talk to Big himself, Jess suggested to Wetherby and Burbank, that *they* say something to Big.

Wetherby hissed, "No way I'm telling that cracker it's all right to give up that dinger." He widened his eyes. "Piece of shit."

Instead, Burbank approached Big, said a few words, and patted him on the back. Jess hoped Big felt better, even though in almost every way he was a total shithead. But he was a teammate, and if there was one thing Jess had been taught his whole life to love and value, it was being on a team. Teammates had each other's backs. He hoped his teammates still felt that way about him after the press conference. He watched Big nod and grin up at Burbank, then Burbank returned and sat again beside Jess. Together with his fellow starting pitchers, whom Jess now thought of as friends—they'd adopted him as sort of a kid brother—Jess watched Rah's leadoff double in the bottom of the eighth with such pride and love, that he was afraid he'd give away his special relationship with Rah, except that the entire bench of Mets players was screaming and shouting, slapping high fives, and letting themselves hope that maybe, just maybe, they could come back from three runs down.

The rally fizzled. After Rah advanced to third on an infield single and scored on a ground out with the Nats' infield playing back, Pete and Squirrel struck out, stranding Nimms on second. When the Mets went back to the field for the top of the ninth, they still trailed 3-1, and Gallagher summoned Domingo Fuentes, the Mets' closer, to try to keep the game close.

Fuentes did his job, retiring the Nats in order, and the Mets jogged off the field; they needed two runs to tie and three to win or they'd be flying to Milwaukee. The Nats brought in their closer, Gillespie, to secure the win, and he walked Sanchez, the first batter, on a 3-2 slider that could have been called a strike but wasn't. Sanchez sprinted to first base, bringing the tying run to the plate.

"Rally caps!" Wetherby shouted the length of the dugout. To make sure it happened, Jess and Wetherby walked up and down the bench, repeating "Rally caps, rally caps."

Passing him on their way back to the right corner of the dugout, Jess locked eyes with Big, who said nothing; didn't smile, but he nodded, and reversed his cap, inside out and backwards, like most of the players, and even one or two of the coaches. The caps seemed to work. Harkness, batting sixth, singled hard to right, and suddenly the Mets had runners on first and third, nobody out, and the entire Mets squad was up and standing on the top step of the dugout.

The Nats' pitching coach emerged from the visitors' dugout to confab with Gillespie, which seemed both to wake him up and calm him down. Gillespie overpowered the Mets' number seven batter, Sean Parker, on three fast balls: ninety-eight, ninety-nine, and one hundred miles an hour. That brought up Vic Villette. As Villette dug into the box, Jess looked at Rah, who was kneeling in the on-deck circle. Unless Villette came through, Rah would bat with two outs and home field advantage on the line. Jess tried to imagine how nervous Rah must be, in what was certainly the biggest moment of his baseball life, kneeling in the on-deck circle. Jess leaned further over the dugout railing and pounded the fence.

"Rah!" he shouted. "Rah!"

Rah either didn't hear him or refused to turn.

Gillespie fired towards home. Villette swung and missed.

Jess shouted again, "Rah, Rah!"

Rah turned towards him. Jess pumped his fist and mouthed, without sound, "*Te amo, Rah. Te amo!*"

Rah smiled his incandescent smile just as Gillespie fired a four-seamer, up in the zone, that Villette popped a mile high in the infield. The first base ump signaled an infield fly, and Villette was meat even before the ball settled in the second baseman's mitt. Villette stopped running halfway to first, fired his helmet into the dirt, and started towards the dugout, ass dragging. Rah embarked on the million-step trek to the batter's box, with every eye in Citi Field watching.

Rah dug in, right foot obliterating the back chalk line of the batter's box. He took two short, precise practice swings and settled into his stance. Gillespie nodded at his catcher, rocked into his motion, and broke off a sick slider that started on the plate, but dove off it. Rah swung and missed by six inches. Around Jess on the top dugout step, his teammates groaned and slapped the top rail.

"You can do it, Rah! You can do it!" Wetherby shouted.

On the field, Gillespie nodded at his next sign, wound up and hurled a hundred-mile-per hour heater that Rah fouled straight back. Jess tried not to lose hope, but with Rah down oh and two, the game was on life support. Gillespie glowered towards home. He was a nasty-looking, unshaven fucker, and in that moment, Jess hated him. Gillespie rocked into his motion and fired another supercharged heater, but it rode high, and Rah laid off. Ball one.

He's setting you up for the slider, Rah, Jess thought. *You know it!*

And Rah did, because this time, when the slider broke off the plate, Rah didn't chase, and though the pitch was clearly outside, just for a micro-second, with the crowd screaming so loudly he could barely hear his own thoughts, the ump seemed to hesitate, and Jess feared, *Oh no, he's going to ring him up!!*

Instead, the ump signaled ball two. On the mound, Gillespie shouted, although Jess couldn't hear what he said. When the Nats' catcher pegged the ball back to him, Gillespie snapped his glove angrily. *He wanted that call,* Jess thought, *of course he did. And now he's pissed off and coming with heat because he doesn't want to go three and two.*

You know that, Rah. You know it!

Jess glanced at Wetherby on his left, and Burbank on his right, their caps inverted and reversed. On the field, Gillespie peered towards the plate, nodded, and rocked into this motion. The pitch sizzled homeward, the platonic ideal of a four-seamer rather than an actual ball moving through space. But Rah saw it, *he saw it,* and the crack of bat on ball, maple compressing rawhide, was the most beautiful sound Jess had ever heard.

The struck ball arced from home plate towards dead center, still rising as it left the infield, rising still as it took aim on the New York Home Run Apple. Rah flipped his bat triumphantly and raised both fists overhead. Every player and coach in the dugout began to scream because he'd done it, he'd done it, he'd done it. His blast flew past the Home Run Apple, landing halfway up the black batter's eye behind it. Mets win, Mets win. 4-3.

Rah took off sprinting towards first. The Mets players and coaches poured out of the dugout. Sanchez scored first, followed by Harkness, joining the mob waiting for Rah to cross the plate so the wild rumpus could begin. Rah rounded third, and Jess, who headed the scrum of players waiting to mob him, could see Rah's smile lighting the way. Their eyes met, and Rah nodded a private recognition. Of what? Who knew? Pure joy. Then Rah leapt up and landed both feet first on home, entering the joyous, bouncing throng. Suddenly, Jess was crying. When he looked around, he saw that he wasn't the only one.

PART FOUR

WILD CARD

CHAPTER THIRTY-ONE

That night, just past ten—as they'd agreed in the clubhouse—Rah knocked, and Jess let him in. Rah wore a t-shirt and jeans, carried his orange-and-blue duffle. He looked exhausted and happy, much like Jess felt. There'd been a great deal of sprayed champagne in the clubhouse. Quite a bit had found its way into the players' mouths too, although everyone agreed they shouldn't get trashed with the Wild Card series starting in less than forty-eight hours. Still, boys will be boys, Jess thought. Even men will be boys. He bet he wasn't the only Met with an aching head, as he stepped back to admit Rah, then double-locked the door behind him.

"Anyone see you?"

"You know what?" Rah tossed his duffle onto the bed. "I doan care."

"Since when?"

"I think, I hit that home run? I doan have to be afraid all the time. They're not gonna send me down." Rah grinned. "They can kiss my ass."

"Who can?"

Rah was still grinning. "Anyone who wants to."

Jess gazed with love at his catcher. "You trying to make me jealous?"

Rah nodded.

"Are you drunk?"

Rah nodded again. "It feels good not to be afraid. Like a thousand pounds off my head." He stepped towards Jess. "Fuck 'em."

"Fuck 'em." And then, taking Rah in his arms, he whispered, "I've missed you so much."

Hours later, with Rah sleeping beside him, Jess flipped his pillow, hunting a cool spot, worrying, as he'd been doing most of the night. Was he making a huge mistake, hanging a curve in the middle of the plate, where anyone could hit it? What would the other players think? Would Rick still be his friend? And Wetherby and Burbank, the other pitchers and catchers, Furillo, all the Latin guys, the coaches, all of whom probably suspected because of the Twitter storm, but didn't know for sure? And what about the evangelicals who prayed together in the locker room after every game? And these were his teammates, who had reasons to like him. Well, not Big, the motherfucker, who would turn out to be Big I-told-you-so, with his broken nose, jealousies, and homophobia. Fuck Big.

What about the Nats? And the players on all the other teams? The fans at Citi Field? What if he pitched like crap and the Mets lost the opening game of the series because he was gay, and everyone hated him? At 4:00 a.m., he almost got up and phoned Mr. Dean, who'd said he could call any time, day or night, to ask him to cancel the press conference. He couldn't get up in front of everyone like that. *He couldn't.* But did he really want to make a scene and mess everything up, with Rah beside him for the first time in what seemed like forever?

Joe woke early and stared at Frannie, who lay beside him sound asleep, softly snoring. The clock on his end table read 6:14 in vampire-red numbers. It was Rosh Hashanah morning, and Joe's soul, like that of other Jews on this first Day of Awe, hung in fearful balance. He remembered Rosh Hashanah the year he was suspended, twenty-five or was it twenty-six years ago? He was already in love with Frannie but hadn't kissed her yet. He had attended services at that strange little synagogue on the boardwalk in Venice, CA. Afterwards, for the first time in his life, he'd taken literally the Old Testament invocation that for sins against God, prayers, repentance, and charity would avert the evil decree, but for sins committed against other people, you had to ask their forgiveness directly. He'd asked forgiveness from the husband of a woman he'd had an affair with, and although he hadn't kissed Frannie yet or told her he loved her, he'd asked forgiveness of Frannie's boyfriend, Des, because he'd been lusting after her.

He'd wanted so badly, then, to get his life in order, and he craved the same thing now. With his cancer returning, who knew what the future held, or if he even had a future? The rest of his life were all Days of Awe. Joe knelt beside the bed and prayed for Frannie and Jess, even for Jack: may they all be inscribed in the Book of Life. A sweet year, a healthy year. May Jess do well at his press conference. May everyone accept him, except for the jerks and assholes who never would. May he throw lights out tomorrow night, and may he be kept safe from harm. May he win the Cy Young someday, though I never did. As for me, God, grant me time enough to enjoy the many gifts you've given me, however long that may be. But I'd sure like to see Jess take home the Cy Young.

Then he climbed back into bed to wait for Frannie to wake so he could ask her forgiveness.

After she returned from the bathroom in a monogrammed terrycloth robe, wet cheeks glowing, mind likely not yet clear despite the coffee Joe had fetched from the lobby—she'd had an awful lot of Chivas yesterday—Frannie said, "Are you crazy? What do you have to ask my forgiveness for?"

"It's the Days of Awe."

"I know that."

"If I hadn't stuck my head in the sand last winter, the cancer might not have gotten so bad."

"*That's* why you're asking my forgiveness?"

He nodded.

"That's all you've got?"

"Well, I did have horny thoughts about that golf pro before she told me she was a lesbian."

"I forgive you, Joe, I do. Now it's my turn."

Uh-oh. "But you're not even Jewish."

"I'm a Jew-lover." She smiled. "Wait here."

She returned to the bathroom, and when she emerged, still looking a little crispy about the edges, as if maybe her head hurt, she carried a black velvet drawstring bag: too small for shoes, too large for jewelry.

"Open it."

"Is it a present?"

"Not exactly."

Joe un-snugged the drawstring and extracted an eight-inch pink, slightly soft to the touch, bendable piece of plastic. The *object* was as big around as the base of his electric toothbrush, and there was an on-off switch near the bottom with different speeds and settings. Its shape and the embarrassed smile on Frannie's face left little doubt of its function.

"What's this?" Joe asked.

"An Unbound Bender. It's a kind of vibrator."

"I can see that." He felt himself getting upset. "Why are you giving me a vibrator?"

"I bought it last spring when you wouldn't have surgery. I was so mad, Joe. I wanted to show you, and myself, I could replace you and your penis, no problem. Thirty-nine, ninety-five."

He would have guessed it cost more. "Does it work?"

"Not as well as you. I want you to forgive me for being so angry. And so afraid. It's not your fault you got cancer."

"But if I'd gone to the doctor sooner..."

"It might have made a difference, maybe not."

She took the vibrator from his hand and touched the power button. The Unbound Bender hummed. Frannie pressed its tip into his palm, and his whole hand vibrated. *Creepy.* Frannie replaced the Bender in its drawstring sack.

"So, Joe, do you forgive me?"

This is too weird, he thought. "I do."

Jack boarded the elevator and pressed fourteen, which was Joe and Frannie's floor. He'd gotten in late, no problem with the flight or thunderbolts from an angry Yahweh for flying on His holiday, but Jack didn't reach the hotel until 1:00 a.m., so too late to call. He'd tried Two-J's cell this morning, no answer. He'd tried Joe and Frannie's room a bunch of times through the hotel operator, but it kept ringing busy, and they weren't answering their cells either. Worried and a little agitated—he'd come all this way, risked a lightning bolt, and no one was talking to him?—he descended to the lobby and sweet-talked reception into divulging Joey's room number, which he knew was against policy. He didn't know where MLB headquarters was located, and though he could have found out, he didn't fancy showing up by himself because they might not let him in.

The elevator doors opened, and Jack started towards 1408. He was wearing his one good winter-weight suit. It was October, frost on the pumpkin. He rapped three times, hard, on 1408. No footsteps, no voices. *What the hell?* He raised his fist to rap again, and right then the door opened.

"We'll be right out," Joey said, and closed the door.

Ten minutes later, Jack was getting ready to knock again, or give up and catch a cab by himself, when the door opened, and Joe and Frannie came out looking like their best friend had died.

"Good Yom Tov," Jack said. "Happy New Year."

"Good Yom Tov," Frannie answered, but Joey pushed past him, headed for the elevator.

"What's wrong?" Jack asked.

Joey was moving too fast to answer, while Frannie, from her great and beautiful height, just shook her head. "Not now, Jack."

Then she took off after Joey, and all Jack could do was hustle after them.

At ten-fifteen, which was fifteen minutes and a year or two later than it should have been, Jess sat down at the small table at the head of the boardroom of MLB headquarters. The spacious room was jam-packed with reporters and camera crews. Jess was flanked by Davey Dean, MLB's vice president of diversity, on his right and Bill Abbott, the Mets president of baseball operations, on his left. He'd never met Abbott, though he knew Abbott was a friend of Dad's. A small forest of mic stands was arrayed in front of him. Somewhere in the back of the room, Rah sat with Jack and his parents. Emmy had texted from class to say she could come in for tomorrow's game if he wanted her there and if he could get her a ticket (smiley face). She sent her love.

Jess wore his Mets number 32 jersey, the traditional white version with pinstripes, blue and orange stitching, and a blue Mets cap with orange letters. He wasn't wearing his full uniform, that would be ridiculous. He'd selected the blue cap because the blue matched his eyes, and he wanted to look his best because he felt so incredibly nervous. He couldn't keep his left foot from tapping under the table, same with both hands, which seemed to have minds of their own and wanted to tremble and dance unless he folded them together in front of him. So that's how he was meeting the press: like a dutiful schoolboy in the first row, baseball cap and melded fingers.

Mr. Dean leaned closer. Hiding his lips behind his hand like a catcher visiting the mound, he whispered, "Ready, Jess?"

Jess nodded. Mr. Dean nodded. The television lights came on.

"On behalf of Major League Baseball, I'd like to introduce Jess Singer, one of our game's brightest young stars. As most of you know, Jess is starting tomorrow night for the Mets against the Washington Nationals. Bill Abbott, the Mets president of baseball operations, is seated on the other side of Jess. He'll speak afterwards. Joe's father, former major league pitcher, Joe Singer, is seated in the back of the room with Jess's mother and grandfather. Jess will read a short statement, then answer a few questions. His statement is not explicitly about baseball. But at this time of year, when you're as talented a pitcher as Jess, it's always about baseball."

Mr. Dean faced him and smiled.

"Thank you, Mister Dean." Jess tried to keep his hands and voice from trembling. He couldn't do anything about his tapping foot. "Thank you, everyone, for coming out today." He looked down at his printed statement, realizing what he'd just said had made his statement irrelevant. He looked up at the cameras. "Actually, I'm the one coming out today."

There were whispers around the room, maybe even laughter.

"As some of you know, there have been rumors on social media about my sexuality for the past few weeks, ever since I threw a no-hitter and appeared on *The Colbert Show* with my good friend and catcher, Rah Ramirez. I chose to ignore those rumors and concentrate on the pennant race, thinking that in America, where gay marriage is the law of the land, what did it matter? And whose business was it, anyway, except mine? In the heat of the pennant race, I thought only my on-field performance should matter, and I didn't want the focus to be on me, instead of my team.

"I was wrong. Some people don't think athletes should be homosexuals, or maybe they don't think homosexuals should be athletes. There have been death threats, with the FBI providing protection. I've come to understand that by refusing to address the issue of my sexuality, I've encouraged the haters and given the impression that I'm ashamed of who I am. That's not true.

"Worrying about the 'rumors' has divided my attention from what is most important to me, not only today and yesterday, but especially tomorrow, when I'll open the Wild Card series against the Nats. I've had two of my worst pitching performances since the no-hitter because I've been more worried about the rumors than the opposing hitters, and I'm tired of it. So I've decided to say this where everyone can hear it. I'm proud and I'm gay, and I pitch for the New York Mets. That's who I am. If anyone doesn't like that"—he looked up, he hoped, straight into the cameras—"that's too damn bad."

Jess stopped. There were other things on his written statement, but he'd said enough. He wished he hadn't said, "Damn," but he supposed it was all right because Mr. Dean was smiling at him.

"Thank you, Jess," Mr. Dean said. "I wish I'd had the courage to say the same thing thirty years ago." Mr. Dean turned towards Bill Abbott, who still looked like the Marine he'd once been, Jess thought, though he was white-haired and old, even older than Dad.

Abbott cleared his throat. "On behalf of the New York Mets, I'd like to express our organization's admiration and gratitude for Jess Singer's maturity and courage, both on and off the field. It's rare for a young player to be both as talented and articulate as Jess, and he has the Mets' full support."

After a short silence, Mr. Dean said, "Jess will take a few questions now."

Reporters raised and waved their hands to be first.

Jack was wedged between Joey and Rah. Frannie sat on Joey's far side.

Rah, Jack thought, must be a nervous wreck. Now that Two-J's had dropped the bomb, reporters were buzzing like a hundred million bees, and Rah needed to get the hell out of here. Just yesterday, he'd saved the Mets' season, and that should have been all she wrote, but sooner or later, and likely sooner, some douchebag was going to quiz Two-J's about his *personal catcher*, and unless Two-J's knew enough to say, *No comment*, and even if he did, from the ardent look on Rah's face, Jack feared the kid was going to jump up and say, *Yes, Jess, it's true.*

Jack rapped Rah's knee, leaned close, whisper-shouted, "Get out while the getting's good."

Rah shook his head. "No, Grandpa Jack."

Some reporter up front, whom Jack couldn't see but could certainly hear, a nasty talk-radio prick from WFAN, whose voice Jack recognized, said, "Those social media rumors you mentioned were started by someone who called himself Flushing Fred."

"That's right," Jess answered.

"Flushing Fred alluded to a relationship between you and your catcher, Rah Ramirez."

"Also right," Two-J's said.

No, no! Jack could barely see his grandson—there were too many reporters between them—or even hear him clearly. And there was a roar building in the packed room.

The nasty prick asked, "Do you have any comment on that rumor?"

"No comment," Two-J's answered, with a smile in his voice.

Two-J's, Jack thought. *What are you doing?*

Rah stood, and just for a second, Jack considered throwing his eighty-two-year-old shoulder into Rah's tree-trunk thighs, then he thought, *What the hell? They planned this!*

"I do," Rah said. "I have a comment."

Jack peered past Rah at Frannie and Joey, who looked as dumbfounded as he felt.

Rah said, "It's true. All true."

Two-J's stood up at the table in the front of the room and shouted over the reporters' heads, "*Te amo,* Rah!"

"I love you, Jess!" Rah shouted back.

After that, Jack thought he must be having a heart attack, or some sort of psychic conniption. Or maybe he'd entered an aural hallucination because it soon sounded as if half the room and then everyone in it was clapping. But that couldn't be, Jack thought. Until it was.

CHAPTER THIRTY-TWO

By the time Jess and Rah reached Citi Field, everyone knew. At least Jess assumed they did. The story had been blowing up on Twitter and Instagram, and most players were all over social media. On the ride out, they'd discussed how to handle their teammates. Their friends. Their enemies. Fucking Big Barnes. They entered the clubhouse separately, changed, went out on the field, and stretched. No one said a word. Jess ran sprints with the other pitchers, and Rah joined batting practice, which was already going on. Watching him disappear in the dugout to get a bat and a helmet, Jess wondered how the other Latin players would treat him, and if Rah would tell him if they were terrible to him. Rah was so brave, he thought. It had been his idea to come to the presser and make it their coming out party.

"I'm tired of being afraid, Jess," he'd said, last night in bed. "And maybe because I hit that home run and save the day"—he grinned— "they won't give me so much shit."

Jess started towards the bullpen to do a little light throwing, as he did the day before every start. Halfway to the pen, so lost in thought he could have been on the dark side of Jupiter, he didn't hear or see Rick Heynen come up beside him, until he was already there.

"Hey, stud muffin." Rick grinned. "You guys got a special handshake?"

"Nope."

"And all this time, I thought you and Rah were just discussing balls and strikes."

"We were."

"What about that pretty Emmy who's been hanging around? Sherry sure likes her."

"So do I." He looked up into Rick's frank brown eyes—Rick who was the only pitcher on the squad taller than he was. "Just not that way."

They were almost to the bullpen gate. Gib was inside waiting and so was Mac. Rick said, "You know Davey Dean is coming to make a presentation to the team tomorrow afternoon. They're calling it *sensitivity training*."

"Oh shit. I won't be there."

"I believe you will." Rick grinned. "A lot of the guys will be a whole lot more *sensitive* if you pitch lights out tomorrow."

"What about you?"

"I'm there for you, no matter what."

"Thanks, Rick."

"Just put up zeros, little brother. And get your mind right."

Jess nodded. He'd never had a big brother but had always wanted one. "I'll try."

Heynen jogged back towards the infield.

That afternoon, at four o'clock, Jack was returning to the hotel from the Bagel Barn on First and 62nd. He'd had a three-hour nap, then ventured out for sustenance. He felt all stirred up, as if his guts were in a blender. Maybe he shouldn't have traveled on New Year's after all. It hadn't signified that he attended the press conference. Two-J's barely noticed, and the shit about to hit the fan was going to hit it anyway. Jack had a bad feeling and wished Jess had kept his big mouth shut. Whose business was it anyway who he was screwing? And there was something else. He missed Glad something terrible—who would have guessed?—and wished he was with her in Delray, or had somehow convinced her to fly north.

He was feeling every one of his almost eighty-three years. In his Bagel Barn bag, he carried the unfinished half of his bialy with a schmear, as well as half-price, day-old bagels he planned to throw in the East River. Although he hadn't attended High Holiday services in almost seventy years, and he had not only walked but run away from most things Jewish, he still remembered accompanying his father, Izzy Singer, a ragpicker from Bialystok by way of East New York, to the Sheepshead Bay piers, on the afternoon of the first day of Rosh Hashanah to throw away his sins.

"Good riddance," his father would say, in the Hymie accent that had embarrassed Jack, his old-world father, who never had two dimes to rub together, and called him *Yakob* till the day he died, another thing Jack hated. Izzy would pitch crusts off the pier into the dark waters and spit, "Good riddance!"

Tashlich, the word had come unbidden while he was ordering in the Bagel Barn. *Tashlich*, Jack thought, crossing to the east side of York Avenue. *I'll knock on Joey's door and see if he and Frannie want to come. From the look of things this morning, I bet there's things they want to throw away.*

When Jack invited them to the river, more than anything, Joe felt grateful. He was worried about Jess. It was one thing to tell the truth inside an interview room. It was something else again when you had to face jerks and haters, and there would be plenty of both. He remembered the father who'd sent his little boy to his table before he'd fled New York: *Say it ain't, Joe. Say it ain't!* And the thinly veiled anti-Semitism he'd faced even before and especially after the gambling accusation. Jews and money. *Hey, Jew-boy.* Even his nickname, *Jewish Joe.*

Joe hoped Jess would be able to keep all this out of his mind tomorrow when he got up on the bump. Right now, riding the elevator to the lobby, he was having trouble keeping Avi's final warning out of his mind. *Since your cancer came back once, it's more likely to come back a second time. If it does, it won't kill you right away. There are new treatments. But if it comes back a second time, there are no cures. Just a battle.*

They left the lobby, headed for the East River. Joe wore a Mets cap, Jack his fedora. As a *shiksa*, Frannie didn't need to cover her head. When they reached the river walk, they turned north. A cool wind blew, and small waves mottled the surface. Joe remembered Frannie running here last spring when they first met Avi and Stu. He still believed Stu was interested in Frannie, and if something bad happened, Stu could be an option. Frannie said no. Stu was too short. And she refused to consider bad outcomes, as if they'd switched roles, and she was now the positive thinker.

Joe walked farthest from the railing, Frannie between him and his father. He was only an inch or so taller than Frannie, while Jack, who'd been shrinking fast, was a full head shorter. They passed several knots of *yarmulke-d* Jews holding prayer books, some of them tossing bread on the water. The ceremony, Jack had explained when he knocked on their door, was called *Tashlich*.

"Don't ask what it means," he added. "I don't *sprechen* the Hebrew."

They stopped at a wide place on the river walk. Overhead, cable cars shuttled back and forth to Roosevelt Island. Frannie fished her cell phone out of her purse. Jack had asked her to look up *Tashlich*, which was weird, Joe thought. His entire childhood and in all the years since, Jack had never gone to *shul*, never fasted on Yom Kippur, or did any of the other things Jews did. And now, *Tashlich*? Then it occurred to Joe, *This is because of my cancer.*

Jack reached into the Bagel Barn sack. "You want the everything, Joey, a salt, or a plain?"

"Everything."

"Makes sense," Jack replied. "Cover all the bases. I'll take the salt, cause I'm the saltiest, which leaves the plain for you, Frannie."

Jack distributed the bagels, and Joe, Jack, and Frannie tore them into pieces.

Jack said, "This is about casting your bread upon the waters."

"Throwing away your sins," Frannie said.

"Hoping the seagulls don't eat them."

"And praying that next year." Joe looked at Frannie. "Is a healthy and happy one."

"Amen." Then Jack added, "And that Two-J's pitches lights out."

Frannie unlocked her phone. "I found this on the internet about *Tashlich*. It's from Micah, Chapter Seven, Verse Nineteen. 'He will take us back in love; he will cover up our iniquities. You will cast all their sins into the depths of the sea.'"

"Joey," Jack began, suddenly serious. "I never said this to you, back when. I'm sorry for introducing you to those goombahs. I know how much it cost you not to give the commissioner my name, even though I told you that you could have."

Jack hesitated. His lower lip and then his whole chin were trembling. "You done right by me, Joey. But I didn't do right by you. You've been a better son than I've been a dad. I want you to know that. And, and, I'm so sorry."

Jack started to sob. Frannie caught Joe's eye, and he stepped forward, hugged his father, and held on.

Joe said, "I forgive you, Dad." And to Joe's surprise, he felt lighter.

When Jack stopped crying, which Joe was sure he'd never seen him do, not once, the Singers pitched their bagels into the East River, where they floated on the gray water. Then Frannie reached into her purse, fished out the black velvet bag, which contained the Unbound Bender vibrator. She threw it as far as she could across the river. The bag floated for a moment, then sank.

"What the hell was that?" Jack asked.

"My fears," Frannie said.

Joe took her hand, grateful that the vibrator hadn't floated up for all the world to see. Then they started back to their hotel.

CHAPTER THIRTY-THREE

Tuesday dawned bright, cool, and clear: perfect October baseball weather. In addition to the start of the playoffs, Jess was acutely aware Tuesday marked the second day of Rosh Hashanah. Technically, he wasn't Jewish because Mom wasn't. But when your dad was known to millions of fans as "Jewish Joe," everyone assumed you were a Jew and expected you to act like one. There was nothing he could do about that. But by the time the game started, Rosh Hashanah would be over, so it wouldn't be wrong to pitch, and he could still be inscribed in the Book of Life, the Book of True Love, and the Book of a Great Post-Season. Or maybe, because he would be warming up and getting ready before sunset, it would be wrong to pitch, and as Jack liked to say, he was headed for the crapper.

No matter. Nothing could have stopped Jess from pitching. It wasn't Yom Kippur, the Holy of Holies. He wasn't Sandy Koufax; and it wasn't the 1960s. Jess just hoped he didn't get booed off the field for being gay. He hoped his teammates wouldn't be pissed at him for coming out. He prayed no one was mean to Rah, that no one threw glass or verbal bottles at either of them. Above all, he hoped he could follow Rick Heynen's advice and put the world and its demands out of his mind. *Just put up zeros, Jess. Just put up zeros.*

Above an inch-high boldface headline—*Setting Off the Gay-dar Gun*—the back page of the *Post* had re-run the picture of Rah lifting him after the no-hitter. Jess loved that picture, was glad he no longer had to deny what the picture so clearly showed, and—he was really entering Fantasy Land now—if he and Rah ever got married, he'd have the picture blown up life-size outside the entrance to the reception hall.

Jess rolled over and gazed at Rah, who was fast asleep with his head on the next pillow. Man, his batterymate could sure sleep.

At two o'clock, Jess and Rah stood outside the Mets' players' entrance at Citi Field. On the car ride out to Queens, Rah had suggested they enter the locker room holding hands.

"Are you crazy?"

"Crazy for you, Yess."

Jess kissed him. It was an excellent kiss.

"Once the *gato* is out of the bag, Jess, it's *out*."

They entered the locker room together, but not holding hands. Jess felt everyone's eyes on them, but no one said a word. He changed, then headed to the trainer's table for his pregame massage. There was barely enough time before the team meeting that included a visit from Davey Dean. Mr. Dean, Jess had been told, was also meeting with the Nationals. A historic occasion. Not only was Jess the first rookie pitcher to start a Wild Card game for the Mets, he and Rah were the first openly gay baseball players to appear in the post-season, to play for a New York baseball team, to play for any team since anyone could remember, and MLB and Mr. Dean wanted to make sure nothing went wrong.

While Jess lay on the trainer's table, Gallagher came into the room.

"You ready Jess?"

"Yes, sir."

"The Mets have gotten about a million interview requests."

Jess raised his head and looked at his manager, whose eyes focused on a spot two inches past his head.

"A lot of them are not what you'd call sports publications."

Jess could feel his stomach getting tight.

"You're probably wondering why I'm telling you now."

"Yes sir, I am."

"We're turning down all requests. I thought you should know. And after the game? Baseball questions only. Don't worry. We've got your back."

Jess closed his eyes. *Just put up zeros*, he thought. *Zeros.*

Jess called from the locker room to say he'd left four tickets at Will Call and hoped that he and Mom wouldn't mind, but Emmy would be joining them.

"Of course, we don't mind. How are you doing, son?"

"Nervous as hell."

"I used to throw up sometimes before I pitched."

"You told me."

"Just remember, the most important pitch is strike one."

"I gotta go."

Joe wished he'd told Jess he loved him. Or how brave he was for holding that press conference and saying what he'd said. But no, he hadn't said any of that, just, *The most important pitch is strike one*, which Jess already knew. *Sometimes*, Joe thought, *I just don't know.*

Jack decided to call Glad before heading to Citi Field with Joe and Frannie. He wished he'd tried harder to persuade her to come to New York. He'd never been great at talking about his feelings, and he was a pretty goddamn old dog to learn to fetch a new stick. But he had asked Joey to forgive him. Twenty-five years too late, but still. And he'd cried, when was the last time that happened? He must be getting in touch with his feelings. Because there was no denying, he missed Glad's skinny behind and sharp mouth. So he dialed her house phone, but she didn't answer, and he declined to leave a message. What would he say, *I miss you?* Then he tried her cell, but she didn't answer that either. Maybe she was pissed. Or asleep. Praying, or *boinking* some *alter kocker* because he was not only out of town, but had flown on the holiday, so he wasn't worth spitting at.

He didn't believe the part about *boinking*.

He decided against leaving a message on her cell and went into the bathroom to shave. While he was trimming his moustache, his phone rang.

"What do you want, Jack?"

"Happy New Year to you too."

She didn't answer.

Exasperated, he asked, "How do you know I want anything?"

"You called both my phones."

"How do you know that?"

"Stop horsing around, Jack."

"I wish I'd done a better job of asking you to come with me."

"I wish you had too."

No one said anything for a long goddamn time. "Me, Joey, and Frannie, we threw our sins away in the East River. Bagels, we used."

"What are you saying, Jack?"

Like an old dog learning to bark. "I miss you, Glad. And when I get back, I wanna see more of you."

"You've already seen all there is."

"Then I want to see it more often."

"I already told you. I'm not going to be anyone's nurse. I've buried too many men."

"You don't have to worry about that. I'm gonna outlive you."

"We'll see about that."

Jack smiled. The conversation was going better than he'd hoped, so he figured it was time to get off. Just as he was thinking about saying goodbye, Glad said, "I watched Jess's press conference last night."

"Whaddya think?"

"He spoke well. Looked good too."

"You were right about him and Rah."

Glad laughed. "I'm always right, haven't you learned that yet?"

He almost said, *Maybe you being right all the time killed your husbands.* But Jack was no dummy. "I gotta get off and go to the game."

"Happy New Year, Jack. Come home safe."

After the meeting at which Davey Dean presented the Mets with Pride/ Equality t-shirts with rainbow lettering and an official MLB logo, the team went out on the field to stretch, practice fielding and batting, as if it were a game like any other, which, of course, it was. Jess, as was his habit on days he started, rode the stationary bike for fifteen minutes, then reviewed video and scouting reports of the Nats. Before putting on his uni and heading through the tunnel to the bullpen to warm up, he sat in front of his locker, eyes closed, with his black Bose headset on, visualizing his opening sequence of pitches. Pick off the corners. Put up zeros. Top of the zone four-seamers. Low and outside changes to righties. Throw the two free and easy, play catch with Rah. Nothing hard about it.

Then he slipped into his uni and started down the tunnel to the bullpen. Halfway there, so lost in thought and visualization he didn't hear the approaching footsteps, he nearly banged into Big Barnes. They both drew back as if they'd smelled a skunk.

Big grinned. "I was right about you all along, Singer."

"Can't fool you, Big."

"You think you're so high and mighty. And maybe you are. But your fuck-buddy Rah better watch his back. The amigos got something special planned."

Could that be true? Jess wondered if he was going to have to fight Big again, if not today then later. They looked hard at each other, and then Jess admitted Big was right. Compared to Big, he was high and mighty, and if Big kept making trouble, maybe he could get Mr. Abbott to trade him to Pittsburgh. Or KC. Some losing, small market team.

"What's a matter, Singer, got nothing to say?"

"Not to an asshole like you."

"For a fag," Big said, "you talk big."

Here goes, Jess thought. "And even for a stupid asshole, you're really, really stupid."

Just then, Jess heard footsteps approaching from the locker room, the direction he'd been walking. Big heard them too. A heartbeat later, Rick Heynen and Marcus Wetherby rounded into view, the Pride/

Equality undershirts Davey Dean had distributed at the team meeting showing under their half-buttoned game jerseys.

"Hey, Jess," Rick said, and a moment later, "Hey, Big."

"Hey, Jess," said Marcus, and nothing more.

Jess could hardly believe Rick and Wetherby were wearing those shirts.

Rick asked, "You warmed up yet?"

Jess shook his head.

Pointing at his own chest, Marcus asked, "Big, you wearing your t-shirt?"

"No fucking way."

"You stupid motherfucker," Marcus said. "If you ain't Flushing Fred, I'll eat my hat."

Jess could see that Big didn't know what to say. *I am Flushing Fred? I'm not?* What did it matter? Marcus rolled his eyes and set out through the tunnel towards the bullpen. Jess fell into step after him, beside Rick Heynen.

Waiting for the Mets' starting lineup to be introduced, with Jack on his right, Frannie on his left, and Emmy on the far side of Frannie, Joe wished he had a drink to settle his nerves. But he wasn't drinking, just in case it made a difference with the cancer. Frannie, who'd been drunk in the owner's box two nights ago, wasn't drinking either. She'd sworn off for a month, she said. Sober October. Not Jack, who'd ordered a beer for Emmy too, though Joe doubted she was twenty-one.

It was probably okay he wasn't drinking. Multiple eyes and cameras would be trained on their little group. Not just the starting pitcher's parents, but the *gay* starting pitcher's parents, with his sometimes girlfriend. Who knew exactly what Emmy thought; she was such a brave girl, decked out in Jess's number 32 and a Mets cap. She must love Jess, Joe thought; of course, she did. This must be hard for her. But Jess had shared that Emmy's brother was gay, so it wasn't a complete surprise, and yet, this can't be what she dreamed of. You can't choose who you love, Joe thought. Jess loved Rah, while he'd loved Frannie almost from the day they met. Hell, he even loved Jack, who'd given him so many reasons not to.

When they walked to their seats located just behind the Mets' dugout, Jack had said to all three of them, "The cameras will be all over us, so try not to show emotion, especially if things ain't going Two-J's way."

Joe had nodded, but doubted that he, Frannie, or Emmy could keep their game faces on. They were only human; well, maybe Jack wasn't. He and Frannie were Jess's *parents*, and Emmy, a girl who loved their boy. Anyway, the cameras would mostly focus on Jess, and Rah too, but at least Rah would have his catcher's mask to hide behind.

The Mets' PA announcer read out the Nationals lineup, and predictably, every starter was booed, with the loudest boos reserved for the Nats' young stars. Then the announcer intoned, "And now, starting for your New York Mets..." and the capacity crowd rose to its feet and began stamping and shouting for the Mets' starters, with the loudest cheers for Pete the first baseman, the superstar shortstop, then Rah, and finally Jess, although with both Rah and Jess, Joe feared he could hear an undercurrent of boos.

He looked at Frannie, concern in his eyes. He took her hand and squeezed hard. Then Jack leaned past him and hissed, "There's assholes everywhere, ain't there?"

Emmy laughed. "Sure are!"

Joe tried to toss it off. Fans paid good money, and that bought them the right to boo. He'd been booed plenty in his day. But that was his son they were booing, not because of how he pitched or what he threw, or how many runs he gave up, but because of who he was, and that was hard. Then a broad-chested African American came onto the field wearing the white shirt, tie, and dress uniform of the NY Fire Department. He stepped behind the microphone set up at home plate and began a full-throated, no-frills, just thrills, rendition of "The Star-Spangled Banner."

The crowd cheered. The fireman bowed. The mic stand was removed, and Pete, the first baseman, who was Jess's height but forty pounds heavier, began rolling grounders to the Mets' infielders. Then Jess climbed up on the mound and began his final warm-ups.

On the field, Jess toed the rubber focused on Rah's mitt. During introductions, he'd heard the cheers and undertow of boos, a black slash in a blue sky. On the bench, before their names were called, he sat beside Rah, who'd told him in the clubhouse that his mother had called from Cuernavaca to say she loved him.

"And your father?"

Rah shook his head.

That was trouble for another day. Jess delivered his last warm-up. Rah fired the ball to second, and it darted around the infield from glove to glove before settling in Jess's. He stepped off the rubber and walked behind the mound, bounced the resin bag twice on his palm and twice on the back of his left hand, then returned to the slab. Hiding his face behind his glove as Jack had taught him, Jess gripped the ball in his mitt and picked up Rah's call through PitchCom. Jess swept into his motion, raised his right leg, curled his knee, and with the baseball gods and good fairies who'd blessed his crib so many years ago silently cheering, Jess released his curve and watched it break down and in towards home.

THE END

ACKNOWLEDGMENTS

'd like to thank the H-team of early readers: Lamar Herrin, Jim Heynen, and Ron Hansen. Thank you, Leslie Wells, for your sharp eye and sound advice. A shout-out to my editor, Jacob Hoye, for your general savvy and impressive knowledge of baseball, even though you started out a Yankees fan. Thank you, Mike Mungiello and Michael Carlisle, friend and agent for forty-one years, my second longest marriage. Very special thanks to Dr. Zvi Fuks, world-renowned radiation oncologist, for your generosity and guidance in all things medical. If I've gotten anything wrong, it's my fault not yours.

Finally, and once again, thank you to my first reader, wife and lover, Susan Morgan, who has watched and mocked but more than tolerated my life-long affair with the Mets.

Also by Eric Goodman

High on the Energy Bridge
The First Time I Saw Jenny Hall
In Days of Awe
Child of My Right Hand
Twelfth and Race
Cuppy and Stew